THE INHERITANCE

PETER STEPHAN JUNGK

THE INHERITANCE

Translated by Michael Hofmann

PUSHKIN PRESS
LONDON

First published in German as *Die Erbschaft* 1999
© Peter Stephan Jungk, 2010

English translation © Michael Hofmann

This edition first published in 2010 by
Pushkin Press
71-75 Shelton Street
London WC2H 9JQ

Reprinted 2012

British Library Cataloguing in Publication Data:
A catalogue record for this book is available
from the British Library

ISBN 978 1 906548 20 9

The translation of this work was supported by a grant from the Goethe-Institut
which is funded by the German Ministry of Foreign Affairs.

Cover Illustration: *Caracas Venezuela* Zigy Kaluzny © Getty Images

Set in 10 on 12.2 Baskerville Monotype
and printed in Great Britain by the CPI Group (UK)

www.pushkinpress.com

THE INHERITANCE

For Luc Bondy

We live in continual strife, but I love him extremely, almost more than myself. The same stubborn audacity, limitless emotional softness, and unpredictable lunacy— the principal difference between us being that Fate has made my uncle a millionaire, and myself the opposite, which is to say, a poet.

Heinrich Heine

Quitt charges head first into the block of granite. He gets up and charges into the rock again. Once more he gets up and charges into the rock.

The Unreasonable Are Dying Out Peter Handke

TABLE OF CONTENTS

THE INHERITANCE

1

NOISE

HELICOPTER DRONE SPINS HIM OUT OF DEEP DREAMS. On the bedside table the red numbers of a digital alarm clock—it is 05:33.

He gets up, pushes the heavy nylon curtain aside. Looks down from the twelfth storey onto the city and the overcast, still dark November sky.

A squadron of jet fighters thunders above the hotel. The supersonic bang of the engines leaves the windows shaking. There is nothing extraordinary about air-force exercises in this country. He draws the curtains. Is careful not to leave a chink open, otherwise the light will come flooding in after sunrise. In the bathroom he takes out the box of *Quies* from his sponge bag, plucks a couple of wax balls out of the cotton wool they are embedded in, and shoves them deep into his ears.

He sleeps through until eight o'clock. Takes the pink wax balls out of his ears. Reaches for the remote control, for no particular reason, switches on the television. At the top of the hour, the speaker of a worldwide news station announces that a military coup had failed only hours before in Caracas, Venezuela. The government is once more in control of the situation.

He jumps out of bed, crosses the darkened room. Pulls back the curtain, looks down on the sun-drenched city beneath.

Three of the four domestic television stations are off air. The remaining programme screens a weather chart, with the predicted highs and lows for the day ahead.

17

The traveller struggles with the window lock, even though in the forty hours since his arrival here, he has been forced to realise several times already that the window cannot be opened.

He gets dressed. Yesterday, not far from the hotel, he found an espresso bar. In the company of a gang of earth-encrusted construction workers, who were digging the tunnel for a new subway line, he drank one of the best coffees in his life.

As he hands in the key, he remarks to the concierge: "Well, I guess it's all over now?"

"No, señor, by no means … "

He thinks: the concierge is mistaken. And pushes through the revolving door on to the palm-lined street. Thick humidity settles on his body. He directs his steps to the workmen's café. The steel shutters are down. The building site is quiet. Explosions can be heard, coming from not far away. The doors of a small car are wide open. A group of passers-by surround the parked car. From the car radio comes the sound of frantic voices.

In the bright neon of a restaurant, excitable men in short-sleeved shirts are hurling phrases back and forth. There's a smell of fish and stale oil. The manager has a transistor pressed to his temple. The stranger, his shirt soaked with sweat, orders a *pequeno*. The manager doesn't move the radio from his head.

After downing the last drop of the painfully bitter coffee, and choking down a piece of dry sponge cake, he heads out onto the street again.

He goes to the subway. The station on the Plaza Venezuela is barred with metal barriers. He asks a man who is carrying two suitcases where the nearest bus stop is; he must get to Avenida Urdaneta. Every ten steps or so, the muscular man has to stop and rest. " … *Hoy?!* No bus!"

In the middle of the Plaza the stranger waits—he doesn't know what he is waiting for. A couple of helicopters circle overhead. A taxi stops, the cigarillo-smoking driver leans out of the window, asks him where he would like to go. He tells him, it's five stops by subway. The driver names the price: "Hundredandtwentydollars." He doesn't see why he should pay more than ten for so short a distance, whatever the particular circumstances of the day.

The night before, he set up an appointment for this morning with the executor of the estate of his uncle, who had died at the age of ninety. He considers going on foot to the offices of the import-export company Kiba-Nova, where Julio Kirshman is waiting for him. More explosions fill the air. He decides first to call from his hotel room, and ask the executor to put off their meeting, scheduled for nine-thirty, to a later time when things might have settled down.

It had been imprudent of him to leave his Austrian passport in the safe of the Kiba-Nova company, but Kirshman, the junior manager and co-proprietor of the import-export business, had warned him that US and European passports were highly sought-after items for the criminal class of the city, and his passport would be worth a fortune. The hotel safe offered absolutely no security for such a precious item. It was only in the company safe that he could leave it with an easy mind.

Back in his room again, the telephone rings. "Herr Loew? Dr Johannes here." The lawyer recommended to him by the Austrian Consulate, to whom he had initially turned twenty-four hours before. "You must under no circumstances leave the hotel," Friedrich Johannes warns him. "Did Kirshman not call you? A detachment of rebels is bombing the Presidential Palace as we speak. There are almost a hundred dead. I hope you're carrying your passport with you at all times? Even in the hotel! I'll call you later."

A look out of the window. Everything seems quiet. It's ten in the morning. He waits to see whether Kirshman will call. How will the executor, a close friend of his uncle's, behave towards him?

Daniel Loew sits cross-legged on the soft wide bed, with his notebook open in front of him. He tries to find words to describe the atmosphere and the colours of this day, the situation on the street, the almost palpable sense of fear in the city. He manages nothing.

Kirshman doesn't call.

Two hours later, Dr Johannes warns him again—not to leave the hotel. Daniel says he still hasn't heard from the executor.

"That doesn't surprise me. Remember what I told you last night?" replies the lawyer. "Have you thought some more about whether you'd like me to take on the case of Loew versus Kirshman?"

"I'd just like you to be … a little patient."

At one o'clock, Loew calls the Kiba-Nova office. A recorded message with a woman's voice gives the business hours of the company—Monday to Friday, eight-thirty to six-thirty pm, no break for lunch. He goes through his papers, looking for Kirshman's home number. Julio picks up: "Well, so what do you say?! All this drama in our country, did you hear about it?"

"How could I not have heard?"

They speak German together—the mother tongue of Kirshman and Loew. Julio was born in 1948 in Caracas, Loew in 1954, in Vienna.

"You still there?" asks Kirshman.

Daniel doesn't answer.

"Well, I guess the two of us will just have to sort it out tomorrow," says Julio. "I expect the shooting will have stopped by then … "

2

ARRIVAL

ALEXANDER STECHER BRAVO'S SOLE RELATIVE, apart from Daniel's father, Jacob Loew, had come to Caracas to resolve a few outstanding issues relating to the inheritance with Julio Kirshman. He had sent his flight number and expected arrival time from New York.

No one was there to meet him at Maiquetia Airport. In the arrival hall, he was mobbed by self-appointed helpers, tearing the suitcases from his grasp, offering him highly competitive exchange rates, promising cut-price deals for hotels, sightseeing visits, bordellos. He hardly succeeded in ridding himself of the helpers and supplicants, even chasing some of them away, finally subsiding in the back seat of a 1966 spaceship-sized Dodge Polara. The ride to the hotel took an hour. It went by jungle-covered hills, and through long unlit tunnels. He passed slum dwellings in all shapes and colours, assembled from corrugated iron and all kinds of other materials, gradually becoming denser as they approached the city centre. He was surprised by their seeming robustness, in view of their fragility. Petrol stations, auto-repair workshops, bus depots, oil pumps all around the metropolis.

The clouds were like gleaming anthracite.

As soon as he had installed himself in room 1244, he called Kirshman at home. It was Sunday afternoon, four pm. An employee told him Señor Julio was in the office.

"Ah!" the executor sounded surprised, "you're here already? Exhausted? Want to come by the office tomorrow?"

The flight from New York to Caracas hadn't been particularly tiring. He didn't see why he shouldn't set off immediately.

"All right then—come on over. Take the subway, the B-line. Watch out for pickpockets, they're on every corner!"

He found his way to Cuji a Romualda, not far from the Avenida
Urdaneta subway stop, without any trouble; it was in the middle
of a pedestrian zone full of textile shops, cheap dressmakers,
carpet stores, all of them closed. High white metal gates separated
the Kiba-Nova premises from the street. Loew watched three
workers, their loud voices breaking the Sunday quiet, loading
and unloading goods, calling out jokes and obscenities to one
another.

And then he went inside.

Behind a massive table sat a short and heavy-set old man, hands
buried in his trouser pockets, a cold half-cigar between his lips. He
didn't get up. He motioned him with his chin to sit down. They
didn't shake hands.

"So there you are!" Coughing, shortage of breath accompanied
the words. He steered the cold cigar from one corner of his mouth
to another. "Well, you've really dumped us in it, haven't you!"

Daniel stood up: "That's not going to get us very far."

"Siddown, Professor, and calm down, it wasn't meant like that!"
They were silent.

In his trouser pockets, Konrad Kirshman drove his long nails
into the palms of his hands.

The stranger looked around. On shelves were stacks of half-
opened boxes and dozens of ripped-open cartons, some full of
goods from Asia, Europe, North and South America.

A door creaked behind him. A wiry individual, short military
haircut, clean-shaven, mid-forties, walked into the room, as though
stepping onto a variety stage to a little personal drum roll. He
bounced up to the visitor, all jolly and cheerful: "At last! We meet!"
They shook hands. "I'm Julio. I take it you've already met Papa?"

Daniel had brought along his newest book of verse, and handed
Julio the slim, black-bound volume. Julio cast his eye over it, and
immediately stowed it away in the drawer of the enormous desk,
locking it twice afterwards. In the instant that the deep drawer was
open, Loew could see that it was brim-full of banknotes.

Julio turned to his father. "Dad? Will you leave us alone for a
minute?"

" … You got secrets? Secrets from *me*, little fellow?"

"Will you leave us alone?"

The octogenarian slowly got to his feet, reeled towards the door with his hands in his pockets. As he left the room he barked instructions at the workers hanging around outside.

"Sorry about my father, I overheard what he said … I'm sure it wasn't meant like that."

Loew studied Julio Kirshman's face. It looked relaxed to him, and mild, in contrast to the anger in the eyes of his father.

Julio looked at Daniel in turn. The tall visitor, with black shoulder-length hair and pale, delicate features didn't look like the man he'd expected to meet. On his visits to Stecher, he would often ask to see pictures of the nephew. In the flesh, Loew looked more confident, more grown-up, and more serious, than in Kirshman's impressions from photographs. The stranger's manner had something oddly ceremonious about it, a kind of aura that didn't permit one to play fast and loose with him, as he might have wanted to otherwise. He had used the intimate '*Du*' form with Daniel, and was now wondering briefly whether it wouldn't be more judicious to use the more respectful '*Sie*' instead.

"Well, so how's about taking a look over the warehouse?" asked the executor, having resolved to stay on '*Du*' footing after all.

He led Loew from storey to storey, showing him vast expanses, the size of sports arenas, full of import-export goods. The first floor housed guitar strings and baseball bats from Taiwan, the second scissors, nail-files, and knives from Solingen, the third children's violins, Hammond organs, and ping-pong balls from South Korea, the fourth table-tennis nets, dolls, fishhooks, and pocket-calculators from China, the fifth, sixth, and seventh more and more new and varied and colourful products from all five continents. On the eighth floor there was a very faint smell of cigar smoke. "Just you wait! If I catch the freak who dares to smoke up here!" swore Kirshman. "Among the fish and butterfly nets! I'll string him up from the nearest lamppost!"

A slow goods elevator took them back down to the ground floor. "So, now that you've seen all that, do you still seriously think that *we* would want to take something away from *you*? We've got enough

23

of our own here, we don't need any of dear departed Alexander's money."

"Which is why I'm all the more surprised you've refused to give me what is mine," the inheritor remarked, in the peaceable tones of someone praising a good cigar.

"Don't worry! It'll all be sorted out in no time. Down to the last cent. You know, you don't have to stand on ceremony with us, just say '*Du*', we're practically family after all—Papa and your uncle, they were best friends for half-a-century! So now do you want to see the apartment?"

They drove in a black SUV to the Avenida Altamira, in the San Bernardino section of town, parked outside the apartment block that Stecher Bravo had moved to twenty years before. He had sold a large piece of land on the edge of the city, on which his pretty single-storey house had once stood in the middle of a mango orchard, to the municipality for a huge sum—and, for a fraction of the profit, acquired the modern apartment.

On the twelfth floor, they rang the bell next to the lift. They hadn't called ahead, or announced they were coming. A high voice asked: "*Quien es?*" and Kirshman replied, "*Sono yo*, Julio!" But not until the executor had added that the nephew of Señor Stecher Bravo accompanied him was the door opened a crack. And then, still holding on to the doorframe, the old lady admitted the two men. Stecher had talked to her about him often, the stooped woman tried to explain to Daniel. His uncle in turn had told him not infrequently about Perpetua, his loyal housekeeper of the past thirty-five years, and described her to him regularly in his letters. He could only guess at the content of her verbal cascade.

Alexander's black leather gloves were on a rickety wooden stool next to the fridge, along with a colour brochure on the South Tyrolean spa town of Meran.

Julio led the way into the drawing room. It was late afternoon. Kirshman hurried out onto the balcony, to check that his car was safe. Daniel followed him outside into the dusk. The air was fragrant with sweet tropical blossoms. Lights were coming on all round, in other blocks along the avenues and boulevards. A swarm of birds flew by, at a great height. Hundreds of pairs of wings were dancing synchronously.

"We can't stay long," said Kirshman, "otherwise I'll be short one jeep."

They went back into the drawing room. The furniture, among which Stecher had lived for more than five decades, ever since his emigration from Hamburg, without ever replacing any of it—skewed tables, peeling wallpaper, sun-bleached bookcases. The chaise longue, bought in summer 1940, with the last of his savings. A large, dark-brown radio from the nineteen-fifties, RCA, made in the USA. No TV. The sofas and armchairs, covered in coarse material, with patches of wear and tear. Perpetua pointed to the grey recliner, in which Alexander had spent every day in the years before his death. Even as a ninety-year-old, she said, he never stopped reading, with his legs on the red leather footstool. Loew sat down in the armchair, put his feet on the footstool. How extraordinary, he thought, to be sitting on my uncle's chair, to be standing in the apartment that was home to him for decades. To be visiting these rooms for the first time, where for so long Alexander was hoping I would come, and I never went to visit him, all the many times he invited me. Perpetua brushed away a tear with the rough back of her thumb.

Julio sat down to the right of him. "This," he said and cleared his throat, "is where I always used to sit, next to your dear uncle, when I visited him, I was the only one he wanted to see, the only one he allowed to come near him, those last years of his life—it was *me* he turned to for help, me he used to call in the middle of the night, over all sorts of nonsense, he wanted to see me, because he was frightened. Just me. He was stone deaf. Refused to put in his hearing aid. I used to have to yell to make myself understood. And where were you all that time? Did you ever come and see him? But the fact that you will inherit this apartment, that's something you owe me, Daniel Loew, because let me tell you, he wanted to leave it to Perpetua, not to you, not at all!"

Kirshman ran on to the balcony, leaned far over the railing. Came back into the dark sitting room, head aggressively thrust forward, like a bull's. Switched on a standard lamp. And picked up where he'd left off: "We're left with the problem of Perpetua's granddaughter, because our Sasha—I always used to call him Sasha, you know, Alexander—he was in love with her from when she was nine or ten years old, and now she turns round, the lying bitch, and says he promised the apartment to her, and right after his death she moved into the room behind the kitchen. Anyway, Manuela's inherited your uncle's little 1962 yellow Chevy, it's in the will and all; anyway, she went around after his death, changing all the locks, and cutting the phone line, and performing voodoo ceremonies, right here in the apartment. The floors were all littered with cigar butts. Getting little Manuela out of the flat, ha!—that's going to be your next challenge."

Perpetua unlocked her nineteen-year-old granddaughter's room. She had gone to the coast for a week, to Maracaibo, and wouldn't be back. The room smelt strongly of incense. Pictures of Jesus, Mary and the angels decorated the dirty walls, the floor looked as though it had had soot on it, and blood. In a corner were a couple of battered saucepans with a few yellowish chicken bones in them.

"Didn't I tell you? Voodoo!" Julio ran across the apartment, back out onto the balcony.

They said goodbye to Perpetua. The housekeeper gave Daniel both hands. He kissed her sunken cheeks. Her swollen palms felt like wood, a consequence of the care she had given Stecher. In the months before his death, he had developed fungal growths on his arms and legs. They had given Perpetua an eczema, which she couldn't manage to shake off.

Julio dropped Daniel in front of the Hotel Presidente. He didn't invite him back to his house. He didn't introduce him to his wife or his three children. Didn't advise him where to have dinner. By way of farewell, he said: "Bet you're tired now!" Rolled down the window once Loew had got out. "Quite a nice place here, isn't it? How'd you find it? I bet it costs a packet. I'll see you in the office, tomorrow at eleven, and then we'll get everything sorted out."

3

ESTHER MORENO

N O-ONE IS ALLOWED TO LEAVE THE HOTEL. There is a long line of people in the lobby of the El Presidente, waiting to be admitted to the restaurant. Daniel joins the hapless ones, as they shuffle forwards. He listens to their conversations—the missed flights, the postponed trips, the delayed business meetings. A captain, whose cruise ship is at anchor in the port of La Guaira, is unable to join his crew. An eye specialist expected back at her clinic in Los Angeles tomorrow has had to cancel all operations for the next several days.

It feels unbearable to Daniel to stay in the queue of people, waiting like cattle to be fed. He goes back up to his room, and drapes himself in a couple of towels. Walks down a long passage in the basement, and finally reaches the swimming pool. The surface of the water is absolutely still. There is no one there. Deckchairs, parasols glimmer dully in the light. A smell of chlorine and heat.

He slips into the water. He has always felt in his element in a swimming pool. He swims on his front, mechanically repeating the simple, unchanging movements of arms and legs that he learnt at eight or nine under the turn-of-the-century cupola of the Diana Baths in Vienna, long since demolished. He swims with stamina from end to end, and back and forth. Overhead, twenty stories soar into the sky. The palms creak in the hotel gardens. Two parrots fly back and forth in a spacious cage, and shriek, as if their lives were in danger.

Daniel keeps seeing the picture of his uncle in front of him, smiling. Always smiling. Not just when he was being photographed did Alexander Stecher Bravo smile, he smiled in every conceivable situation. A slender man, always clean-shaven. Glasses, from early boyhood. Every day he wore a clean white shirt, and always a tie, even when it was very hot. His hair was white and kept short.

"*Muy bien! Muy bien!*" squawks one of the parrots.

He was just four; his uncle Alexander, fifty-two years older, was sitting at the foot of his bed, on the eighteenth floor of the New York hotel, the St Moritz, on Central Park South. His parents were going out that evening, to the world première of *West Side Story* on Broadway. They had left the relative whom Daniel had met for the first time a couple of hours before, never having seen him before, with the task of babysitting. For more than half-an-hour you were shaking your head, Stecher was still telling his nephew decades later, just incessantly. I thought you must be some kind of idiot. But then you suddenly stopped, and you blinked, and you saw that it was me who was sitting beside you, as always immersed in the stock market reports in the *Wall Street Journal*, the *Washington Post*, the *New York Times*. You sat up, looked at me, and said: 'Oh, *you're* here, so there's no point in my still shaking my head!' And minutes later you were blissfully asleep.

Calm strokes, from end to end of the pool. The creaking of a rusty deckchair.

In a legal sense, Daniel Loew is not Alexander Stecher Bravo's nephew, even though he has always felt and described himself as such. Daniel's father, Jacob, had two cousins on his mother's side, the sons of his mother's only sister—Arnold and Alexander. Arnold, a high-school teacher, and a passionate ornithologist in his free time, died without having married or left any heirs. Alexander, another obdurate bachelor, had no children either. Stecher spoilt his second cousin from when he was born. Almost every year he travelled to Europe from Caracas, either flying or taking ship to Le Havre. For Jacob, his first cousin, Alexander had little interest. Whenever they would meet, both were lost for words.

His hair is still wet from the pool when he walks into the windowless dining room. There is barely anything left to eat on the long buffet table. Twenty neon lights give off a chill light. In the middle of the ceiling there's a mirror ball. On gala evenings it's set in motion, scatters lightings over the room.

From the almost empty platters he picks up a few withered lettuce leaves, an end of cheese, some greyish slices of sausage and dried-out pieces of white bread. A copper saucepan contains three bony pieces of oxtail in a black gravy. He sits all alone in the hangar-sized room. Gulps down what little is on his plate. Gets up to hunt for a piece of fruit.

A woman enters the room. Her eyes put him in mind of a deer's caught in heavy nets. Her long white neck thrusts out in every direction. "I'm hungry!" she calls out. And once more: "I'm hungry!"

He gives her two oranges, the last there are.

"Let's share," she says.

He returns to his place, the round table is littered with leftover food, crumpled paper napkins, dirty cutlery, empty bottles and glasses. The unknown woman sits down at his table with him. Tears the peel off the oranges. Daniel becomes aware of a mild heat spilt by his solar plexus over his thighs and groin. A black Alice band holds the woman's reddish, wiry curls back. She has beige fluff on her upper lip. Her suit, which is made of expensive material, is a little crooked on her, it's too big for her, inherited, as it might be, from a heavier, broader relation. Her high heels are a little tight on her feet. He takes her to be roughly the same age as himself, late thirties. Her skin seems dry, her lips cracked, as though the climate were ice and snow. She has tiny, soft, blonde hairs on her cheeks and her prominent cheekbones. She gobbles up the orange he gives her.

Years ago she experienced a coup in Caracas, the woman says. "The rebels barricaded themselves into the fifth floor of the house I was living in at the time, and fired at the government troops until at the end of two days they were overpowered, and finished off there and then with shots to the head." Stray bullets and pieces of shrapnel found their way into her apartment on the fourth floor, and damaged the Chagall painting she'd inherited from her grandparents called *Leoncin in Winter*, shattered her wardrobe, sideboard and a two hundred-year-old clock.

She picks the last few lettuce leaves off the metal dishes on the sideboard, and goes back to the table. She moved to Miami after the last government crisis, it was only a week ago that she returned to Caracas for the first time, to sell her apartment. "Ever since emigrating, I've kept trying to sell it, but my attempts have been unsuccessful," not least because some distant relatives settled in it, and refused to be dislodged. Finally, she decided she had to take her family to court, and had already got in touch with a lawyer. But now the military coup would put an end to all such efforts for an unknown length of time. She stops to draw breath. "What about you? What are you doing here, who are you, what's your name?" Her nasal voice has something whiny and plaintive about it, the torrent of her long sentences something oddly tired and bored.

The white plates reflect back the light of the neon tubes. There's commotion in the background—a group of hotel guests are complaining because the telephone is down. They demand to be driven to the airport. The people on reception tell them the airport will be closed until further notice to all national and international flights. It was not possible to call a taxi, because naturally all taxi drivers were themselves subject to the citywide curfew.

"You don't need to tell me if you don't want," says the woman. "I just thought, from the way you were sharing your oranges with me, that I must have known you before, even though I suppose we have never met before and might never see each other again. Time isn't chronology, as people generally suppose. Time is the great everything-at-once, yesterday-today-tomorrow-always, if you know what I mean."

In the lobby, the commotion is settling down. People are returning to their rooms.

"This is my first visit here … I arrived the day before yesterday." He speaks very softly.

"On business?"

"My uncle lived here, for over fifty years … "

"I see! You're visiting your uncle! … "

"He died a few months ago … "

"And before that … I mean, while he was alive … did you never visit him? Or did you have a quarrel?"

"He came to me. Almost every year."

"I'm sorry, but … weren't you at all curious about his life, his place?"

Daniel does not reply.

"And now? Why are you here now," she continues, "now that he's dead?"

He remains silent.

"I've got time, a lot of time, thanks to the circumstances of this peculiar day. What am I to do? Sit in my room and ponder? Think about my husband? He died of a heart attack when he was just forty-nine. We were happy together, very happy, if I may say so."

She puts out a leg, her pointed knee touches his knee, as if by accident. Now she looks simultaneously pert, pretty and sad.

"Do I … remind you of anyone?"

He shakes his head.

"What's your star sign?" she asks.

"Sagittarius."

"Just like mine—December the eighth."

"What a coincidence—mine's the ninth."

She smiles contentedly. "You said your uncle passed away five months ago?"

"He was over ninety … " Loew is gathering up the breadcrumbs on his plate into a little pile the size of a fingernail. "What do you do … in Miami?"

"When my husband died, he left me enough money that I can live in comfort till I'm a hundred and fifty." Her half-embarrassed grin gives her a strangely sluttish air that Daniel hadn't noticed before. Her uneven teeth show like a small animal's, a marten's, maybe. "And you? What do you do?"

"I'm a poet."

"Can you live off that?"

"I live modestly," he says. From time to time he garners literary awards, most recently one called the Hildesheim Rosenstock, a very long-established prize, which is awarded by German industry every ten years. "My works have appeared in several languages. Also I translate plays from English into German. Just lately I've started teaching seminars in creative writing at an American University in Bristol, which is work that, to me, pays remarkably well."

"And where do you live?"

"In London."

" ... Alone?"

He gets up. "My wife is expecting our first child next year."

She looks down at the ground. "Well, I won't ask you any more questions."

He grips the back of his chair with both hands.

"You haven't told me your name—"

He tells it to her.

She nods appraisingly, as though the sound of his name separated him from other mortals. "And I'm ... " she seems for a fraction of a second to falter, "I'm ... Esther Moreno. Your uncle you were telling me about before ... " She hesitates again: "Oh, never mind ... It's none of my business really."

A waiter moving back and forth along the back wall of the dining room, like a wild cat in a cage, turns out the lights. He turns them on, then off again.

4

ALBACEA

O N HIS UNCLE'S NINETIETH BIRTHDAY, his nephew had decided to ignore Alexander's wish not to have any more telephone conversations. The celebrant was not happy: "I'd rather you wrote me a letter. What? Can't hear a word. I know it's my birthday, thank you very much! I'm deaf! Who? Oh, it's you! I'd much rather you wrote. Save yourself all that money you spend, finding out whether I'm still alive. Don't worry, I'm tough. If she can't feel my breath one morning, then Perpetua will see if my hands are still warm, because even in this monkey country they don't put you in the ground if your hands are still warm. Anyway, if I do kick off, I'm sure you'll be told soon enough … "

Since their last meeting, some years ago now, they had been corresponding once a month. Eight weeks after the ninetieth, the regular rhythm of letters stopped. Daniel waited another three weeks before deciding to ignore Stecher's pleas once more. After many rings, the housekeeper picked up. *"Muerte! Muerte!"* she wailed, repeated "Kershenbohm! Kershenbohm!" several times, impatient that he didn't know the name, and gave him a telephone number, where he would be told more.

"Hello?!" The voice of an old man.

"I'd like to speak to Mr Kershenbohm, please."

"Kirshman. Konrad Kirshman."

"Daniel Loew, I'm calling from Europe."

"You're the nephew of Alexander. We can speak German. I was his closest friend, for over fifty years. We cut a swathe through the whorehouses, your uncle and me, when he arrived in Caracas, back in December 'thirty-nine. That's something you don't forget! What can I do for you?"

"I wanted to know—"

"Whether you stand to inherit anything?!"

"No, when and how he died."

"Stroke. A week ago. He came back from hospital, routine check-up. And then it happened. He didn't suffer. My son Julio will tell you more. He's not here at the moment. Your uncle nominated him as his *albacea*. You know what that is?"

Daniel said he didn't.

"Executor. Call back next week, and then we'll have more news for you. You're the heir. But just before his death, Alexander changed his will. Now his housekeeper's to get the apartment, did you know that?"

"I think that's absolutely fine," announced Loew. "He was forever going on to me about how wonderful she was, and how he worried she might leave him one day … "

"You must be out of your mind? Well then, whatever, nephew of the late lamented Alexander … call back next week."

After the conversation was over, he was surprised never to have heard of Kirshman and son. His uncle had never mentioned the import-export business Kiba-Nova to him.

"In case anything happens to me, I'm going to leave you my current accounts plus securities held in the German Bank of Latin America in Hamburg, and in their branch in Panama City," it said in one of his uncle's letters two years before his death, a letter whose next sentence went on to rave about the intoxicating scent of a South American mountain grass that only flowered for four days of the year. "I'm going to leave you my current accounts plus securities held in the German Bank of Latin America in Hamburg, and in their branch in Panama City." That was it. And the heir had been content to leave it at that. That was enough detail. He didn't ask for any more information.

Eight days after the conversation with Konrad Kirshman, he called Caracas again.

"Ah, it's nice to hear from you, Papa told me about your conversation … Your uncle changed his will shortly before his death—the apartment is to go to *you*, and not Perpetua!"

"That's exactly the opposite of what your father told me a week ago."

"He's getting a bit old. The apartment is worth quite a bit. And in the late Alexander's account here in Caracas, on the day of his death, there were four hundred thousand bolivares, which is roughly six thousand dollars. Which you'll get as well. Any questions?" Julio's voice echoed on the line.

There was of course every chance that his relative had used up all his savings, as a consequence of his extended travels, and the numerous visits to hospitals and doctors that had become necessary in order to cope with a recalcitrant bowel condition. "Of late, I've had to undergo four operations and six stays in hospital," it said in one of Stecher Bravo's last letters, "which is not exactly an inexpensive hobby in this country. I really couldn't have anticipated this ridiculous inflation. Just imagine—my car insurance has gone up sevenfold from last year. *Time Magazine* was just one bolivar not so long ago, now it's an incredible sixty. It's so extreme that I'm unable to protect myself against it. Well, I suppose I do have the comfort of not being immortal."

"Hey!? You still there?" Julio called into the telephone.

Daniel's heart was thumping. "Do you have any information about his bank accounts? … "

"What bank accounts?"

He took a deep breath. Then resumed: "Well, in Hamburg, for one … do you have any knowledge of that?"

"Hamburg?!"

"That was the one thing that Alexander dinned into me from when I was thirteen years old, from my bar mitzvah, I was to be sure to remember that in case, God forbid, anything ever happened to him—"

"Don't worry. We own an eight-storey building here full of merchandise, we really don't need his money. Now if you'd been lumped with an executor who was hard up, then you wouldn't have seen a penny! He'd have pocketed the lot, you can bet on

35

that! I just have to pay for the funeral, and his housekeeper and one or two outstanding bills. The rest is yours!"

"It seems to me that Perpetua should be treated a little more generously," Daniel demurred, "especially as the apartment—"

But Julio had already hung up.

On the assumption his uncle's friends knew as little of him as he did of them, the heir sent an express letter to Caracas, to Kirshman and son, to introduce himself to them a little more:

Dear Kirshmans, how happy I am to have spoken to Julio on the telephone today! I can sense that Alexander has chosen the right man to be his albacea. As you may know, my uncle had no relatives beyond my father and me. My father in turn has no relatives except Alexander and me, the rest of his family died in the war. He is a struggling architect, barely able to feed his family. Alexander used to make fun of my father (did he do this with you, I wonder?), disliked the few buildings he did manage to put up in the course of his career. My mother comes from Vienna, almost all her relatives were also put to death in concentration camps. My wife, Valeria, is a clothes designer. We have been living in London for the last few years, in the house of an Austrian émigrée, at a very low rent, I am happy to say. Should you be at all interested, I would be only too happy to send you one or other of my books. I am very grateful to Alexander for leaving me something. I'm sure he's done the right thing, in entrusting you with the responsibility for it. I send you both my very best wishes …

5

ROOM 1813

E STHER MORENO IS LYING ON THE COVERLET of her unmade double bed. The day after the coup the maids at the El Presidente have failed to show up for work.

"Your wife may have heard the news, and she may be worrying about you. You ought to give her a call."

Room 1813 looks over the other part of the city. After they left the dining room together, the unknown woman suggested that Loew go with her. He hesitated. She persuaded him. He is standing by the window, looking down at the swimming pool. A breeze gets up, and tousles the palm trees. A quiet wail of sirens rises from the depths.

She picks up the telephone, and, for the umpteenth time, presses the number nine, to try and get a line. "Dead. Nothing at all ... It's very disconcerting, your way of standing there." She throws off her shoes. Perfectly straight toes shimmer through her silvery tights. Not bent, he thinks, the way they are with so many women over the age of forty. She slips off her jacket. Through the silk blouse, he can make out the mild curve of her bosom.

Every sentence he speaks, every word she says, every movement of his body, every stirring of hers, adds to the number of threads binding him to the room, and the woman. He is getting tangled up in Esther Moreno's presence.

"I should say you're ... what? Mid-thirties? Your behaviour, this afternoon, at any rate, was more like a seventeen-year-old kid's."

He pulls up a chair, not far from the edge of the bed.

37

"My people are from Poland." Esther is looking past him, now that he's finally agreed to sit down. "They survived Treblinka. After the war, they emigrated here. I was born not long after, in Caracas." The telephone rings. She picks up. "The lines are open again," she says then. "You can call anyone you like. The porter says the situation's worsened. The curfew's been extended at least to tomorrow evening … "

Daniel doesn't want to call in the woman's presence. He tells her he will call home later, from his room.

Esther insists that he call his wife from room 1813: "That way you won't have to pay for it, stay here. I'll give you some privacy."

He declines. She gets off the bed, stalks out of the room. He calls home.

"I've called you ten times," Valeria's voice sounds upset. "The hotel answered each time. It's nonsense to say the lines are down. They put me through to your room each time. You didn't answer. Where have you been the whole time?"

He flicks through the passport he finds on the bedside table. The Venezuelan document gives the date of birth of Señora Moreno, Esther, as the fifteenth of August, which is his mother's birthday, not the eighth of December.

"What's going on?" asks Valeria, on the other side of the world.

"I went swimming, and I've just now got back to my room." There was a curfew, and he wasn't seeing or talking to anyone. "I'm sorry I left you with no news for twenty-four hours." He asks her to call his mother for him: "Tell her I'm safe. Nothing else really matters."

"I will definitely not call her." She brings the conversation to an abrupt close.

Esther enters the room. "You could have told her you've met someone who said it was all right for you to call from her room? That you accepted the offer, in order to save a little money. What century are we living in? Can't people be open with one another? Why is everything always automatically shrouded in lies and more lies?"

He walks out of room 1813 without a word. Pads along endless, thickly carpeted corridors. When he pushes the button in the lift, he receives a violent electric shock. Riding down from the eighteenth floor to the twelfth, he takes his left hand in his right, and solemnly promises himself to ignore Esther Moreno should he run into her again, whether in the lobby, the restaurant, or the swimming pool.

He turns on the television: "Soldiers closed one of the capital's main streets, to deactivate bombs dropped in the morning when rebel aircraft attacked the presidential palace … "

There's a knock on the door.

" … and other strategic sites in Carac—" He cuts the volume, stands completely still in the middle of the room.

More knocking. "I'm sorry. I didn't mean to upset you. I think I can help you … "

The phone rings. She was not one, his mother says, to share her daughter-in-law's concern for his safety. "But what are you doing there, what possessed you even to go there? Is it on account of Alexander? But he's dead."

Before his departure, he told his mother the Austrian Cultural Institute had invited him to give a reading from his works. Now he repeats the claim.

"Don't lie to me—there's been no such institute in Caracas for years. You've gone to collect your inheritance, and you don't want to tell me about it."

He puts down the receiver.

"I promise you I won't offend or upset you again". Daniel hears Esther whisper. "Please let me in."

A minute later, he's looking through the peephole.

She's walking, head down, back towards the lifts.

He opens the door. "Come on then," he whispers.

She sits down on the edge of the bed, bolt upright, hands folded in her lap. "You ought to confide in me. What have you got to lose? Tell me your story. I'm experienced, I know a bit about life. I can give you good advice. Trust me. It's not in your nature to try and keep things secret. You want to share, give yourself, open yourself to others, don't you. A Sagittarian … "

"When did you say your birthday was?"

"How could you have forgotten that so quickly?"

39

6

SIMONE VON OELFFEN

T WO MONTHS AFTER STECHER BRAVO'S DEATH, Daniel's repeated questions concerning the accounts in Hamburg and Panama were still unanswered. All that had happened was that Julio had sent the nephew a photocopy of the will, in which it was declared that Loew was indeed sole beneficiary. Somewhere, there was a sub-clause to the effect that he was entitled to all the property that the uncle had accumulated *in Venezuela*. That, the executor surmised, was Stecher's way of implying either that there was no property outside Venezuela, or, in the surprising eventuality of there being such property, then it would not fall to the nephew. He requested full mandatory powers, to enable him to close the Caracas account in his name, and, further, to put Alexander's apartment up for sale, again on his behalf. "Otherwise, you'll have to come over, and I don't expect you want to do that. Let's try and save you the bother."

Rather than giving Kirshman the desired powers of attorney right away, he decided to wait and see whether he might not come up with some information regarding holdings in Hamburg and Panama first. Once more, several weeks passed. There was no more information forthcoming from Julio. Then, one day, it was a mild autumn afternoon, he decided to get in touch with Stecher Bravo's Hamburg bank directly. That day he had managed to compose a few lines, sitting on a park bench on Hampstead Heath, that he was pretty pleased with. On his way home, passing the small post office on South End Road, he watched a young beggar playing a broken recorder, and getting only one very high note out of it. ("Never give to a beggar!" Alexander had always enjoined him. "With us, in Caracas, the beggars have the most money of anyone.")

His heart beat harder than usual. He stepped inside the post office. He succeeded in getting a number for the headquarters of the German Bank of Latin America. Presuming he wouldn't be given any information over the telephone, he nevertheless dialled the number, and asked to be put through to the bank's legal department. He was, he explained, the nearest relative to a man who had been a good customer of the bank, who had died three months before, and had made him his sole heir.

"The name of the party in question, please?"

"Alexander Stecher Bravo."

"One moment." And then, after a silence. "The account was active till the beginning of July this year. When was it that your relative died?"

"The twenty-eighth of June."

"Someone with bank clearance closed the account on July the third."

He reacted with incredulity as never before in his life. His suspicion fell on a family living outside Hanover, of whom Stecher had often told him, descendants of the owners of a cotton and industrial garment factory. Johann Stecher, Alexander's father, had from his youth worked as a representative for the well-known North German firm of Nischen & Abel. Following the death of his father, Alexander had been a trainee in the textile industry, and had finally succeeded his father as a representative for the very same firm. Even though Jews were no longer allowed to work for Aryan firms after the mid-Thirties, the behaviour of Nischen & Abel was exemplary. They helped Alexander, his mother and his brother to leave for France, and were instrumental in Stecher's subsequent emigration for Latin America. Out of gratitude, his uncle had, each time he was in Europe, made a point of visiting the children and grandchildren of the Nischen brothers. Each time, Daniel responded with jealousy and anger when Alexander announced: I'm on my way to Gutersloh, to see the Nischens!

"Well, I suppose that's the end of it. Thank you for telling me … "

"You shouldn't resign yourself to it so readily, Herr Loew, if you are the heir!"

An employee of a German bank, a lawyer, someone he had never met, allowed herself to exhort him not to abandon his pursuit, merely from the sound of his voice on the telephone?

"Well, I mean … Is it worth it? … " He was loath to say more.

"What do you mean?"

He forced himself to say: "Is the sum in question … large?"

"I'm afraid I'm unable to give you any information about that over the phone." And, after a pause, she went on: "Aren't you curious to learn who it was who collected the money?"

"Are you allowed to give me the name?"

"Well, maybe a little hint will help you. It was a gentleman from South America. He came with power of attorney."

The news spun round his head. He could feel the ground rolling under his feet in the phone booth. At the very time he had first spoken to Konrad Kirshman, his son was already in Europe, plundering Alexander's Hamburg account.

"Herr Loew?"

He could not speak.

"Come and see us in person. Bring a copy of the will with you. And your passport. I'll help you if I can … "

He rang Caracas from the same booth. Kirshman and son, he was told, were on an extended business tour of the Venezuelan provinces.

Simone von Oelffen received him in a mahogany-panelled conference room on the ground floor of the German Bank of Latin America. The lawyer wore her long blonde hair braided in a plait. She had light-blue eyes. As soon as she began to speak, he sensed that she was driven by a sense of adventure. He was sure he saw a spirit of fight flickering up below the professional discretion. She had spent some time in Sao Paolo, been unhappily married, and had travelled extensively through Latin America. She saw in Julio Kirshman's conduct a pattern she had

43

often seen in Colombia, Chile, Argentina, Paraguay, Venezuela, Brazil: "Deception. Lies. Fraud. Bribery. Corrupt states, corrupt men. The few exceptions merely confirm the rule. Justice? There isn't any. The whole continent is corrupt to the bone. Whoever pays the biggest bribes wins. No matter who has right on his side."

She set a document before him that showed quite unambiguously that at the beginning of July this year Julio Kirshman had withdrawn one hundred and five thousand marks from Alexander's security account. The spidery threads of the figures trembled in front of Daniel's eyes. The balance on the day of his death was much smaller than the imaginary fortune he had seen in his mind's eye for decades. He was quite stunned.

"Herr Kirshman was not acting altogether unlawfully." Frau von Oelffen moved her tapering fingers over the papers that were spread out before them. "He had a general power of attorney vested in him by your uncle, you see, here—Stecher's signature. On the other hand, such a power is of course not valid beyond death, Kirshman was duty bound to inform us of the death of your uncle. In his role as executor he is under obligation to inform you of each one of his steps, and then to make the moneys under his supervision available to you immediately."

"My uncle wrote to me a few years ago … " it wasn't easy for him to continue, "that he also … had an account in a branch of yours … in Panama City. Would you be able to tell me anything about that?"

Frau von Oelffen's eyes lit up. It was as though he had lifted the lid of a treasure chest in her presence. "I'll certainly see what I can do. Will you come and see me this evening. At home. I can't speak to you here … not as freely as I should like. If you see what I mean." She pushed a piece of paper with her address across to him.

He had the knack of winning people over right away by his shy, and yet intense manner. He did it without any particular effort, with his open, smiling expression, and he was courteous, a trait that was especially effective with women.

A few hours later, he was standing in Frau von Oelffen's whitewashed terraced house in Teufelsbrück, where she lived alone. It was dark outside. On the wide Elbe diesel barges puttered by. The window had a view of the river. He saw a little beer garden next door, with white plastic chairs and tables. Every so often, a large plane landing or taking off filled the apartment with noise; in the immediate vicinity was a factory of the Airbus Consortium—the next biggest, in fact, after its headquarters in Toulouse. Prototype jets undertook test flights over Teufelsbrück and Simone von Oelffen's house, even late into the night.

She had cooked dinner—octopus in red curry sauce, served with an Argentine Cabernet Sauvignon. Daniel spread a large, snow-white linen napkin over his knees.

"I've been thinking about your case," she began. "You must go to Caracas in person, to oversee the selling of the apartment there, the one you mentioned to me earlier. You can on no account leave Kirshman general powers of attorney, otherwise he will sell the apartment dishonestly, and keep at least half the profit for himself. You need to take charge."

He didn't have the money, he replied, to hang around in Caracas for weeks. Nor could he leave his desk for so long.

She insisted: "It could be an important experience for you as a poet—the foreign land, the inscrutable behaviour of an executor. Please! I admit we in Hamburg have little notion of what a poet's life is like—this is a hard-headed city, people who have chosen a path for themselves that doesn't ensure a comfortable living will always meet with incomprehension. Even so, I think I can guess what being a poet may feel like, may look like ... The first step, which we take tomorrow will be to open an account in your name. You ask Kirshman for the return of the one hundred and five thousand marks he has taken from you. And you give him the number of your account, so he can transfer the money back to you."

Now, after two glasses of wine, it seemed easy enough to approach his main object: "What about Panama? Were you able to find out anything about Panama?"

45

She looked over to the window. A narrow passenger steamer was throwing up a little wake. Had she not heard his question?

"I guess you weren't able to."

"Your uncle had several accounts in Panama, as I was able to discover from my documents." She spoke slowly, with a certain formality. " … All of them numbered accounts. As you may or may not know, there is the strictest confidentiality in Panamanian banking. Much stricter than, say, in Switzerland. If I were to lift the least little veil, I'd be out of my job tomorrow. Until you've gone before a court in Venezuela or Panama, and had your title as heir approved, there's nothing to be done. The law is the law."

Never before in his life had he felt as money-drunk, wealth-hungry, fortune-crazed as on that October evening in Hamburg. "I should like to … let me … " he stammered, "I should very much like to … repay you in some way … see that I can—"

"Go to Caracas. First, try coming to some amicable agreement with Kirshman. Do not antagonise him, otherwise he'll avenge himself on you. I know the type, believe me. You must on no account cross or anger him prematurely. Sell the apartment while you're there, don't leave that to him. As soon as that's done, mention Panama. On no account any sooner, otherwise he'll obstruct you. And then we'll see."

After dessert, she asked her guest to sit with her on the green sofa. Before he knew what was happening, her hand was in his. Her cold fingers were rubbing against his palm. Her black clothes had a smell that reminded him of cleaning rags during his school days, the ones used to erase the blackboard—sourish, and stale damp. Simone was trembling all over. She pressed herself against him, communicated her trembling to him, his chest, his belly. Her hand crept around his waist. On the bridge of her nose he made out a tiny, purple blue vein that bothered him strangely.

He held her tight round her shoulders, stroked her upper arms, her back, her neck, her earlobes. And stood up. Went back to the table, emptied his glass, filled it up again. "Please don't be upset with me. It's just that I don't want to … hurt you … " he managed to say.

46

Then, a little later, she whispered: "You're so incredibly tender to me, Daniel. Will you stay with me? I promise to leave you alone … "

He stayed in her house, on the guest bed. As soon as Simone guessed he was asleep, she positioned herself in the doorway, and watched every one of his breaths.

The next morning, Daniel accompanied his host into the city. They said goodbye at a safe distance from the bank building, in a drafty tunnel of the Jungfernstieg subway station. Simone's colleagues weren't to observe them together. Half-an-hour later, Loew entered the German Bank of Latin America, made his way to Frau von Oelffen's office, and there, in the presence of her secretary, and without exchanging a single word of a private nature with her, opened an account in his own name.

Right next door to the bank's white façade is the Hotel Vier Jahreszeiten. After leaving the bank, he sat down in the hotel lobby. (Some thirty years before, he had once stayed there with his parents. For a while, his father must have had a little money. Daniel often remembered, a little mournfully, those moments in his childhood when Jacob Loew had struck him as relatively carefree, as he had then, when he spent the earnings for designing an H-form high-rise block in the Viennese working-class district of Favoriten in seemingly no time at all.)

On a sheet of handmade paper, which he had asked for at the reception of the Vier Jahreszeiten, he wrote out a memo to Kirshman:

Have this morning opened an account at the German Bank of Latin America, Neuer Jungfernstieg 16, Hamburg. Number of account is 495-190. I request that you transfer the sum of DM 105,250 (one hundred and five thousand two hundred and fifty German Marks) back to me IMMEDIATELY. If you should have any questions, please ask the bank's legal adviser Frau Simone von Oelffen. She is informed about everything. Further, I ask you urgently to tell me why you withdrew the above sum on 3rd July this year, from the account of Stecher Bravo, when it should have been mine? And why, in spite of repeated questions from me concerning Hamburg, did you never tell me you had long ago closed that account? I am sure you have an explanation for these circumstances, which otherwise I am at a loss to understand. I send you and your father my cordial greetings, and trust that the said sum will be transferred back to me as soon as possible.

He asked a member of the hotel staff to fax the note to Caracas, paid a staggering sum for the service. He folded the sheet in an envelope, and took it to the nearby post office on the Gänsemarkt, where he also sent it registered delivery.

He had four hours till his night train left for London. A few minutes after five o'clock a taxi set him down at the main entrance of the Portuguese Sephardic Cemetery on the Konigstrasse in Altona. A rusty sign on the fence announced that the day's opening hours ended at five o'clock. Thick chains barred the entrance. He could see no warden's hut. An ancient woman passing raised her stick at him: " … 's shut. Has been for ages. G'night." He looked for an unobserved spot, waited in case anyone came by, and then scrambled over the fence. The high barbed wire seemed to offer him little resistance.

In the cemetery, bushes, trees and grasses were flourishing as if in a hothouse, though the leaves had already taken on autumnal colours. It grew dark. Years ago, Stecher Bravo had once taken him to the grave of their legendary forefather Yehuda Mordechai Cassuto. Daniel thought he could remember the way to it. Alexander's great-grandfather on his mother's side was a highly respected rabbi, a zaddik, a wise man of whom, a century after his death, people still spoke with reverence. Loew stumbled, fell on a gravestone and cut his elbow. Trod on broken stones. The weeds and shrubs grew up to his belly. The birch trees and the tablets with the names of the dead glimmered a whitish grey. He got more and more lost the darker it got, and the further he ventured into the overgrown park. He stopped in the thicket, tossed fragments of the Kaddish to the air: "*Yisgadal weyiskadasch, schemei raba*," he cried out, " … In his greatness and holiness may be recognised the great name of God in the world that he created according to his will … " It was all he could remember. It had grown very dark—there was no moon. He shivered. He directed

48

his words towards the heart of the cemetery, where he supposed the grave to lie: "Yehuda Mordechai Cassuto, teacher, rabbi, forebear! I am unable to find your resting place. I, Daniel Loew, your descendant, beseech you—help me to gain the inheritance of your great-grandson."

7

FIRST AID

"I CAN'T BEAR IT IN THESE STUFFY ROOMS ANY MORE." Esther Moreno heads in the direction of the door. "The ceiling's going to fall on my head. If only I could open the window!"

It's three in the afternoon. He suggests a stroll in the hotel grounds, and up and down along the side of the pool. They make their way along the unlit basement passage. Esther slips her hand between his chest and upper arm. They emerge into the daylight. They come upon a ring of people surrounding three half-naked men lying on sun-loungers adapted to emergency beds. A group of hotel guests are administering first aid. Fine traces of blood form on the stone slabs. The wounded are soldiers loyal to the government, a room-service waiter reports, who were lured into an ambush near the hotel, and wounded. The rebels killed their commander. The three survivors managed to crawl as far as the grounds of the El Presidente, where a guest discovered them a few moments ago, by the garden fence. An ambulance was called right away, but in the circumstances it might take a while to arrive. Since the morning, there have been numerous such incidents all over the city. The youngest of the three unconscious men has lost a lot of blood. He is fighting for his life.

Wherever there were more than three or four gathered together, from childhood on, Daniel had felt the desire to join in, watch and listen. Esther tugs at his shirt, pulls him away, past the parrot cage and on into the heart of the park. Near the tennis court with its reddish clay surface, there are some stone seats. They sit down. He feels the cool of the stone through the thin material of his light trousers. And, quite abruptly, yields to the desire of his chance acquaintance—he plays, in fact, a game of chance. As though he had the choice between red and black, or odd and even numbers, the choice of whether to confide in Esther Moreno or not. And he does. Records his arrival in Caracas, and his first meeting with Kirshman and son. He tells her about visiting the apartment in San Bernardino, and about Perpetua. He describes his journey to Simone von Oelffen, even his search for the tomb of Yehuda Mordechai Cassuto is not left out.

Esther lays her hand on his: "But you don't look at all Jewish! … " It was not the first time he had heard that. He wanted to pass for a Christian among Christians, but also to be recognised by his own people as one of their tribe. If he was forced to give away his origins, his people almost always reacted by thinking of him as a *Ger*, a convert to Judaism.

"But why didn't you tell me right away? Then we could be so much more open with each other." The woman strokes his hair. "Isn't it a delightful chance that we met?"

To his chance acquaintance, he fills in the course of the past six weeks, between the pilfering of his Hamburg account and his arrival in Caracas, two days before. While Julio had first promised to return the money right away, he wrote to the heir two weeks later:

In his will, the late lamented Sasha only mentioned property in Venezuela. He wanted me to have the Hamburg money, and not you, otherwise he would have mentioned Hamburg in his will. Show me the will that Alexander sent you, and the passage in it that gives you the right to Hamburg. I'd like to see it.

There was no such second will. Stecher Bravo had only once, in one letter, told his nephew of his accounts in Hamburg and Panama.

"But now you've met him," interjects Esther Moreno. "And … were you able to agree something with him?"

"I met a lawyer yesterday. I can only hope that Dr Johannes will be able to help."

"But didn't that … Kirshman … give back what he took from

you?!" She picks up a dried palm frond, and fans herself with it. "I think money stories are so exciting, don't you? There's nothing in the world as sexy as money!"

Ambulance personnel run past them. From close up, shielded by leaves, they watch the injured being taken away. "Getting in touch with a lawyer in your position doesn't seem to me the most sensible way to go necessarily. It might be cleverer to see the man I've asked to help me with my difficulties with my apartment," says Esther Moreno. "I've known him since the time when I was living here: the *arbitraje*, the senior arbiter of the Jewish community in Venezuela. He's much more reliable than the Chief Rabbi of Caracas, who has the reputation of being thoroughly corrupt. You will tell Francisco Shatil everything you've told me. And he will summon Kirshman, hear what he says, and then come to a decision, to which your opponent will have to agree, if he's not to be expelled from the community. We can ask Señor Shatil to come to you as soon as the curfew's lifted. If all goes well, you can give me a little bit of your share one day. Of course you don't have to do that, unless you want to; but I think you ought to offer Shatil ten per cent in any case, I mean that's obvious. Ten per cent of the sum at issue, if he's able to help you."

8

RED MEAT

O N THE SECOND DAY OF HIS STAY IN CARACAS, the day before the military coup, Daniel found his way to the Kiba-Nova offices at eleven in the morning. Two employees showed him to a small office on the second floor. They asked him to wait, Señor Kirshman would be along any moment.

A little later, a young, somehow equally bashful and arrogant-seeming woman came in and shook his hand: "Monica da Silva."

"She's my lawyer," Julio followed her in, with a friendly smile. "Now listen closely, my dear fellow. I want you to sign this document, which will allow us to wind up Alexander's account here in Caracas. Will you give me your passport? I need to take a copy of it. Thanks. You know, you shouldn't carry your passport around like that, passports like yours are just exactly what our gangsters love to take. Why don't you leave it here in my safe until you go? Have you any idea how often your uncle was robbed by pickpockets! Or me, I tell you, it's more often than I can say."

The lawyer opened his passport flat against the glass plate of a photocopying machine.

"Why the three copies, that's what you're asking yourself, am I right or am I right? Well, one's for the court, one's for the lawyer and one's for me, we all need to have one, right?"

Daniel took back his passport. Signed the paper that was put in front of him, it was to do with a savings book of Stecher Bravo's with a bank in Caracas, current balance estimated at six thousand eight hundred dollars.

"Was there anything else to discuss? Believe me, the sale of the apartment is going to be a real headache. I'm sure we'll be kept waiting for ages while the tribunal decides how much tax you'll have to pay on it." Monica da Silva nodded earnestly. "We'll have to slip the court people a little something, otherwise they'll just let it lie for months, what am I saying, for *years* … " He allowed a moment to elapse. As he went out, he murmured: "Is that it, then?"

Loew thought the manner of Kirshman's question was humorous, so he replied lightly himself: "Oh, we just need to clear up the business of the Hamburg money that you still owe me."

Julio puffed out his chest, and called, as if for a dog: "Gabriel Miranda!" whereupon a slight man of middle age, who had been listening and waiting quietly outside the door, stepped in.

"My number two lawyer," explained Kirshman, and then for the benefit of the sweat-soaked lawyer put on the charade of only just having heard of alleged events in Hamburg. Thereupon, not without talent, Gabriel Miranda played the role of the surprised, inflexible legal adviser.

"Well now," the executor resumed, "what my advisers tell me is that Hamburg isn't mentioned in your uncle's last will. As I wrote you a month ago, then, it's all for me. That's the way your uncle wanted it, and he told me so often enough. But listen, I'm not a monster. I'll split it with you, I'll even go fifty-fifty. You're not to think the late lamented Sasha's friends want to keep it all back for themselves. You'll get your slice too."

From childhood on, whenever Daniel felt himself the victim of an injustice, his habitual reaction was silence. Outbursts of rage were not in his nature. He would have appeared to himself like an actor if he had given vent to his feelings in the Kiba-Nova offices with loud shouts of pain. He simply said, "You know you're wrong. Alexander told me about his bank account in Hamburg from when I was thirteen years old."

Julio smirked. And the executor's skewed smile finally goaded Alexander's nephew into error, into the uneven, unpredictable terrain he had wanted above all to leave untouched for now.

"What about Panama?" he yelled (how shrill the words suddenly sounded!). "What about Panama, you, you … You must be out of your mind, Julio Kirshman, he told me about the Panamanian accounts in his letters of the last years time and time again, and every time we saw each other, he told me! … "

Only mention Panama, Frau von Oelffen had sternly urged him, once the first few steps have been irrevocably taken. Listen to me—I've been around in these places, I know what they're like.

The executor was struggling for breath. He had suddenly turned very pale. "But you don't know anything about Panama!" he blurted out. "He never told you that! That was just between Sascha and me! That was never anything to do with you, never!" The bare walls echoed like steel. "You can't know about that. Unless the woman in the bank in Hamburg blabbed to you! Curse that damned woman!"

"It's not from her that I got the information."

"Well, who else could it have been? Not Sascha!" The lawyers shot meaningful glances at their client. He should come to his senses. And, just as quickly as he had exploded, he got a grip on himself again. "All right. Calm down. You'll be staying an extra couple of days, we'll sort it all out together, the pair of us. Feeling hungry at all? What about a bite of lunch together, the two of us? Come back in an hour. I'll treat you. Wait, before you go—leave your passport, you'll only get it nicked!"

Loew handed it to Kirshman. It was probably advisable at this point to give Julio a signal that he trusted him, to quell his panic.

Julio opened the safe, pushed his visitor's papers in it, and locked up the complicated security system of the steel chamber.

Daniel walked through the narrow lanes around the company premises, feeling strange and dizzy, as though slightly anaesthetised. The day before, all had been quiet here, but this Monday blue-uniformed postmen kept crossing his path, market vendors were flogging window-cleaning sprays, a little boy staggered along in front of him, with long, straggly hair, clearly blind drunk. A shoe-seller kept calling: "*Rápidamente! Rápidamente!*

Rápidamente!" An ancient crone was trying to sell a grey wool carpet, holey, used, and stinking of mothballs.

He found himself in front of the massive cathedral, which seemed to pulsate in the heat. Next to it the equestrian statue of Simon Bolivar, the hero of the nation, the son of the city of Caracas, the victor over the Spanish conquistadores, the liberator of Venezuela, Colombia, Ecuador, Peru and Panama, the founder of Bolivia, the man whose courage and resolve had inspired Loew to write one of his earliest poems—surging and grandiloquent in his early style. It was his uncle who had got him to write it: "Compose a hymn for him, an ode, a ballad! And make it rhyme. A good poem rhymes."

There was a phone booth in the shade of Bolivar. He had asked the hotel porter to write down the number of the Austrian Consulate for him, now he went through all his pockets looking for the piece of paper. If he couldn't come to an agreement with Kirshman, Plan B was to involve the embassy. He finally found the crumpled scrap in his breast pocket, so sweated through he could barely read it. He dialled the number, just as the deafening pealing of the midday bells filled the whole city centre.

When the ringing finally stopped, he called the consulate again. A female assistant of the Consul's, who was just out of the country, put him on to a man trusted by the Embassy; Dr Friedrich Johannes handled work for them from time to time, she told him.

They made an appointment for the following afternoon.

Back in the company building, he encountered Kirshman and son at the desk that dominated the ground floor room like a fortress a small town. They were stowing money into deep drawers— banknotes in one, bundles of cheques in another, discussing blank acceptances and debentures. There was talk of the expected remittance from a metal-working business in Bogota, which, it was hoped, would arrive denominated in dollars, and not in Colombian pesos.

How Daniel was startled to hear Kirshman and son conversing not in Spanish, but in German. In the language of my poetry, he thought, of my work, of my seeking after word and sentence, rhythm and melody! Almost sixty years had passed since Konrad Kirshman had first set foot on Venezuelan soil, having fled from Speyer on the Rhine in October 1934, but he had remained loyal to his mother tongue, had brought up his son speaking German, hardly ever used Spanish with him. They were discussing what form of care Julio's mother should have. Kirshman senior had decided to book her into a home on the southern edge of the city.

"Mama should have someone who's there for her, round the clock!" his son disagreed.

"Come on, she doesn't know her own name!"

"I want her to stay at home, among her own things! And someone should come in and look after her."

"Home care's twice as expensive, come on, son, you know how it is!"

"She needs her own familiar surroundings. Her kitchen, her bed, her chair. Leave her where she is!"

"That's all very well for you to say, but you don't have to live with her!" Konrad coughed violently, and went purple.

Just then Julio became aware of Loew's presence. "So there you are already! Come on, let's go. Papa, you stay here."

They sat facing one another in a small Argentinean steak restaurant not far from the company. Over their heads dangled copper pots and pans of all sizes.

"You know," Julio began, "when I was a boy I was lazy. Self-satisfied and lazy. My father wasn't happy about that. And as I didn't show any signs of changing, he packed me off to the US—to a military academy. Westminster, Maryland. That's where they made a man of me. And from that time, I haven't let anyone kick me around. Since then, I've been my own boss. And Papa's happy. What will you have? Medium? Rare? Well-done?"

A small old waiter, who in the nineteen-fifties had been a reasonably successful jockey, so Daniel learnt, took down: two filet steaks, medium rare.

59

"In other words, after your return from Maryland you could show your father," Loew put in, "that you're a man. In business matters as well. Suddenly you were just as capable as he had always been. If not more so! ... "

"That's right, wise guy!" Julio smacked the table with the flat of his hand. "You know, nine months of the year I'm on the road, selling our merchandise in the countryside and in provincial cities and villages where I don't have Papa on my back the whole time, that would be insufferable. So I'm away a lot, which is good for me. We couldn't give up our business, even if we wanted to, it comes along after us. The wholesalers in the five major cities are dependent on our merchandise from Caracas. But now Mama's ill, you heard, she doesn't know if she's coming or going, can't tell noon from night. And Papa's just not up to dealing with it, I mean you've seen him, you know what he's like."

"Do you have any brothers or sisters, Julio?"

"That's all I need!"

"How old are your children?"

"Nine, five and three."

"I'd like to ... meet them."

"And so you shall, so you shall. Only you're not to forget ever that I had power of attorney. If I'd wanted, you would never have gotten a thing! If you'd had a poor *albacea*, you'd have come away empty-handed. And you need to remember too that there was another will, eight or nine years ago. In that one, there was no mention of you. It was *me* that got Sascha to change his testament, in your favour! Now tomorrow morning you come to me in the office, nine, half-nine-ish, and we'll hammer the whole thing out. What do you reckon?"

Back in the El Presidente, Daniel called the Austrian embassy's lawyer, Dr Friedrich Johannes, again. Asked him to move their appointment forward to this evening. In the morning, Kirshman would, he presumed, lay before him documents to sign that, as far as he was concerned anyway, would finally settle the issues relating to Hamburg, Panama and the sale of the apartment. It seemed advisable therefore to him to get in an expert opinion first.

"Do you like fondue bourguignon?" asked the lawyer.

"I can't eat meat twice a day."

"I'm almost a vegetarian myself, though I do have a weakness for fondue. If I'm to see you, I'll have to cancel two other appointments. So give me a simple answer—yes or no."

"I have to see you."

"Eight o'clock. The Le Chalet is only a few yards from your hotel."

Dr Friedrich Johannes had the bearing of a politician. He wore a dark-blue three piece suit, and a green tie with orange stripes. He was fifty, perhaps a little older.

Red cubes of meat, on short metal skewers, were sizzling away in the oil pan.

"Don't be offended," the lawyer interrupted Daniel's account of an early childhood memory of the Golden Gate Bridge in San Francisco, "autobiographical details are not at issue here. I'd have nothing against exchanging personal information with you, once we've known each other for a few years. But for now it's enough if you tell me the contents of the case … "

Loew was offended. It seemed far from unimportant to him to tell this man something of himself and the facts of his life, before setting out the case.

"Were you born in Germany?" he asked Dr Johannes.

"I'm a Chilean, sir. Born in Santiago. My mother was a refugee from the Nazis, in Chile she met my father, who was a Christian from Heidelberg, who had immigrated to Latin America a few years before the debacle. If you're not happy with me, you're welcome to look for someone else. There are thousands of lawyers in this town."

"Alexander Stecher Bravo was the son of a Jewess and a German Christian. That connection between the two of you makes you in my eyes the more suitable to advise me and, if need be, to represent me in court."

"Well, that's an artist's way of looking at things. It wouldn't necessarily be mine. But let's not argue about that. Tell me. Plain and simple. Just the facts, please. No emotion."

No sooner had Loew finished summarising the facts, as far as his meeting with Julio earlier that day, than Dr Johannes leant forward, as though to make certain of not being heard by anyone except his vis-à-vis: "What sort of sums are we talking about with these Panamanian accounts?"

"I don't know."

"What's that?"

"I don't know."

"Your uncle … your father's first cousin … he never told you how much he was going to leave you?"

Daniel shook his head.

The lawyer leant back in his chair, pulled a perfectly pressed grey handkerchief out of his pocket, and mopped his brow. "Well, I won't thrust my services upon you. Apart from everything else, having a legal adviser is an expensive pursuit. From what you've told me, you don't seem to be exactly loaded. I charge two hundred dollars an hour. Plus fifteen per cent of the total, if you win. I can only tell you—the man's cheating you."

"Kirshman and son were Stecher Bravo's closest friends."

"You tell me your uncle never mentioned them to you, ever. How can you explain that inconsistency? And why did Stecher never shed any light on his financial arrangements with you, while evidently keeping Kirshman informed of his every step?"

A pause ensued.

"I suppose," said Loew, and then again hesitated, "I suppose he didn't want me to depend entirely on what he was going to leave me. I was to make my own way in life, go into a profession, not bank on my inheritance."

"But then, if I may say so, he would hardly have whetted your appetite on these sums from when you were twelve or thirteen years old. You know, after all you've told me, I'm hardly surprised Kirshman's tried to lead you up the garden path. The first letter you sent him, in which you had the goodness to tell him how badly off you were—you couldn't have done anything more harmful to your cause. It's as if you'd lain down and waggled your legs in the air like a dying beetle. Instead of creating the impression that he was dealing with a man of influence like himself, you tipped him off that you were pretty

62

much someone struggling for existence."

The meal in the expensive fondue restaurant, half of which they left, Daniel paid for with a credit card from an English bank, to which he was heavily in debt. His hotel bill at the El Presidente he planned to pay from the same smoke-and-mirrors source.

"Thank God—you must at least have a bit of money, otherwise you couldn't have afforded to take me out to such a meal, nor could you pay for a hotel like that. If you want to take me up on my offer of services, let me know. Go and see Kirshman in his office tomorrow morning, as agreed, let him show you what he has. Don't sign anything he gives you. Tell him you've instructed a lawyer. That will take him aback. I'm convinced of that. He doesn't think you're capable of such a step, after all the grievous mistakes you've made thus far."

Dr Johannes walked him as far as the hotel's revolving doors. "One more piece of advice," he said as he was leaving. "Don't discuss your case with anyone. I've learned from experience— the Devil never sleeps."

Early the following morning, the city of Caracas and its immediate environs found itself in the firm grip of a military coup.

9

THE MONEY-BELT

O N THE AFTERNOON OF the first day of the coup, machine-gun
salvoes come bubbling up out of the distance, and ebb away
again. Formations of fighter jets streak past the El Presidente,
like nimble fingers grabbing at the skyline of the five-million-plus
city. A band plays evergreens in the hotel bar. A rota has been
introduced for dinner with reserved tables and times, to avoid a
repetition of the chaos at lunchtime.

"Johannes? Friedrich? What was his name? He could have a
point." He feels Esther Moreno's breath caressing his eardrum.
They are sitting under palm fronds, on their stone bench by
the tennis courts. "I think it's just wonderful that you're so
open with me. I take it very personally, let me tell you, your
trust in me. It's so rare that you meet people nowadays who
are prepared to talk about themselves, who are willing to open
their hearts to you." She squeezes his hand, which, in spite of
the heat, feels strangely chilly. "The lawyer's right to ask. Why
did your uncle leave you without any more detailed information
for all those years? In his seeking for justice, Señor Shatil, the
arbitrator will certainly give voice to the thought that perhaps
Kirshman was preferred in some way by your relative? You
don't seem to ponder things very hard, Daniel. Don't you enjoy
Talmudic discussions? Are you happy with the first explanation
that comes along? Contradict me, go ahead, tell me I'm being
unfair. Am I being unfair?"

He regrets ever having told the woman about his case. He says:
"You're asking too many questions. Slow down, Esther, slow
down, your incessant questioning is making me *nuts* ... "

"We'll be apart for an hour or so, I'll be seeing you at supper again. We've been given the same table at the same time. I think Señor Shatil needs to understand what passed between you and your uncle. Otherwise he won't agree to be involved. If I heard him correctly, the telephone line was very bad, then his property backs onto the hotel grounds. That would mean that, in spite of the curfew, he could meet with us at any time."

He often did what people suggested, what people told him to do. Prompts, rebukes, suggestions from his parents and teachers, recommendations from his wife, he always considered. Tips from magazines, radio programmes and daily newspapers he would always take seriously if they seemed to offer any practical advice. It was only in his writing that he followed his own promptings. There he didn't listen to instructions or appeals. Pursued a flickering will o' the wisp objective; groping forward, looking for signs, unfixed, at large. *Fata Morgana* orientation, his entire life.

Round-the-clock news fills room 1244—a typhoon in Thailand, plane crash in Southern Kenya, the detonation of a car bomb in the heart of Johannesburg, fourteen dead. He lets the images flicker by without sound, waiting for news of the city where he's been for the last two days.

He is lying naked on the double bed. Grips his cock like the metal handrail on a shaking bus.

His circumcised cock cupped in his hand, he summons the spirit of his uncle.

How often did we meet,
Alexander Stecher Bravo,
Over the past thirty-eight years.

Not as often as all that, my boy, you were four when I saw you for the first time, in the St Moritz Hotel, Central Park South, eighteenth floor; while you were going to sleep you kept throwing your head from side to side as if there was something wrong with you. You looked at me, and said: "Oh, I'm so funny!" I didn't think you were that amusing, I thought you

were more of a sad little fellow! I felt sorry for you because you
didn't have any brothers and sisters.

> *How many times did we meet,*
> *Stranger, relative?*
> *Not so often,*
> *No more than thirty times,*
> *Oh, less, much less than that.*

It's not true to say that we met every year, not true at all, I only
came to Europe every two or three years, we didn't see each
other more than fifteen times in my life. Once on the corner of
Fifth Avenue and 42nd Street, that was twenty years ago now.
You were passing through, you and your parents, I was in New
York for three days, at that time New York was where I kept my
money, I had all my accounts almost without exception in the
States, and I would go and visit them every couple of months
or so, to check up on the interest, see how they were doing.
Ran into you by chance near my Chase Manhattan branch on
Fifth Avenue, of course you weren't to know that my fortune
was kept there, I had six different passbooks in my jacket pocket
with six different code words, and we fell into each other's
arms, and celebrated our unexpected reunion at a Howard
Johnson's on 44th Street, over Coke and a cheeseburger. At that
time, we weren't yet writing monthly letters to each other, that
correspondence only began much later, it was only in the last six
years of my life that we wrote to one another so regularly, don't
kid yourself about that, or me either. I invited you several times
to come and visit me in Caracas, my boy, three times we got as
far as me wiring you the air-fare, and still you didn't come, three
times you cancelled, each time at the very last minute, *bueno*,
I don't want to reproach you, but I still felt hurt, felt like an
idiot. What really made me angry though was a letter you sent
me two or three years before my death. With all innocence, it
was a pretty unambiguous sign of your unreliability. You had
been to see your mother, and as you were once again hard
up, she had given you five hundred dollars, well, all right, five

hundred dollars. You got home, and you left your money-belt containing mother's cash and your passport lying on your car seat. It wasn't till the following evening, you were going to the movies with Valeria, whom I was never allowed to meet, and you saw the money-belt lying there, you hadn't even given it a thought. You hadn't missed it a second! You tied the belt around you, not telling Valeria what had happened. In the cinema, it got to be too tight, and you loosened it again. An hour after leaving the movie theatre, you realised you didn't have the belt any more. You went back to the cinema, it was already shut. The next morning, following a sleepless night, you drove to the cinema, the cleaners had just finished their work, and they had found nothing. You looked for the doorman, but nothing had been handed in to him. It might have been more sensible if you hadn't told me anything about that whole episode. Of course discipline can easily turn into rigidity, into pedantry. But some sort of halfway house would have been right. And that in turn puts me in mind of your continual moving. Your globe-trotting bothered me. Vienna, Basel, Tel Aviv, New York. And now London? I never knew where you were, and how long you'd stay. You change apartments, cities, countries, the way normal people change trousers, you could never decide on any one place. Nowhere and everywhere was home to you. You couldn't settle on a woman either. How often I wrote to you, my boy, start a family, a man without a family isn't a man. Don't take me as a model, please. Those love affairs of yours, all pitiful, damaging to your dignity and the good name of the family, they did you a lot of harm. You were just wild in the way you went after women—a sailor. You were a whore and a pimp, both at the same time.

(The Caracas skyline, with swathes of black smoke over the city centre. He turns up the sound: " ... Five officers in the armed forces are believed to be leading the uprising, working with civilians whom officials described as left-wing extremists ... " He turns the sound down again.)

You never asked me who my friends were. If you'd come to Caracas, you'd have got to meet them, I'd have introduced you, but you never saw fit to come here in my lifetime, not once, but now, after my death, here you are. Can't you feel how strange your behaviour must seem to me? Twelve years ago, in Meran, I'd been going to speak to you about my friends, do you remember, you came to me, we had agreed you would come and stay with me for a week or longer, as my guest, and then, after two days, you announce you want to leave. I bet you regret your hasty departure now, don't you? After that, I think we only saw each other once or maybe twice more, our meetings were less frequent than you had the impression they were.

Daniel tries to get a word in: When you gave Kirshman and his son unlimited insight into your financial arrangements, gave them power of attorney over your money, was that to punish me for only staying three days with you in Meran, instead of the week I'd promised?

Did I say that, my boy?

There's a knock on the door. "Will you let me in?" She clutches the door frame. Her voice sounds foggy. "The days when a woman of my years could wait to be seduced are over. I can't wait till tonight … "

He holds his breath.

"You're a silly boy, blue-eyed Daniel. Too bad. Too bad for you and too bad for me."

He hears her tripping walk, swaying and uncertain.

He breathes again.

10

MERAN

A S SOON AS THE LOCOMOTIVE of the Italian railways had pulled
in to the station at Meran, Daniel was shaking his uncle's
hands through the open window, holding them tight, very tight.
They hadn't seen one another for six years. The nephew was
struck by how healthy, how strong, his relative looked. He was
wearing a white short-sleeved shirt, his skin was evenly tanned,
his large hands felt soft and cared for, the nails well-manicured.
Alexander didn't like to be kissed hello or goodbye, for him
the euphoria of meeting and the sorrow of departure were best
expressed in the pressure of the hands.

"Welcome, my boy. The Golden Plough is very nearby. We can
easily walk there … is your rucksack heavy?"

Daniel shook his head. During the short walk to the Golden
Plough, he imagined a solid inn, sunk in time, panelled with
fragrant cembra pine, furnished with massive armchairs and
yielding sofas. The hotel on the busy Europa Allee turned out to
be a brand new four-storey prefab construction.

The room on the ground floor, number 14, looked out on to a
little allotment patch full of molehills, planted with gooseberries,
raspberries, apricots and pears. A little further back ran the
lines of the Meran-Bozen railway. The nearby vineyards were
without colour in the hazy light of late summer. There was a
smell of compost. The smoke of a bonfire blew over from a
garden nearby.

On the bed was a parcel wrapped in coarse paper, which Daniel
opened right away. Alexander had brought him his old prayer
book. The pages were yellow, some of them torn. The *Siddur*

followed the Sephardic ritual, to which Stecher Bravo belonged through his mother. The little book had a greasy-earthy, sweaty smell, and the binding reminded him of a mourning-service book.

In the early evening, they wandered into the town centre. Found an extensive beer-garden, *Zum Försterbräu*, not far from the wellness and therapy centre. For the first time that day, the sun broke through the clouds.

"Light like this has always struck me as being 'Catholic' in some way," said Stecher while they found a place in the shade of a lofty chestnut.

At the time Daniel was slowly approaching the idea of rigorously observing the Bible, and living in accordance with the six hundred and thirteen injunctions and prohibitions of the five books of Moses. For some years now he had had the feeling that the pattern of his days, his weeks, his months, was lacking rigour. Having grown up without a sense of religious ritual, with the single exception of his bar mitzvah, he had begun to keep the Sabbath, to observe the laws of diet as much as possible, he fasted on Yom Kippur, mourned on the ninth of Av, the anniversary of the destruction of the first temple at Jerusalem by Nebuchadnezzar, and didn't sleep with women during the days of their cycle.

"I'm so relieved!" cried his uncle. "Because if you eat what you're eating, in a place like this, you really can't be that serious about your new-found religiousness! After a year, or two at the most, you will see that it's only possible to be devout if you've had a devout upbringing. Then it's not a burden—it's just the way things have always been for you. But becoming pious halfway through life, that doesn't seem to me a very good idea. It's like trying to slip into someone else's skin. It doesn't come from the heart. Just try it, and prove to me that I'm wrong, observe the rules, keep the holidays, every one of them, wash your fingertips with nail water, to shake off that one-sixtieth portion of death that every night's sleep represents. Observe the law with every step, with every word, with every gesture. I don't think you're cut out for such a rigorous manner of life. And yet, you'd have every

72

reason to try to adopt this ludicrous idea. Both on your mother's side, and on mine, which is your father's, you are descended from celebrated rabbis, one from Prague, the other from Hamburg. Yehuda Mordechai Cassuto from Hamburg, Rav Shmuel Hirsch from Prague. Write down our family history. That way it will be preserved for you and any descendants you may have!"

"I've done that. Obviously. Many years ago."

"So much the better. By the way, I wanted to please you, so I made enquiries whether there's a synagogue here, so that we could go to a service on Sabbath eve, the day after tomorrow. It seems there isn't. Only on high holy days the Palace Hotel temporarily converts one of its restaurants into a prayer room, for the dozen or so guests of Jewish origin who have patronised that establishment year in, year out, from before the War ... "

At some of the surrounding tables, the broad skulls of old men shifted. Stecher looked across at them in embarrassment.

It was still light when they strolled back to the Golden Plough through the palm avenue of Garibaldi Park, past groups of seventy, eighty and ninety-year-old spa guests. The tangle of canes and walking sticks was like a thicket of bamboo.

Under a pavilion roof a small orchestra was playing Johann Strauss's *Lilac Waltz*. The melody pierced the bags of bones. With his increasing deafness, Stecher could only hear the top notes, but even so tears came to his eyes that he quickly blinked away. He hoped Daniel hadn't noticed.

He stooped to pick up sweet wrappers and empty crisp packets that were blowing over the gravel paths, and binned them. Tapped an old lady with purple hair on the shoulder. She blushed, bent down and picked up the brown apple skins she had dropped a moment before. Stecher showed her where the rubbish bin stood.

"Meran, you know, has been my favourite place in Europe since 1911, that's why I wanted us to meet here at least once," he said, walking on. "As a nine-year-old I first came here with my parents on a grape cure. We lived at Castle Labers, in the Obermais part of town, so badly damaged later during the First

73

World War. I chased and caught the mice that ran around my parents' room, and played with them till they were dead. Like my parents, I ate—no, not mice—muscatel grapes for days on end. Not until I was twenty did I stop accompanying my father and mother on their autumn trips to the South Tyrol."

"And today the whole of Meran appears to be just one big old people's home! … "

"What did you say?"

"It's lovely here … "

"Didn't you say something about … an old people's home?"

Daniel looked shamefacedly down.

Stecher Bravo, however, agreed with him: "You can say that again."

They stepped into the hotel lobby. "How many days," asked his uncle, "are you going to stay with me?"

"Can we talk about it tomorrow?"

"But not less than a week?"

"How long have you booked my room for?"

"As long as you want."

The following morning, they took the post bus to the village of San Pietro, high above Meran. The place was peopled by stick-swinging, German-speaking oldsters and oldsterettes in red-and-white gingham. They were as indistinguishable as poodles.

Every pension, every hotel, every private residence looked as though it had been built of neither stone nor wood. A Potemkin village, put together from outsize construction kit pieces. Windows like arrow slits, roofs like turrets.

"When I see people my age, I think every time—they should all have been under the ground long ago!" Stecher barely avoided falling under the wheels of a double-decker tour bus with the legend *Sonnen-Express*, which was spinning round in front of the funicular station, looking for a parking spot.

They went into an inn. Ate cheese rolls to strengthen themselves, drank prior to setting out raspberry syrup with soda from half-litre jugs that had lipstick stains on them. A group of old girls were belting out Austrian folksongs into the room in a polyphonic choir.

Ever since getting up Daniel had been wondering how he was going to break it to Alexander that he didn't want to stay in Meran any longer than three days (instead of the agreed seven). Before setting out, he had started working on a new cycle of poems, a work that was going to treat the subject of hunger in all its aspects. He yearned to return to his writing table. It couldn't be soon enough.

They had left the village of San Pietro far behind them, and hardly encountered anyone. They started to sweat in the morning sun, on the meadows and in the vineyards.

They were crossing an ankle-deep carpet of flowers.

"How long are you staying with me?"

"A bit less, maybe … not quite as long as we originally planned … "

"I would be very upset, if that were the case."

They were walking towards the little market village of Riffian. Steep paths on which they sampled wild strawberries, plucked raspberries and blackberries. Stecher seemed stronger and fitter than Daniel, fifty-two years his junior. "And yet when I was a boy, I was a weakling," he cried, leaping like a goat over tree roots and rock outcrops, "before me my parents lost two other boys in infancy. I was their first surviving child, even though to begin with I didn't look promising—I was born prematurely. I was supposed to put on at least fifty grams a week, but I had no tolerance for milk, and had to be carried around for nights on end. Because I had a double hernia, I wasn't supposed to cry. There's a number of things that can be explained about me that way, because by the time I was your age, late twenties, I was terribly spoilt. I was always the smallest in any company, it was only after my school-leaving exams that I finally started to grow. I was never beaten, not even when I played pranks at school. Once, a teacher gave me a choice between detention and a smack. I chose the smack. Because I was perfectly sure the man wouldn't smack me. And it's true. He stroked me!"

"I was hit once by one of my teachers at grammar school in Vienna ... "

"What did you do?"

"On a slide of the Sahara, I drew a rain cloud in biro. When the picture was put in the projector, the whole class started laughing ... "

"He was right to hit you, then."

" ... An ex-SS man, as I later discovered."

"The two things are completely unconnected."

"They stroked you. And you think it's fine if they hit me?"

"You weren't such a delicate child."

They were walking along the Passer, jumping over streams. The din of the water made conversation impossible. Alexander pointed to a group of children in the middle of an apple orchard who were bathing half-naked in the icy river.

On the Tappein Way, a promenade that loops high above Meran in its bowl, they rested. His mother had instructed Daniel to walk on the Tappein Way, on the traces of her past. It was there that she had fallen in love half-a-century ago, as a fourteen-year-old.

"Who was the lucky fellow?" asked Stecher.

"A touring actor from Brno. Twenty-five years older than my mother. They got married on her sixteenth birthday."

"A forty-year-old hits on a little underage girl, seduces her, takes her virginity, and marries her two years later! Charming story! Your mother's parents must have wished the earth could swallow them up. How long did the marriage last? Were there children, heirs? Is the man still living?"

The nephew felt exhausted. Three hours had passed since they had headed out of the village of San Pietro.

"What happened to the man, Daniel?"

Loew had forgotten to take his cap with him, he couldn't cope with the piercing sun. Ideally, he would have lain down just where he was on the wooden bench on the promenade, and had a nice long sleep. He closed his eyes.

"In Caracas, there are mountain grasses that flower with such a wonderful sweet aroma! It makes me homesick to think

76

of it. You'll experience it when you come and visit. You must wonder why I stayed there all those years, don't you? It's not possible for me to feel well anywhere else. And so I stay. Only occasionally am I reminded that I live in the tropics—say when I see a reference in the paper to apples as an exotic fruit. Are you in a bad mood? ... "

"Caught the sun, I suppose."

"Make yourself a covering for your head from my handkerchief, here, you tie a knot at each corner, it's every bit as good as a hat, looks stupid, but it serves its purpose. Maybe it'll cheer you up if I tell you about Franziska, my first great love? My only great love. I was the age you are now. Franziska, a Christian girl from Mönchengladbach. Her father was a shoemaker. Such a sweet girl! I invited her back to Hamburg, to introduce her to my parents. And I lost courage. I took her to the seaside for two days, to Travemünde. She said: 'All your life you will regret not having married me.' *Bueno*, enough of that. Have you got a ... a woman, at the moment?"

"She's slender, tall and black-haired, like an Indian. People stop in the street and stare at her."

"No wonder you're in such poor condition."

"She's exhausting."

"I hope you didn't ring her from your room?"

"Don't worry ... "

"That would have cost me a fortune!" wailed Stecher Bravo.

"She takes all my strength. She despises God. In the same breath as she claims he doesn't exist. Her fury that she will have to die is endless. To be buried, to be put in a box and lowered into the ground ... "

"Do you mind changing the subject?"

"I'm sorry ... "

"So it's on account of her that you wanted to leave ahead of time."

"I want to get back to my writing. That's all."

"I was so looking forward to our time together. The departure from Caracas was ghastly—my housekeeper had already left, gone to her relatives in Spain for the summer ... Come on, get up, let's go on, otherwise our legs will seize up. Perpetua was already gone when I heard that my flight to Europe was being put back two whole days, as you may imagine I fly charter, it's much cheaper than any regular flight, but then you get things like that happening. I had to go back home, and I'm not used to being without my Perpetua … At home it looked as though a plague corpse had recently been taken away. All the curtains were drawn. Everything dark, everything shut away. The wardrobes locked, the plugs out of the walls. Every room smelling of mothballs. Without Perpetua, I'm useless, I can't cook, I can't make up the stripped beds. *Bueno*, I don't even know where she keeps the linen. No hand towels or bath towels. Once I got to Europe, I vomited in the bus from the airport, and the two ladies in front of me, well, you can imagine the situation … and then in a hotel lobby in Bologna. And then a third time when I arrived in the Golden Plough four days ago. Only since you've arrived have I begun to feel a little better. A little."

They were approaching the edge of town. Across the railway tracks lay the cemeteries of the spa town, right next to the municipal slaughterhouse. All the gates locked. Through the railings of the Jewish graveyard, Daniel could make out the weathered plaque bearing the names of those Meran troops of Israelite descent who had fallen in the First World War. Right next to the Jewish cemetery was the large German military graveyard.

"How strange … "

"What's strange about that?" his uncle asked.

"The two cemeteries … side by side!"

Stecher saw no significance in it. He had no interest in these 'super-sophistications' as he called them, he lacked the 'equipment' to register them.

Alexander did not like to be in the vicinity of the dead. They turned back. A woman approached them, heavily made-up, in an evening dress. Her eyes looked sad. She almost brushed Daniel's shoulder. Uncle and nephew both stopped to look at her, turning their heads like children who see grown-ups they happen to like the look of.

"One day you will inherit everything I own," said Stecher Bravo as the unknown woman disappeared from sight, "and not just half of it, as was once my plan, and as I once wrote in my will, because at that time I felt under obligation to Perpetua, but she has relations in Spain who have money, and I don't need to worry about her. You are to have everything. As I told you at your bar mitzvah."

"Don't let's talk about it please ... I'm sure you're going to go on living for a long, long time. And ... I'm really not desperate to inherit from you!"

"No, no, quite right, you shouldn't be desperate. I just wanted you to understand that everything that is mine will one day be yours. And it's not so little either."

Loew thought it might offend his uncle if he showed interest in what he was planning to leave to him. To indicate curiosity about the places and the banks where he kept his accounts. He wasn't to know that his relative was disappointed by his very reticence. Because Stecher Bravo took his nephew's apparent lack of interest for true indifference. Whereas in fact he would have been more than willing to talk to him about money.

"I don't like to talk about death," he tried once more. "But you really could ask me about what I intend to leave you without any modesty ... "

"I don't want to talk ... money ... with you ... I'm sorry, I can't ... "

"Why can't you?"

"It's unpleasant to me. It's the way I was raised. I can't change my nature ... "

"Well, I must say, I have quite a different memory of your mother, not at all as lofty and unworldly as her only son would have me believe. Nothing fastidious about her, when money was involved. The things I could tell you!"

"Look over there, see the dying light on the Harzer Spitze!" his nephew distracted him.

"Alpine glow. Very romantic! ... " growled Stecher Bravo.

They were sitting on a park bench close to the hotel entrance, on the edge of the traffic-thronged Mazzini Square.

"That young woman who just passed us, she looked exactly like my Franziska. After we were finished, I pretty much stuck to dancing girls. There's one I think of in particular, she can't have been older than fifteen. I wanted to rescue her! She had been drinking, and I dragged her right across the dance floor, to the fresh air. I couldn't do anything for her ... Well, it's all forgotten now, all forgotten."

He looked down at his wristwatch, a Waltham from the nineteen-thirties. The little bunches of white hairs sprouting from his nostrils trembled ever so slightly. "Nine o'clock already! Bedtime!" He jumped up and disappeared into the Golden Plough.

That night Daniel called his mother from his hotel room. She felt lonely, she told him, as soon as he wasn't in the same city as her. (He was still living in Vienna at the time.) "If you want, you can use me as an excuse, maybe he'll let you leave earlier than planned. And try and get something out of him. That man has so much money, believe me. Tell him you'd like to work on something for a couple of months undisturbed, tell him your idea of the hunger-cycle, say you need his help! ... "

"Mother, please, stop!"

"He could have helped your father and me so easily, at a time when we were really badly off."

"I know, Mother, now please—no more of these stories ... "

"Avarice is one of the worst diseases there are. For decades I've known him to be an incredibly mean, and sometimes morbidly tight-fisted man. Did you go to the Tappein Way? ... "

Before going to sleep he picked up the prayer book Stecher had given him. It lay on the nightstand, next to the hotel issue of the New Testament. He sniffed at the greasy yellowed pages of the Siddur, opened it, read words of Hebrew without understanding them. And decided to take the present, which gave him the creeps, and bury it early next morning, in the garden of the Golden Plough. He got up and washed his hands thoroughly.

He awoke after ten hours of sleep.

Felt much more tired than he had the day before.

Wrapped the prayer book in one of his sweaty undershirts, and stowed it away in his rucksack with his other things.

"I'm glad to say my digestion is working properly again," announced Stecher Bravo, when they met in the windowless breakfast room. "When I'm alone, I often imagine: this is the end! But now I see—it's not so bad at all! Having you with me is a huge help!" "My mother ... she's not doing too well," said Daniel. "I talked to her yesterday."

"You don't have to play games with me, my boy, I wasn't born yesterday. You want to get back to your exciting Indian girl. We see one another so rarely. I have so much more I want to tell you. I'm not going to live for ever!"

"I want to leave ... tonight ... "

"Tonight? But what for? Tell me what for!"

"I just need to get back ... "

"You mean to take a train at the beginning of Sabbath?!"

In silence they chewed their rolls which tasted of cardboard.

They spent the day near Castle Labers. The town was at their feet, half-obscured by haze. The drizzle didn't bother them. They walked on paths that smelt strongly of mushrooms.

"Can you improvise a poem?" asked the uncle.

"Only with the greatest reluctance ... "

"If you're a poet, you have to be able do that sort of thing!" insisted Stecher Bravo.

"Walk—
Many-footed
Heavy-booted
Step on it
Dogshit."

"Not at all bad. For an improvisation. What about the shortest poem you've ever written?"

"It's called *Hero's Death*:

Off with his head

81

Chapeaux!"

Alexander laughed.

The biggest snake Daniel had ever seen in his life slid across the path. Vanished like an arrow into the grass. "Strike me pink!" cried Stecher, whistled through his teeth. His nephew hadn't heard the expression.

"There's nothing that big even in Caracas!"

"Strike me pink!" The poet pulled a palm-sized notebook out of his jacket pocket, with a pencil affixed to it. He wrote down his uncle's phrase.

"How do you think you're going to make a living in future? Why don't you write a play! You can make a packet in the theatre! If you want to please me in my old days, try writing a play. What are you going to feed a family with?"

"Well, in the first place I don't mean to start a family, please God, and secondly just leave me in peace! I've got my work, which means everything to me ... I'm satisfied, I don't need more. I'll get by. Somehow or other."

"Somehow or other! Exactly. Well, I hope you're not mistaken. Or that you're not banking on your expectations of an inheritance from me. I might live a long time yet, you know?"

"Alexander, please don't talk that way ... "

"You carry on as if you're more Catholic than the Pope, my boy!"

They collected Daniel's luggage from the Golden Plough.

When the official quoted the price at the train station's ticket counter, Loew pulled out his wallet.

He had decided he would pay for his travel expenses himself, but allow himself to be Stecher Bravo's guest where board and accommodation were concerned. Secretly, he hoped his uncle would not permit him to pay for his ticket. (For that reason, he hadn't bought himself a slightly cheaper return ticket in Vienna, but just the ticket out.) But Alexander didn't intervene.

In the underpass on the way to platform three, his uncle remarked: "You spend money like a millionaire!"

"I think if you don't have much, you spend it more easily than if you do."

"Could be, could be. Reminds me of one of my oldest friends, in Caracas, a multimillionaire, dollar millionaire, mind you, who last year refused to pay the ever so slightly higher contribution to remain part of the Jewish community. Threatened to resign, if they insisted on the hike. He arrived fifty years ago, an émigré from Germany. For decades he's spent every day in his grim business, in the darkest corner, watching over his employees, never takes a single day off. Not once … "

"What's he called, your friend?"

"What's it to you?"

"If I hear the name, I find it easier to imagine the man."

"Nonsense … What about your girl, just now, what's her name?"

"Maria Magdalena."

"Couldn't find a more Christian name, I suppose?!"

"And your millionaire?"

"Ah, you'll forget this story anyway, just as you forget everything you're told. You lose the important things in your life, as if it was small change out of your pocket."

"What surprises me is how persistently you try to offend me … What have I done to you?"

"Well, be that as it may. If you like, I'll be only too happy to introduce my friend to you, next year, when you come to Caracas."

The slow train to Bozen got in half-an-hour before its scheduled departure. Daniel and Alexander sat down in one of the empty carriages. They took off their shoes. Rested their stockinged feet on the opposite seats.

"So you're travelling on the Sabbath. How can anyone take you seriously? Either—or. Either you strive for piety, which in my opinion is nonsense, or else you forget it. But this mixing and matching? I don't like it a bit."

"Let's not have an argument before we say goodbye. Thank you for these lovely days together."

"Be healthy," said his uncle, "everything else will look after itself. Or not."

They shook hands.

"Next year in Caracas!" Stecher called out to his nephew, and then he went out onto the platform.

Loew wound down the window.

"Did I ever tell you," Alexander said, "that the model for Heinrich Heine's character Hyazinth Hirsch was an ancestor of ours? Isaac Roccamora, lottery messenger in Hamburg, of whom it is said he was endlessly honest in money matters, and an expert in the removal of corns, and the valuing, buying, and selling of jewels. He was the uncle of my maternal grandmother, who also knew Heine well."

"No, you never told me … I'm sure I wouldn't have forgotten that … "

"Hyazinth Hirsch … read the travel piece on Bagni di Lucca. Quite something; it will surprise you!"

A short whistle. The train moved off.

They waved to each other—until the track curved, and the train swung out of sight.

11

THE ARBITRATOR

ON THE MORNING OF THE SECOND DAY of the coup, Francisco Shatil, arbitrator of the forty-thousand-strong Union Israelita de Caracas, appears in the restaurant of the El Presidente. He has entered the hotel grounds by a garden gate. His property is indeed immediately adjacent to the hotel.

Esther Moreno said the night before that Señor Shatil had given her his agreement over the phone to hear Daniel's case.

"To me it makes more sense to proceed with Dr Johannes," the heir demurred. "He's going to move things forward as soon as the coup is over."

Esther disagreed with her chance acquaintance—recourse to the *arbitraje* was, she said, the only sensible next step in the solution of the dispute at this moment.

Shatil, bony, with a prominent nose, the owner of a tyre factory, is also the general representative of a big US insurance company. At first, the seventy-year-old man gives every impression of being a retired geography teacher. As he says by way of introduction, he collected antiques, and highlights a find he made a few months after the end of the Second World War in a little flea market in the Vienna Prater—it was a pub sign, *The Happy Metternich*, that dated from 1848, the year of the wave of revolutions throughout Europe.

Shatil asks to be told everything that has happened so far, from beginning to end. Esther slithers about on her upholstered chair. Hotel guests stream into the unaired room, captives, stranded for the past several days, they hurl themselves on their scanty breakfasts as if it were the last meal of their lives.

"Shouldn't we go out in the garden?" suggests Loew after finishing his account of what has happened to him. "It'll be a bit quieter there … "

Francisco Shatil doesn't budge.

"I'll be right back," Esther leaves the men to themselves.

The heir observes every quiver of Shatil's thin lips, impatiently awaiting the arbitrator's verdict.

After ten minutes, Esther Moreno is back at the breakfast table.

In the meantime, not one word has passed between the two men.

In the middle of the room, a woman taps a fork against a glass: "Ladies and gentlemen, dear guests of the El Presidente, in my capacity as deputy director of the hotel, I don't want to keep the following news item from you any longer than I have to—the situation is being stabilised. As of eight am local time, forces loyal to the government have regained control of the situation." There is a smattering of applause. "The curfew will be lifted tomorrow morning, God willing. In emergencies it may be possible to leave the hotel this afternoon already for short periods. Does anyone here feel themselves to be such an exceptional case?" Four women raised their hands. "Then, ladies, may I ask you to come to me individually, so that I can decide your cases. Are there any other questions?"

An ever larger group of guests surrounds the lady. The noise level increases, under the neon lights.

"Come on, shall we go outside," it is now Esther's turn to suggest. Shatil doesn't react. Daniel and Esther get up, push their chairs against the table. Shatil follows them out into the hotel grounds. They make for their stone bench under the palm fronds.

The arbitrator pulls the squeaking back of a deckchair into the vertical position. It is very hot, this day of late November, with high humidity.

"Konrad Kirshman may have a rough exterior," the *arbitraje* finally begins, after a further silence, "but he has a good heart. A good heart. The man is one of the pillars of our community." He

86

stops, brushes his fingertips over his pencil moustache. "I admit, he keeps his hand in his pocket, jingling with his money. But is that to be a reproach to him? Does that mean he or his son have done something wrongful—"

"Sorry for interrupting," the carotid artery is throbbing along his jaw to the point of his chin, "but we are talking about someone who has tried to take my inheritance from me!"

"Oh, has he? You know that for a fact? How much did your uncle possess? And you're accusing Kirshman and son of taking something away? If your uncle left you no precise information regarding his accounts, he will have had his reasons. Perhaps others were to have his money, and not you. Konrad Kirshman was the head of the Chevra Kadisha for decades here in Caracas, the holy burial society that escorts the dead to the point of their burial. It's a voluntary work, unpaid. It is accounted a great honour to be admitted into that brotherhood. I would be only too happy to be invited to be head of the Chevra Kadisha! The members of the Chevra Kadisha are responsible for washing and clothing the dead, they take the body to the cemetery, put it in the coffin, lower the coffin into the ground, cover the place with earth and stones. Have you any idea of what it is to wash a corpse? To comfort the nearest relatives of a dead person? To make the first cut with the point of a knife into the clothing of a survivor, whereupon the mourners begin to tear their jackets and shirts, as instructed by the tradition? Señora Moreno told me you were a poet? The body of the deceased is first washed from head to foot in lukewarm water. Everything must be cleansed— the fingers, the toes, the sex, the anus. The hair is combed, the fingernails and toenails are clipped. One may not lay a corpse on its front, face down, because that would be to disrespect the dead person. After the thorough cleansing, the corpse has nine bushels of water poured over it. How do you suppose the members of the Chevra Kadisha feel when they must bury an infant boy who died after just a day or two, and they have circumcised him, as our law requires? Or when they wash a three-year-old girl, a beauty with long black curls, who died in a car accident, as happened only last year? So nine bushels of water are poured over the head of the upright naked corpse, and then a raw egg and shell are stirred together with wine, as an emblem of the eternally spinning wheel of fate, and the head of the corpse is anointed with the mixture. Finally, the body is dressed in a white shroud—"

"*Buenas dias, señor!*" The lady from the hotel directorate who spoke before in the restaurant, strolls past. "Tomorrow we'll have withstood it, neighbour! … Thanks God!"

He nods and smiles to her.

"Show me your uncle's will," he says then, "I should like to see it."

Daniel has a photocopy of the will. The original is in Julio's hands. He gets up to go and fetch it. While the lift glides up, he is picturing the washing of Alexander's corpse. On the corridor of his floor he whispers to himself: "Chevra Kadisha! You set foot in houses and apartments of the dead, the first to do so after the doctors have gone. Chevra Kadisha! You move unobserved through bedrooms, bathrooms, studies. It's child's play to pocket, to collect whatever falls into your hands, whatever isn't nailed down."

As he approaches the stone bench again, he hears Esther Moreno laugh out loud.

The arbitrator of the Jewish community of Caracas studies the testament.

It is my last will that at the time of my death all my property, all I own now and shall own in future in Venezuela, whether it be in the form of property, shares or assets of any kind shall be divided as follows: A) All my estate to Mr Daniel Loew, adult, Austrian citizen, currently a resident of London, at 16 Agincourt Road. B) Sole exception to this distribution: my Chevy II, 1962, yellow, serial number 469AB62V759. This is to be given to Miss Manuela Ferreira, born 1973. I hereby appoint Mr Julio Kirshman, born on 1st July 1948, to be my executor …

"Chevy driver. I like that. I always recommended Firestone tires to my customers when they drove sixties Chevies. You see, here it is: 'all my property ... *in Venezuela*.'" The tire dealer hands back the copy of the will. "Your uncle didn't write that by chance. He had something in mind. Everything he had abroad is not necessarily to go to you ... "

Esther Moreno twists her big mouth into a grimace.

"Even if that were so, respected Señor Shatil," Daniel has difficulty breathing, and can hardly speak, "that's still a very long way from saying that my uncle's possessions outside Venezuela should fall to Kirshman and son. I am Stecher Bravo's sole heir. And so everything he had in other countries is mine too, except the Chevy. Everything."

"I think he's right about that," remarks Esther Moreno.

For a while only the *plock* of a tennis ball is heard.

"Of course I fully understand your anger," the *arbitraje* finally resumed, "but that's all I have to say. I can't intercede here. This is my community, I live among these men, I meet them on high days and holy days, and on various business occasions. I won't start a quarrel with people of the calibre of Kirshman and son. The reservations you entertain about these two members of our community sadden me."

"Well, that does it for me as well," Mrs Moreno speaks up. Daniel assumes she's about to double cross him. "I don't want you, señor," she continues, however, "to continue to help me in my own case with my apartment. I'm going to leave it with the lawyers—"

"But my dear, respected madam, your case has nothing, but nothing, in common with that of our young friend here ... "

She raises her right hand, index finger pointing upwards, thereby motioning to Francisco Shatil to speak no more.

He doesn't immediately succeed in levering his long, gaunt body out of the deckchair. As upright as he was two hours ago on entering the breakfast room, so stooped is he now as he leaves.

Loew accompanies Shatil to the fence of the hotel grounds, in a loose interpretation of the Talmudic instruction, "Take your guest on his departure as far as the threshold of your house."

The arbitrator turns to face him: "I have only a dim recollection of your uncle. I saw him two or three times in synagogue, years

ago. On Rosh Hashanah, Yom Kippur. I'm no longer certain …
He lived a withdrawn life, kept himself to himself, wasn't a figure
in the community, or outside, if I'm not mistaken. He was proud
of his Sephardic ancestry on his mother's side, that was the first
thing he spoke about with me. Didn't he come from Hamburg?
Showed me an ancient prayer book of the Sephardic ritual,
printed in Livorno … "

"I've got it here with me, my uncle gave it to me twelve years
ago!" Daniel imagined he could change the arbitrator's mind
now.

"Very good, all right now … " Shatil pulls a heavy bunch of
keys from his trouser pocket, and unlocks his garden gate.

"*There* you are! Mama and I had no idea where you were!" the
tender voice in the background remains unseen. "You never told
us where you were going. You know how Mama worries."

"Mairah. My youngest … "

"Papa? Are you alone?"

"Here I am, my darling!"

"Goodbye, señor." Daniel raises his voice deliberately, in the
hope that the unknown girl might be curious and come out from
her hiding place behind the rhododendron bush. He imagines
her smell, sees himself thrashing about with her on the unmade
bed in room 1244, feels her tongue on his, her soft neck held in
the palm of his hand.

Shatil locks his garden gate, disappears behind the screen of
bushes, beyond which the outlines of a tall and spacious villa can
be discerned.

"You've probably saved yourself some money. At least you
won't have to show Shatil any gratitude," Esther murmurs. She
is sitting on the stone bench in the same twisted position in which
he left her minutes earlier. Now she presses her hot cheek against
his hip.

12

AFTERNOON STROLL

"COME DOWN TO THE LOBBY. Hurry!" Dr Johannes calls a few hours later, on the afternoon now of the second day of the coup, into the mouthpiece of the old-fashioned hotel phone. "I've got to see you right away."

He is wearing blue jeans and an open-necked shirt. The curfew remains officially in force, he explains by way of greeting, but it has been considerably relaxed. He has driven the three miles from his house to the El Presidente in his own car, without encountering a single checkpoint. "Let's take our chances, and go for a walk," the lawyer proposes.

Daniel is only too glad to be able to leave the hotel for the first time in a day-and-a-half.

The revolving door continues going round after Esther Moreno, such is the force with which she dashes after them onto the street. "Are you going right now? Can I come with you?" She introduces herself to Dr Johannes. "Daniel's told me all about you. I'm so glad you're taking on his case."

"Forgive me for being blunt with you. I should like to be alone with Mr Loew."

She shows herself to be understanding. Presses a kiss against Daniel's temple, and hangs back.

"Who was *that*? You should be careful—I've been living in this country for forty years, and still experience the most surprising things … "

He said he had spoken to the woman a few times since the beginning of the disturbances, but had no reason to suspect that she was not to be trusted.

"Did you talk to her about Kirshman and son?"

"No. Good Lord, no."

"How is it she says she's heard so much about me, and 'I'm so pleased you're taking on his case!' Why is she pleased? And why does she kiss you? No, I'm serious about this—if you want to lie to me, then it would be better we broke off our talks right away, my dear fellow … "

"I might have said this or that to her. I think she's certainly trustworthy."

"I don't. I don't think you could have done anything more foolish. Who else have you confided in, you genius?"

"Nobody … "

"I hope all our chances haven't gone because of your openness towards this person. Why did you have to take her into your confidence? Who is she?"

Daniel breaks out in a sweat. And then to have talked about the case with Francisco Shatil, a close acquaintance of his opponents! If Dr Johannes knew about that meeting, he would certainly drop him on the spot.

They are crossing the Plaza Venezuela. Forty-eight hours ago there was all the bustle of a metropolis. On the late afternoon of the second day of the crisis, the scene is governed by silence and emptiness, as if some futuristic weapon had destroyed all life, and left everything inanimate intact.

"Do you remember my parting words to you the day before yesterday? Don't talk about your case to *anyone*."

"You treat me like a child, Dr Johannes. That's no way for us to carry on. I know what I have to do … and not do. You'll have to trust me. But perhaps we should indeed … go our separate ways."

"Calm down, calm down, Señor Loew. Please. It's just as I said—the Devil never sleeps."

On the Avenida Abraham Lincoln, one of the main city-centre streets, closed boutiques and travel agencies, an empty café terrace. Metal screens are down everywhere. They meet no one. No bird sings, no dog barks, no cat miaows.

A mild breeze blows, carrying a smell of the sea.

"Now, I must say, I'm a little hesitant to pass on to you what I have managed to discover in your affair. You didn't instruct me to be active on your behalf. But when you told me that Kirshman hadn't called to warn you when the coup broke out, I thought: you have no other choice anyway. You will have to proceed against these gentlemen, and make me your legal adviser. Well, I haven't been idle. I couldn't get to my office, but as soon as telephone communications were up and running again … Oh, you will blab all this out in the hotel lobby the moment you're back—"

"Are you insulting me again? … "

"I'm making the mistake of trusting you." Dr Johannes remained standing in front of a swastika-bedaubed metal screen outside a jeweller's shop. "My good friend Emil Gotthardt—a similar story to mine, he grew up in Uruguay, parents emigrants, albeit Aryans in his case—Emil is the general representative of Citizens Bank in Venezuela. I gave him a call, we thought it wiser to respect the curfew, and we talked the whole thing through on the phone. I began by dangling a little piece of the pie in front of him, in case he was able to find out what your respected uncle's holdings were in Panama, on the day that he died. Well, even though he's a very senior employee with Citizens Bank, no one in the Panama office of the German Bank of Latin America would give him any information. As you know, your uncle kept his money in numbered accounts. And a numbered account is a numbered account, even if it's the Emperor of China who wants some information. But it turned out in the course of further conversations with Gotthardt, and this too I tell you in strictest confidence, Herr Loew—my Emil happens to have had a little fling some years back with that Simone von Oelffen of whom you spoke to me. Strange, admittedly, it probably fits in with your poet's view of the world, how did you put it the other evening, chance rules the world? Well, as chance would have it, my Emil was Simone's lover a few years back. I managed to persuade him to agree to call the lady in Hamburg, after years of silence, because you must know he wanted nothing more to do with her, as soon as she started bombarding him with her affection, thoughts of marriage, children and all the rest of it. Accordingly, her initial reaction on hearing his voice was rather dismissive. By and by, though, she seems to have slightly thawed, especially once Emil used *your* name, whereupon she went into a sort of swoon, as Emil told me. 'Oh, he's so unbelievably affectionate. Meeting him was so good for me,' she apparently remarked as soon as he mentioned you. But she told him that of course she was not entitled to pass on information about any customer's accounts. This morning, though, Hamburg time, middle of the night our time, Frau Simone called my Emil from home and told him something that, if my instinct doesn't deceive me, will occupy us for a long time with its further ramifications. She had, she said, quite against all bank rules, done a little research in restricted files. And had stumbled upon the following find, which I must warn you not to take for hard evidence—we have nothing in writing, I am merely repeating to you what Emil Gotthardt told me from his conversation with Simone von Oelffen. Perhaps you know the children's game called Chinese Whispers? You know the way a message can change as it's delivered from ear to ear? How hallucination can become assassination, or delivery can become beriberi? My piece of news therefore is to be treated with caution—five years before his death, your uncle, Alexander Stecher Bravo, seems to have transferred three-quarters-of-a-million dollars from Hamburg to Panama. Which would mean that, with interest accrued, there should be a million, I repeat a million dollars, on deposit there, that is, unless Señor Stecher acquired some very expensive habits in his last five years of life. My dear fellow, don't faint, as I say, my information is completely unofficial. But it still looks as though your uncle had a little bit more than you thought, doesn't it? Am I right? Come on, man, get a grip! Here, sit down on this stone pediment, I can stand, no problem!"

"A ... a million? ... "

"Yes, a million dollars. Not Deutschmarks. In Hamburg, Alexander Stecher Bravo kept a foreign currency account denominated in dollars. A so-called deposit account. You really are a sight to behold you know, sitting there; you could easily be one of those gargoyles on the façade of Notre Dame in belle Paris. Frau von Oelffen told Mr Gotthardt that your uncle transferred the sum to Panama, to the local branch of the German Bank of Latin America, and thereupon wound up his dollar account in Hamburg. So when he died, all that was left in Hamburg was the giro account, with which you're already familiar."

"But would that mean ... that Kirshman could have grabbed everything in Panama as well?"

"Herr Loew, you impress me with your powers of deduction. Of course we must assume that Julio Kirshman was also given powers of attorney for Panama. In which case, he would presumably have collected everything that belongs to you there."

"I've got to get him!" The heir leaps up. "That crook—a million dollars! I need to talk to him, now, right away!"

"Hold on! We need to get more precise information first, to be able to prove that Kirshman proceeded in Panama the way he did in Hamburg, when he produced his power of attorney. Noon, tomorrow, presumably, the coup will be over, and we can meet him. But before that I want to have found out whether your uncle's accounts are still extant, or ... if they were wound up some time ago."

"But I thought you told me a moment ago that it wasn't possible to obtain information about numbered accounts?" He can't keep his balance. Sits back down on the pediment. His head is shaking with excitement.

"Emil will use inter-bank communications to try and peek into their computer ... "

"But he could have done that right away. Why go the long way round and involve Simone von Oelffen?"

"Since we know how large your inheritance could be, we will be able to hold out the promise of little rewards to all kinds of people if they help us. Emil will offer a present to an acquaintance of his at the GBSA in Panama if he is prepared to access the computer records tomorrow morning, before business opens." And, after a pause: "Why did you never discuss with your uncle

95

how much he was going to leave you?"

"Because it's not done. That's the way I was brought up. It was thought of as very infra dig in my father's house to talk about money. From time to time, my mother violated that basic law of my father's, and that always led to ghastly family quarrels. I'll tell you a story of my childhood, then you'll possibly understand me a bit better—I was about six. We were staying in a hotel near Innsbruck, in Austria. A young couple were playing tennis, and I helped them by running around and picking up balls for them. When they finished, they gave me a schilling by way of thanks—*one* Austrian schilling. I ran to my parents, showed them my earnings, proud and full of myself. Father pulled a face—he insisted I return my wage immediately. It wasn't done for a child to accept money. I trotted in tears back to the tennis courts, gave my benefactors back their coin. They didn't want to take it. Only by telling them repeatedly of my father's rage did I manage to get rid of the schilling ... "

"What an idiot your father sounds, if I may say so. I'm sorry, but it really takes the biscuit for principled stupidity!"

"On the other hand, it really isn't right," Daniel went on, not responding to the lawyer's comment, "to speak to an elderly man, who assumed he still had a fair number of years left ahead of him, about what he might bequeath. It's like counting on his death, the anticipation of coming into his possessions. Don't you think?" Stecher Bravo had once tried to have a conversation with him about all this, but he wouldn't be drawn. "I steered clear of it ... "

"By the way, it occurs to me you haven't yet told me whether you wanted to make use of my services or not? I wouldn't want to put any pressure on you. In view of the new situation, though—"

"I would like to ask you with all due ceremony to be my legal representative in this case," says Daniel.

"As I think I told you, I charge two hundred dollars an hour. And fifteen per cent of the sum at issue, if we manage to recover it one day."

They shake hands.

It grows dark.

In the distance, the wailing of police and fire-sirens.

The streetlights come on.

Shoulder-to-shoulder, they stride back to the hotel.

In the meantime, an armoured personnel carrier has taken up position on the Plaza Venezuela. Two soldiers in battle fatigues climb out of the vehicle. Their heads are concealed under black plastic helmets and opaque visors.

"You do carry your passport with you at all times?" Dr Johannes asks.

The thought of the fortune waiting in Panama City eclipses any other—Daniel is only marginally aware that they are facing the threat of a passport check.

The soldiers allow the two men to pass.

In the humid evening heat, Loew tiptoes along as if on a sheet of thin ice. Keeps his head rigid, staring half-upwards at the sky.

" … We made it!" Dr Johannes gives a deep sigh of relief. Two shrill blasts of a whistle at their backs, like those of a referee at a soccer game.

They turn round.

One of the soldiers has pushed his visor up. The gestures of his arms and hands are further reminiscent of the soccer field. It's the way a referee calls a player to him, before giving him the red card.

They make their way back to the two heavily armed men.

"*Control de documentos!*" The soldier takes the whistle out of his mouth.

A million dollars! It's all Daniel Loew has room for inside him.

Dr Johannes hands the men his passport. The soldier calls the numbers two, nine, four, three, six, nine into a radio. The curfew was still in force, were the two of them not aware of that?

Loew is rummaging feverishly through his pockets.

The second soldier removes his helmet. The officer tells him off, the recruit. The subordinate replaces his helmet, takes a minute till it's back on.

Daniel carries his driving licence, issued in London. The picture even bears some faint resemblance to him. He hands it to the soldier.

"*Pasaporte?*" asks the young recruit, flaps the driving licence open and shut, turns it over.

"*Sí.*"

Dr Johannes is chewing his lower lip.

The officer calls to see the document as well. "*Inglaterra?*"

"*Sí!*"

Where is he staying?

"Hotel Presidente."

"*Habitacion?*"

"What does he want to know?"

"Your room number."

"One, two, four, four."

"*Uno, dos, cuatro, cuatro,*" the lawyer translates. Dr Johannes pleads that he is an attorney, and assumed that the curfew had been lifted. Thereupon the older of the two soldiers objects—where in that case are the pedestrians and the cars and the bicycles? An attorney of all people owed respect to the law, and to a far greater degree than an ordinary citizen. He will allow him and his foreign guest to go, and would not arrest them, though he was perfectly within his rights to do so. But both Dr Johannes and the foreigner will have to present themselves to a court of law tomorrow morning in the city. With a ballpoint pen whose ink has dried out, he writes down the address of the office where they have to present themselves punctually at eleven. Should the men not be there at the said time, a call will go out for their arrest.

They receive their documents back.

A million dollars, thinks the heir.

They carry on walking, shoulder-to-shoulder.

"For God's sake, man, where's your passport? Why haven't you got your passport on you? That could have been very nasty!"

"It's in the safe at the Kiba-Nova offices … "

"I can't believe it."

"It wasn't my idea to go out on the street."

"You're blaming *me*? We agreed we didn't want to stay in the hotel. I'm sure it wasn't a sensible idea. But if we'd stayed, we would have had our hands full of your admirer!" The lawyer wiped his bleeding lip on his shirt cuff. "And how does your passport come to be in Kirshman's safe?"

They reach the El Presidente, walk briskly across the lobby, and retreat to room 1244.

"I'm going to have to spend the night in the hotel," announces Dr Johannes. "And I'd like to point out to you that the hours I spend sleeping here will go down on your bill."

Daniel's hands are shaking. He can see the day when the complete sum of his inheritance will arrive in his Hamburg account.

"Call Kirshman, tell him he has to return your passport tomorrow morning, the earlier the better. And make the following suggestion to him, I thought about it during our delightful passport check earlier—tell him you might be prepared to cede him the rights to Stecher's apartment at a relatively favourable rate, not much below market price, but sufficiently that he gets the idea he's getting a good deal. That way we can lull him into a sense of security. Then, as soon as we've got the Hamburg money back from him as well, we can move onto the next phase."

"I told him in a fit of rage … I told him he owed me the money from Panama as well … "

"No, that's not possible!" And, after a pause: "And when did you tell him that, for heaven's sake?"

"The day before yesterday."

Dr Johannes buries his face in his hands. He wails softly. "It can't be true! It mustn't be! That would mean that during the coup he could have transferred everything by telephone to Honolulu or God knows where, to Switzerland, Norway, Cape Canaveral. Have you never heard of tactics? Or strategy? What's the matter with you? Surely no one in this day and age can be so naive? Are you … a boy scout, or what are you?!"

The lawyer spends the night next door, in room 1246. The walls are thin. The breathing of Daniel's neighbours mixes with his daydream of future freedom from worry. His second-hand car, a Rover, he plans to keep, nor will he move out of the little house on Agincourt Road, he has no plans to splash out on a new wardrobe, or to buy umpteen pairs of new shoes. Valeria could get a piece of jewellery from him, for the first time in their ten years together. A ring. Perhaps a necklace. Or earrings? He intends to go on working as before, with the one major difference—that he won't feel that fear each morning when he gets up, the continual dread in the pit of his stomach, the pressure in his chest, that he might not be able to feed his wife, their unborn child. It seems to him that the lawyer's suspicion is actually baseless, his fear lest Kirshman could have plundered the money in Panama that was his, the nephew's by right. Fate couldn't be so unfair to him. The story of his inheritance will come to a satisfactory conclusion all round.

He didn't manage to get Julio that evening. Left him a message that he needed his passport. Asked Kirshman to bring the document to him in his hotel as early as possible tomorrow morning. "Also, I have an offer I'd like to make to you, Julio, which will please you," he says on the answering machine.

He tells his wife about the treasures waiting in Stecher's numbered accounts that Dr Johannes has discovered.

"Congratulations," replies Valeria, "but isn't your pleasure premature? If the money was still there, wouldn't the executor behave towards you with more politeness, kindness, benevolence? I keep saying to you—you shouldn't count on having money that actually isn't in your account yet … "

"Once we've got the money! I am assuming that Kirshman's intentions are basically good, that he just wants to get everything under his control, in an orderly way, before he springs his surprise on me. That's exactly the way I would do it, if I was in his shoes. What would you like? What can I buy you? I'm so excited, I can't sleep!"

"Come home. I need you near me. You've been gone a week already. Come home … and now go to sleep. Try and get some sleep … "

13

DANIEL IN THE LION'S DEN

H E IS LYING AWAKE.
"I wrote my best poems," Daniel murmurs into the silence, "when I was seventeen and eighteen." He checks his memory for his earliest compositions.

To him, poetry is the crowning glory of literature. It is the music of the earth, and the cosmos, to his way of thinking. However, when he reads the poems of others, his eyes start to spin after a few minutes, he feels, almost invariably, nauseous, dizzy, headachy. Parcels and parcels of books sent to him by publishers, by friends, by strangers, remain unread, if not still sealed up in their envelopes.

As a visitor at Marta Feuchtwanger's, the widow of the writer living in Pacific Palisades, he had once been asked to recite his poems to a small audience of invited guests. One of those present on that evening, Jonathan Glitter, was so impressed by the reading—even though it was in German—that he helped the twenty-two-year-old to secure his first publication in the United States.

"That won't have much to do with your poetry, or your gift," Daniel's mother had speculated at the time—he had proudly told her about his meeting with the famous poet. "You know, that Glitter, I know people who know him, but he's quite partial to pretty young men like yourself ... do you understand what I'm saying?"

A book of his poems appeared simultaneously with Sparrow Press, San Diego, a well-regarded poetry press, and the Edition Manuskripte, Graz, under the title *Mindblow/Seelenlärm*. In a congenial translation by the poet Steven Jennings, it had an enthusiastic critical reception in the US as well as in Europe.

For instance, the British poet Andrew Fimes cheered in the Books Pages of the *New York Times*: "A new music is heard in Daniel Loew's hymnal poems. The simplest, least spiritual things are elevated to the status of richly poetic image by these delicate songs. The author is able, with his supple rhythms, to show each syllable in close-up, as if under a language microscope. And yet, he is no technician, but an eroticist of language. He seeks the nearness of things, and not the being crushed by the lofty and numinous. We won't have heard the last of Daniel Loew, of that I am quite certain."

With his spreading fame, there arrived the first reverse. An influential German daily paper accused him in its weekend supplement of 27th October 1975 of plagiarism, a grave charge that went on to be taken up by other reviewers, before being energetically swatted aside by a large majority of Germanists and literary historians.

"Loew isn't bad at what he does," he read in a piece by Elisabeth Schoeller-Schröder, "he picks up lines of Emily Dickinson, and pertly mixes them with verses by the schizophrenic poet, Josef Bartosch. Rarely, if ever in Loew's poetry, do we meet with anything like an original voice. His externalised inwardness is always questing for something worth questing for, and ends up as nothing more than nostalgia for nostalgia." Paul Celan was cited as one of the main sources of Daniel's inspiration, with mention made of Celan's own alleged poetic unreliability—Celan too was the victim of a calamitous, almost murderous campaign of slander, accused of the theft of intellectual property.

Daniel admired Celan, hadn't read Emily Dickinson since he was a teenager, and had never heard of Josef Bartosch, before the Schoeller-Schroder attack. He was sure he had never knowingly plagiarised any of the three.

After the appearance of the article, he went to visit the mad poet Bartosch in his institution in Gugging, outside Vienna. He brought with him both his volumes of poetry, *Galaxis/Nucleus* from 1973, and *Mindblow/Seelenlärm*, and told him while they walked back and forth in the chill institution corridors, that he had been accused of stealing from him.

The old man, whose speech was hard to follow, tossed his head back in the air, and, without bringing it back down, offered the following: "Never mind, you Daniel in the lion's den, who opens the gates, whose heart was chopping wood in his heart, tick-tack, and where there was a creaking to be heard as well— Don't worry about it!" And when they said goodbye, he called after the visitor: "The beginning and ending of a poem are the most important … " A bee buzzed around him, and he let it.

Now Loew set himself to read all the gently comic, subtly dramatic works of the infirm poet. And saw no similarity between his own poetry and that of Josef Bartosch, beyond the obvious congruence in their writing about nature, and their familial gloom.

In Emily Dickinson, however (after looking for a long time), he did come across one image that appeared in one of his odes:

> *I have never seen 'Volcanoes'—*
> *But, when Travellers tell*
> *How those old—phlegmatic mountains*
> *Usually so still—*
>
> *Bear within—appalling Ordnance,*
> *Fire, and smoke, and gun,*
> *Taking Villages for breakfast,*
> *And appalling Men …*

The metaphor of the volcano had, he assumed, entered his subconscious, and had become part of his own thinking and feeling and writing—the lines:

> *Silent volcano*
> *Sometimes eating*
> *Whole villages for breakfast*
> *By moonlight the drive*

Up Shikoku Mountain

appeared in his early poem, *Kyotokyosaka*. But to make one borrowing or coincidence the basis for a charge of plagiarism seemed excessive. He began to make a study of his opponent, asked friends and strangers to try and trace her history, and finally ordered a book that was produced by the Department for Writing and Book Care, which had been published in 1942 by Schoeller-Schröder's father, Heinrich, on: *Judaism and Intellectual Theft*. The monograph discussed works by Alfred Döblin, Franz Werfel, Joseph Roth, and Arthur Schnitzler, emphasising their "criminal tendency" in seizing on "German cultural property, Aryan inheritance, as if it belonged to them, that bastard race of mingled blood, forever thirsting to plunge Christian peoples to their ruination".

Lying on his hotel bed, soaked in sweat, as if he'd been standing under a shower of warm rain, Daniel exhorts himself—Think of happier days! And quotes from the very first poem he ever published. To see his own name in print for the very first time, and then in a well-regarded newspaper at that—*Heartawake* appeared in the Saturday supplement of the Viennese daily paper, *Die Presse*, 'by Daniel Loew'. On the day of publication, 8th November 1969, the fifteen-year-old high school pupil was living as if in a trance. Kept looking at the creased newspaper. Thought that was fame. From that day forth, people would have no alternative but to see in him the born poet.

How much more clearly my youthful spirit used to absorb whatever it encountered, thinks Daniel. Every scene, every colour, every movement, every shading I could register and put into words, the confusion seemed to want to express itself in form and silence. If only I had a mechanism, he wished, back then, that would take down what I could see and hear in my head! Emotions, he wrote in his workbook, are my capital. He felt akin to the post-chaise overtaking its swift horses. He enjoyed the sparkling in his head, the feeling of inner triumph when something new was created, took delight in the profound quest for essences, the various processes of finding and gauging, reaching and losing. He worked through whole nights. To stay up all night—what a deep pleasure then, and what torment today.

His father and mother spoke warmly of his early poetic efforts, didn't urge him to aim for a financially more secure occupation in later life. They didn't criticise his indecision, when he showed his uncertainty about what to study, and where to go. A year after his final school exams, he began studying Astronomy and Meteorology at Christ Church College. His father, who was barely able to pay the rent on his apartment, paid his way through five terms at Oxford, sent him money for the fees, and most of his living expenses. His mother asked him not to take on any extra work in addition to studying, when he thought he should try to do something to improve his own financial position and that of his parents: "Don't overstrain yourself," she wrote to him. "You are not like the others. You are not as strong. You get tired faster than other people do. Do you want to spend your evenings as a barman in a pub? Or get up at four to work in a petrol station? Better concentrate on your studies. We can manage, your father and I, without you having to scratch around for money!"

Studying came easily to him. Far too easily. He thought of switching to veterinary medicine or molecular biology, architecture, physics or nuclear chemistry, subjects that would have taken more out of him, and pushed him harder. And was far too easy-going to expose himself to the arduousness of such a decision. He didn't finish studying the science of the heavens or the nature of the weather. Broke off his studies as soon as mathematics, since elementary school his weakest subject, emerged as the most critical parallel discipline to the two he had selected. But he was indebted to the years in the astronomy and meteorological departments for what they taught him about colours, sounds, the widening of his perspective that he began to integrate into his work, moments of discovery that enriched his first book of poems, *Galaxis/Nucleus*, published in 1973 by a small press in Austria.

Only Stecher Bravo came forward with doubts. It seemed advisable to him, he wrote to Daniel's parents, to push their son carefully in the direction of a profession that would allow him to pursue his poetic inclinations in his time off, but yet that would afford him some sort of a living. He suggested three possible fields for which, in his view, his nephew showed talent—literature, architecture and languages. If his advice were not heeded, he could see difficult times looming ahead. "You need to exert a more positive influence, listen to me, even if it's only this once. The boy has talent, but he will only gain my respect and the world's good opinion if he succeeds in making his own way for himself, not dependent on your modest income, or on the sum that one day, God willing, he will inherit from me."

Jacob Loew disregarded his cousin's letter. Didn't even think it worth replying, or to pass on the uncle's advice to Daniel. By chance, Alexander's lines fell into the hands of the heir following his father's moving, barely a month after Stecher's death.

"I must write," the then twenty-two-year-old jotted in his diary, at the time he broke off his studies so as to be able to devote himself entirely to writing verse, "it's the only thing I'm any good at."

He lies awake.

14

BEFORE THE LAW

"IT'S ME!" THE VOICE OF DR JOHANNES.
  Three hours after Daniel went off to sleep, a knock on the door of his hotel room.

"It's us!" The voice of Esther Moreno.

He gets up, slips into his dressing gown.

They were having breakfast, they say, at their separate tables, both waiting for him, without paying any attention to each other. Both expected him to arrive in the dining room " … At any moment!" they chime as one. When he failed to show, they started talking.

"She's a backgammon grand master! Like my mother in Santiago, when I was a kid!"

They stand in front of him, like father and mother, Dr Johannes and Esther Moreno.

"What are you grinning at? Get dressed, it's nine o'clock, we need to be in court in two hours. You're on an empty stomach, but we have a number of things we need to talk about. Esther can be in on it; I've got over my suspicion of her," he grabs her round the waist, lets his hand drop again. "Trust, as we say in Chile, is the sugar in the sweet pea."

"Is the coup all over, then?"

"We've survived this time," replies Dr Johannes. "Try and call Kirshman again. You need your passport!"

Daniel shuts the door, switches on the television: " … to normality this morning with the lifting of the curfew. Residents recall with shock startling images—" scenes of the devastation around the cathedral area; also, the Bolivar memorial, badly damaged by machine-gun fire—"of a coup attempt that left two hundred and thirty people dead … "

The phone rings. "It's me, Julio. I'm here. In the lobby. You coming down?"

Most of the El Presidente's guests are leaving Caracas this morning, practically simultaneously, suitcases are piled up, taxi-drivers and minibus chauffeurs are touting for business from the tourists. Those leaving are giving tips to maids, waiters and hotel staff.

Kirshman is sitting in the middle of all the noise, engrossed in a special edition of the *Noticias de Caracas* devoted to the events of the last forty-eight hours. Right next to him, Esther Moreno and Dr Johannes are getting out a backgammon board, throwing dice, moving the counters.

Kirshman jumps when Daniel turns up in front of him. "Ooh, you gave me a shock!"

Dr Johannes looks up, realises who is just shaking hands with his client, whispers to Esther Moreno whom it is. And both pretend to be unconcerned, seemingly carry on with their game.

Loew, sitting at Kirshman's side, is reciting to himself over and over, like a mantra: nothing about Panama! Daniel, be discreet, be quiet!

"Did you bring my passport, Julio?"

"Well, what do you say about my country? The things that go on here!" Hands him his passport, Daniel slides it into his inside pocket, and buttons it up.

"Why didn't you call me when the coup was getting underway? Why didn't you warn me not to go out on the street?"

"Not call you? Because I … didn't have a number for you … "

"Don't you have a phone book at home?"

"Just in the office. What does it matter, you called me anyway. You got in ahead of me!"

"And you couldn't get the hotel number from information—"

"They never answer, those people, and I expect they took advantage of the coup to go on strike too! Anyway, never mind. Forget it. But you were going to make me an offer? … "

"I wanted to ask … whether you might want to buy Alexander's apartment from me … "

108

"There, that's my kind of talk. It's nice to hear you in that vein. How much are you asking?"

Dr Johannes had dinned it into the heir the night before: "Take your time when you're negotiating with Kirshman. Suggest you might be willing under certain circumstances to sell him the apartment. If he shows interest, ask him how much he'd be prepared to pay. Don't begin by telling him how much you'd like. It seems you don't know the first thing about business. Wait to hear how much the apartment's worth to him. Don't be in too much of a hurry! Your uncle lived in a very sought-after part of town. Apartments in San Bernardino go for a lot of money, believe me." The lawyer suggested a bare minimum, below which he should in no case go.

Daniel was unable to bring himself to mention this sum, much less any higher figure.

"How much you want for it, I'd like to know!"

"Seventy-five thousand."

"Seventy-five thousand what? Bolivares, Lire, Dollars, Marks? Pounds Sterling?"

"Dollars ... " He has a sensation of floating outside of himself—like a dead man, looking at his own mortal integument. He feels embarrassed to ask for more, even though Alexander Stecher Bravo's apartment is worth at least a hundred thousand dollars, if not much more.

"Seventy-five? No problem! I'll give you that!"

" ... and also the money you collected ... in Hamburg, a few months ago ... "

"My poet!" His delighted anticipation of Stecher Bravo's apartment evidently soothes the executor: "My, you've become quite the businessman during our little coup! So all in all, you're looking to pick up almost a hundred and fifty thousand dollars from me!"

"Not from you, Julio ... "

"Well, who else? Oh, one other thing. I've been busy, at eight o'clock this morning, I was in court, and I got legal approval of everything I've done, here it is in black and white. The late lamented Sasha's dying wishes have been carried out to the letter, so in case you feel a twinge of suspicion, like you did a couple of days ago, here it is, all in writing: Julio Kirshman has discharged his duties as *albacea* in accordance with the law, and there're no sins of omission or commission. The court confirmed that for me, and now everything's done and dusted. So. Any more questions?"

The heir closes his eyes. Not a word! Not a word about Panama! He opens his eyes again.

"You still tired, I suppose? Jetlag can do that to you. It can take you a week to get yourself back together." Julio pulls out a document studded with three stamps and two wax seals. "The affair will be confirmed at the High Court later today, tomorrow at the latest, and then we'll be quits, you and me, you'll get your money, and then sayonara … "

Esther and the lawyer watch the executor's every move. Dr Johannes is making strange shapes with his mouth. Loew doesn't understand what he's trying to tell him.

"Have you got any more questions then, I asked you? … " Julio repeats.

Finally, he manages to read Dr Johannes' lips: "Would it bother you," he asks, "if I get a photocopy of the document?"

The lawyer nods. With relief, with delight. "Sure, course you can, no sweat, why would it bother me? Ask them at the reception desk, here you go, take it."

Loew asks the porter to make a copy of the document for him.

"All right then—late afternoon today, you come by the office," says Kirshman, as Daniel returns the document to him, and keeps the copy for himself. "There I'll give you your money, two banker's drafts, one for Hamburg, the other for the apartment. The balance in the savings book here in Caracas, you remember, that was about six thou, give or take, so I'll just hang onto them to cover the costs of Sasha's funeral, and a modest recompense for my trouble as executor. You won't have anything against that, I expect?"

"That's … fine." Daniel walks Julio to the revolving door. A hotel employee drives up in the Japanese jeep. Kirshman gets in.

Dr Johannes and Esther Moreno are studying the photocopy of the legal document.

"He must have shelled out ten thousand dollars to get that, first thing this morning!" groans the attorney. "If not more! It takes months, normally, to get a determination like that approved. Months, Herr Loew. But he set off at eight am to the Criminal Courts, a minute after they opened the doors, at the end of fifty hours of a military coup, and in less than an hour—because he was here just after nine—he's managed to obtain a piece of paper confirming that he has acted fully in accordance with the law, and no one can lay a finger on him, not even in future! We need to get moving right away—if a Higher Court judge confirms this one, Julio Kirshman is in the clear, and it won't be possible to bring a charge against him in Venezuela. We have to try and get to the High Court."

"How are we going to manage that?" asks Daniel.

"I don't think we've a chance ... " Esther Moreno shakes her head.

"We try and get a time, right now, I mean lucky we've got our summons, the two of us, then we'll speak about the case, you can leave that to me ... What did he say about the apartment?"

"I sold it."

"You can't have done it as quickly as that!"

The poet is silent.

"For how much then, for Heaven's sakes?"

"Seventy-five."

"Don't you remember what I told you yesterday, you hopeless case—on no account take anything under a hundred thousand dollars!"

"I wanted to show willing ... "

"Has he shown willing to you?"

"No."

"So, why the ridiculous offer? ... "

"I ... I couldn't do anything else."

It takes Dr Johannes, at the wheel of his Mercedes, an hour to get from the El Presidente to the law courts, so dense is the traffic this rainy morning after the lifting of the curfew. Loew sits in the back seat. The air-conditioned interior is heavy with the smell of perspiration. He feels sick. He hasn't had any breakfast, not so much as a cup of coffee.

"We could have got there in twenty minutes on foot," the lawyer says crossly, "we knights of the sorrowful countenance."

" ... But we'd have got soaked," Esther Moreno adds. She is sitting beside Friedrich Johannes.

Daniel sniffs behind the two front seats. The smell of sweat is coming unmistakably from Mrs Moreno. Crowds are already snaking all over the ground floor of the only recently opened six-storey court building. The crush is such, it's as though whole sections of town have been summoned to appear en masse. Dr Johannes charges off ahead, slips on the marble floor in his leather moccasins, spreads his arms like wings to regain his balance. Greets passing colleagues, nods at sentenced and acquitted parties.

On the second floor, outside courtroom 208, the lawyer pushes past the line of waiting people. Once at the front of the queue, he hears from one of those waiting that he has already been waiting for an hour-and-a-half for his hearing.

Dr Johannes calls his two secretaries on his mobile phone, repeats the name Emil Gotthardt several times—they were to try everything to get in touch with his friend. "May I ask you for a favour," he then says. "Esther, would you be so kind as to keep our place for us here, while Herr Daniel and I try and make some headway with the Higher Court."

"I'd much sooner stay with you ... " She sounds tired, drained.

Friedrich Johannes puts his arm on Esther's shoulder. He whispers something to her.

"I promised her," he mumbles, on the wide escalator up to the next storey, "that I would turn my attention to her difficulty with the apartment, as soon as our matter has been solved."

"Would I be right in thinking your initial suspicion of Mrs Moreno has abated? ... When I think back to the horror on your face, the first time you saw Madam! I'm surprised by your change of heart; I wouldn't have expected that from you. There

112

are similar transformations in my poems, quite often in fact—the ending of a poem is a break with all that's gone before. Even turns it on its head, casts it in doubt, makes everything appear in a different light."

"She's a thoroughly decent woman. I like her very much. I hope you have nothing against my seeking her closer acquaintance … "

"Not at all. I'm just surprised … "

"Well, you be surprised then. Life does these sorts of things … "

"And did you … mention Panama to her?"

"How can you say such a thing! The very idea!"

From the third floor, there are only flights of concrete steps leading up. The court building's lifts are not yet in use. The higher they go, the fewer people they see. The further up they are, the more unfinished is the construction of the law court. If the entrance hall had an imposing aspect, by the third floor, not all the doors are in place, and on the fourth there are no windows. On the fifth floor, a whole side of the building is clad in corrugated iron. Through little cracks you can see down over the city.

"Here, do you want to see the house where Simon Bolivar was born, there, see it?" They are standing in a puddle.

The lawyer knocks on a thin section of chipboard.

"*Entrar!*"

Six female court servants are sitting at six wooden desks. They greet Dr Johannes with affectionate familiarity. They are evidently amused to see him in court in jeans. He presents Daniel, asks the ladies to arrange an interview with Magistrada Graciela Collado, the Higher Court Judge, as soon as possible. And lists six makes of French perfume, pointing to one of them after each name.

The youngest, who was promised a bottle of Chanel No 5, disappears into a little cubbyhole. The connecting door is left open a crack. A short woman, dressed entirely in purple, is staring into space. The court servant tells Dr Johannes that the Judge could receive him and his client in half-an-hour. She is terribly busy just at the moment.

Dr Johannes' mobile goes off. The conversation takes half-a-minute. "Emil says his leg-man in Panama is willing to do something for us, if we pay out a certain sum in advance. Are you prepared to do that?"

"I can't … "

"That's really a pity, my dear fellow, a pity. Think it over. I have to go back down to Señora Moreno, I'll be back in two minutes!"

The court servant, to whom Dr Johannes had promised a bottle of Egoiste, now asks Daniel to show her his passport. She copies out the information, typing with black-varnished nails on a 1943 Remington. Loew sets his name to a piece of foolscap.

"It can take hours down there!" Dr Johannes is out of breath. "More and more people in line! I can't hang around here all day! Esther's keeping our place. She's a real trooper. Very rare for women to be so dependable. She kissed me, by the way. A wonderful woman. But no worries—I'm a devoted husband. Have been for twenty-five years … "

"Someone might have seen you … "

"Oh, everyone here has a mistress. Everyone but me. Women … well, you know it's impossible to talk to them. Impossible. It's been scientifically proven—the women of the species are closer to animals than humans."

The prettiest of the court servants calls them in—the judge will see them now.

"My only condition, Herr Loew, for continuing to intervene so generously on your behalf—here, I want you to sign the contract for fifteen per cent that we talked about yesterday—fifteen per cent of the sum at issue in Panama, should you be able to establish your title. Bottom right-hand corner, if you please."

Daniel signs it, on the move.

They are ushered into the little cubby-room. The door is closed behind them. Graciela Collada wears pink make-up on coarse-pored skin. The forty-year-old can barely squeeze her bulk into the soft leather armchair. She extends her oddly small left hand, a signal to the lawyer to begin to speak.

Dr Johannes' résumé of the events so far seems admirably concise to the heir. Señora Collado asks to be shown both the photocopy of the will and of the determination of the lower court this morning; she studies both documents, and shakes her black curly head slightly.

"We petition you, esteemed Señora Collado, not to back up the lower court!"

The judge points to Loew. Dr Johannes provides a simultaneous translation of his brief remarks. He mentions his work, the modest fame he enjoys in Europe, stresses how grateful he would be to receive justice in Venezuela.

"My client would hymn our nation in the highest tones, if his case could be brought to a favourable conclusion here."

The judge nods with earnest mien. Her artificial dress rustles.

"*E dos mil dolares ... como regalo para usted!*" Dr Johannes adds.

With a wave of the hand, they are sent on their way. Graciela Collado has not uttered one word in the course of the meeting.

"It's shaping up well," cries the lawyer, they hurry past the wind-warped piece of sheet metal, "I have a good feeling!"

"Did I hear what you said correctly? You promised her two thousand dollars?"

"*Como regalo*. As a present."

"Without discussing it with me? I'm to give something to your acquaintance in Panama, so that he gives us some information. Esther Moreno expects a certain sum from me, and I'm sure Frau von Oelffen in Hamburg does as well. You yourself will shortly present me with a bill, I assume. And now another two thousand dollars for the lady judge? I feel like a plucked carcass here, with only my bones left."

"Oh, oh, you're poetising again, my dear fellow! Nothing can be done here without presents, you must know that by now. Two thousand dollars—it's the absolute minimum in a case like this. Normally one would have to offer much more, but in this instance the court is grateful to learn of a Venezuelan's accounts abroad. It's not permitted, you should know, for citizens of our state to keep money abroad. But through your case, the authorities will discover what a certain, fairly successful Venezuelan businessman has done, and where and when and how he did it, and how much he kept outside the country. Why have you stopped? Here, down the stairs, can't you walk and think at the same time? Esther will worry about us being gone so long!"

They reach the second floor.

"Now where is the Moreno woman? Right at the front by now, I should think, come on. Esther? Esther!?"

Three voices call out: "*Sí! Presente!*"

The two farmhands who had been standing behind their acquaintance, are only a few yards from the hearing room. The lawyer asks where the woman is who has been keeping a place for him and his client? The men shrug their shoulders. He passes them some money. They let him in the queue. A chorus of whistles goes up from those waiting behind.

"And I always thought women had more capacious bladders than we men," Dr Johannes sighs. "Fine, everyone has to go to the *excusado* some time. It always irked me as a child when I was reading Karl May—the fact that they never needed to go, all those Winnetous and Old Shatterhands!"

In a summary hearing, lawyer and client are fined eight thousand bolivares apiece, the equivalent of a hundred dollars. As they leave room 208, there is no Esther Moreno to welcome them.

"I think I'm beginning, no seriously, Herr Daniel, I'm beginning to worry."

"I expect she lost patience, perhaps she's waiting by the kiosk at the entrance, or she's gone on to the car … "

"Women remain an enigma. An enigma wrapped in a riddle! There's just no relying on them. It's still raining, she's not going to be standing around outside."

"Well, then she took a taxi back to the hotel … " hazards the heir. "If I was in her shoes, I'd have done the same, I think."

They walk over to the Mercedes, and slip inside.

"I'll run you back to the El Presidente, quickly say hello to Esther, and then it's my office all the way."

The traffic has lessened considerably. After a short drive, they're back at the hotel. Daniel hurries on ahead, asks the concierge to put him through to room 1813.

"Who is it you wish to speak to?"

"Señora Esther Moreno."

Dr Johannes has caught up with him.

"Moreno," the man on the front desk slowly goes through the list of guests. "Moreno? We have no one of that name. And the occupant of room 1813 left half-an-hour ago. Ms Eva Singer, from Miami, Florida."

15

PENSION WAGNER

" **M**UY BIEN! MUY BIEN!" SQUAWKS A PARROT.
Daniel is swimming lap after lap of the pool. Over his head are twenty floors soaring up into the cloudy sky. Calm, regular breaststroke. A gentle drizzle slips into the pool.

Dr Johannes made a thorough confession, announced at the same time that he wanted to withdraw from the case of Loew versus Kirshman. He had contravened every guideline of his profession, even divulging to the unknown woman the fact that Stecher Bravo had kept numbered accounts in Panama. He recommended Daniel the services of a colleague very experienced in matters of probate, who would handle the case instead. The heir refused to accept the resignation of his lawyer—had he himself not completely trusted Esther Moreno, even though a soft voice inside him warned him against her, early on? And to put an end to Dr Johannes' tirades of self-accusation, he admitted the day before having met Francisco Shatil, the arbitrator of the Jewish community in Caracas, and having told him everything as well. The lawyer and his client are agreed—the accounts in Panama City have probably been liquidated in the past two days, and Stecher Bravo's bequest distributed among other banks, in other countries, on other continents.

"First we have to see whether the Miami phonebook has an entry for a Dr Eva Singer," said Dr Johannes as he left the El Presidente for his office half-an-hour before, to attempt to trace the real identity of Esther Moreno.

The palm trunks creaked gently in the hotel grounds.

A fine mess, isn't it, my boy? he heard Alexander's voice echoing in his head. But don't worry—it'll all turn out in the end. I just wanted to give you a little fright. I wanted to teach you once and for all that your irresponsibility will have to end. Thirty-eight years of irresponsibility is enough. The way you were when you lost your money-belt, or when any practicalities were involved always struck me as utterly idiotic. Your vagueness was a personal offence to me, perhaps I should have been more explicit about that when we met. But then it seems to me I gave you various indications anyway. You never reacted, you seemed so unworldly, you could have been a hermit, my boy. I should have told you what I thought, but I didn't want to cast a shadow over our meetings, I thought I would let you know when you came to visit me in Caracas. What I said to you in Hamburg was only a fraction of the whole. It's six years now since we met, you arrived at Hamburg Dammtor from London, I had paid both your train ticket and your couchette, naturally, we were to meet on the platform, which was our traditional place. You wondered whether you hadn't got off at the wrong stop, perhaps I had said the Hauptbahnhof, or Hamburg-Altona. In Hamburg, that city with three principal stations, it's easy for misunderstandings of that kind to happen …

As soon as the Heinrich Heine express came to a stop at Hamburg Dammtor, Daniel jumped out onto the platform. It was early October, a day with a blue-white, practically cloudless sky. He waited down in the dirty station hall for his uncle, surprised that he was late, which was most out of character for Stecher. Finally pulled a map out of his rucksack, looked for the street with the pension that Alexander had patronised for decades. Moorweidenstrasse, he saw, was right by the Dammtor. Perhaps, with his increasing hardness of hearing, Stecher had misheard the time of his arrival.

The deserted lobby of the Pension Wagner was papered with a classical frieze of ancient Greek vases on a sienna ground. He rang a little bell on the reception table. Silence, but for the echo of the little bell. He rang again.

"Hold your horses, I'm coming!" a man in his mid-seventies in a pink stripy shirt, with dyed blond hair and a gel-induced bounce. "What can I do for you?"

"My name is Loew … "

"It's a miracle your uncle's still alive, he collapsed here last night. Wagner, pleased to meet you, I've known Herr Stecher for ever, well, he's in Saint Anne's, by the Klosterstern. I'm sure he'll be thrilled you're here. If he's still capable of recognising you, he was this close to dying!"

Alarmed, Daniel asked whether the proprietor could tell him what had caused his uncle's collapse?

"His face was completely blue. The ambulance took him to Saint Anne's … didn't I already tell you that?"

There was no record of Stecher in the private clinic. The woman on reception seemed to remember that yesterday evening, an ambulance had drawn up, but had then gone on to the University Hospital in Eppendorf. She called there: "Will you do me a favour, miss? Stecher Bravo, given name Alexander. No, yesterday, ten at night, say. I'll hold. That's wonderful. Thank you." She nodded, and gave him the address of the Eppendorf hospital.

Alexander was in a ward with five others. He was awake when his nephew entered the room, his cheeks looked fresh, he had drips on both wrists. "Nice to see you, excellent, how did you manage to find me?"

Three old men listened to every word. A couple of younger men were in deep sleep. Their uneven breaths whistled a duet.

"What happened to me, you want to know? Intestines, apparently, the usual story with me, some sort of inflammation, it's not quite clear, nothing too terrible though. They'll discharge me tomorrow, or the day after. I'm only sorry I wasn't able to let you know in time."

"Herr Wagner said he thought you'd be in Saint Anne's … "

At that, Stecher laughed his coarse, cackling old man's laugh. "Well, of course that's where they wanted to take me! Cunning devils. But I've got my wits about me, even semi-comatose as I was, I thought, I can't afford that! First class, who's going to

121

afford that? You can do that just as well here—die or pull through."

"But they'd have given you a room to yourself … "

"And after two days I'd be reduced to penury! … "

The consultant, Dr Stallbohm, took Daniel aside and told him his uncle was suffering from a chronic intestinal inflammation, a so-called diverticulitis, which could occasionally lead to violent attacks such as the one he'd just experienced. What he needed was plenty of rest and a light and balanced diet, two golden rules to which the patient had clearly not paid sufficient heed.

Daniel pointed out to Stallbohm that Alexander hadn't worked for about thirty years, and was basically leading the calm life of early retirement. "He sits in his favourite chair and reads and reads, at least that's his account of how he lives. And once a year, he heads off on long jaunts to Europe. Looks after his investments, builds his fortune, grows his capital. But as far as I know, that's all there is to it … "

" … But something's eating at him, from inside. Try and find out what it is. Some fear? Some anxiety? Some passion that's making his life miserable? Try and take advantage of the time you spend together with him to find out what the possible root cause of his illness might be."

The following day, the nephew sat at Stecher Bravo's bedside all day, only left him to get something to eat himself, at the canteen. Fear spread in Daniel's head, he kept plucking at his shirt and his too-tight jacket, he tensed his toes until they hurt. Experienced the eyes, hands, shoulders, backs of the men who shared Stecher's ward as focuses of absolute sorrow and of the bleakest and most impoverished existence.

On the evening of the day after, Alexander was discharged from the hospital. He protested when Daniel insisted on getting a cab to take him back to the Pension Wagner. "Stuff and nonsense! Of course we're taking the subway to Sternschanze. I can do it in my sleep, we change trains, then it's one stop to Dammtor, and the last little bit we do on foot."

It took Dr Stallbohm's personal intervention to induce his uncle to abandon his plan. The higher the figures climbed on the taximeter, the noisier Stecher's sighs.

As soon as the taxi pulled up on Moorweidenstrasse, his uncle said: "Have you got money on you? Can you lend me the price of the taxi? I haven't got a penny on me!"

Daniel paid. They got out.

He accompanied Stecher to his room, switched on the lights, helped him to get undressed and handed him his pyjamas, stayed with him till he was lying in bed, with the covers over him and only the tip of his nose peeking out.

"You could have taken *my* room while I was in hospital, that would have been fine by me!"

"I'm paying for my own room—please!"

"That wasn't what I meant to suggest, I'm just saying it would have been a possibility. Never mind. Not important."

Daniel made to leave the room and let his uncle sleep. It was nine o'clock.

"Stay with me please, don't go yet. Will you visit the Cassuto grave on this visit? Do you remember where it is? Can you find it by yourself? You always forget everything anyone tells you. Cassuto was descended from Spanish Sephardim who dropped anchor in Hamburg at the end of the sixteenth century, in their own ships and with rich merchandise. They built docks, and helped the hanseatic seaport to a fabulously wide network of trade relationships. You should write it all down, make a note of our family history, it could furnish you with the material for a prose work one day, in case you one day turn to prose. Cassuto had nine daughters—he was so poor, you know his daughters had just two winter coats between them. Seven of them he preferred to give in marriage to Christians, instead of pairing them off with German Jews, such was Rav Cassuto's contempt for the Ashkenazim. So great was your forefather's hatred for German Jews, he is supposed to have said to his wife once: 'Don't sit on that chair, Malkale, or at least wipe it first, there was a *tedesco* on it before!' Only his daughter Sarah found a Sephardic Jew to marry, to the great delight of Yehuda Mordechai's, and that was your great-grandfather Daniel Bravo, the owner of a cigar factory in Altona. And Sarah's first-born daughter, my mother Luna Bravo, married Johann Stecher, a Protestant from Heiligenhafen, a representative from his early manhood of the weavers and clothiers Nischen & Abel. After father died, I followed in his shoes. Once half-Jews were no longer permitted to work, my employers helped me escape across the ocean. September 'thirty-nine seems completely unreal to me now, almost a fairy tale—the steamship Caribia with seventy-four refugees on board set course for Curaçao, once several other South American ports had refused us permission to land. On the high seas, a telegram arrived that gave us leave to stay in Venezuela for thirty days. It was clear that a gentleman who came on board in Trinidad had interceded for us with the Venezuelan government. The ship turned so sharply, we almost all fell over. And brought us back to Porto Cabello, where we landed in the middle of the night. The authorities were extraordinarily generous to us. After just three weeks, I received indefinite permission to remain, and was allowed to work. The Dutch Bank employed me for an absurdly low wage, I accepted because I thought: once they see I'm a good worker, I'll be able to get ahead. You too, my boy, you shouldn't react too proudly if your publishers initially don't pay you what you think you're worth. Unfortunately, the bank let me go when the Netherlands were occupied; they didn't want to have any German-speaking employees—even though everyone knew I was a refugee. A year later they tried to get me back, but I was outrageously proud, and demanded quadruple wages, a procuration payment and a contract of employment. And so I was without work for a time. Gave all my savings to a human trafficker, who promised to expedite the emigration of my mother and brother. The rascal to whom I gave the huge sum of several thousand dollars, held out on me for a whole year. The money was what my brother Arnold had given me as I was embarking in Marseilles, when we said goodbye. He had saved everything I had sent him from Hamburg to Paris over many years. I was beside myself with fear for my family, who were in France waiting for their promised deliverance. What dreadful wretches there are among our people! Finally, but only after I'd threatened him, the monster gave me back the money. Then two days later showed me a copy of a telegram from the Venezuelan government to their consul in Marseilles, giving my mother and brother permission to enter Venezuela. Of course, thereupon I gave him back the cheque, and was grateful to him all my life. Even though he tormented me for a whole year. My two dear ones came, I had barely enough money left to buy a chaise longue and a camp bed for them to sleep on. My landlord loaned us a table and chairs. Even so—we were immeasurably happy. And I was earning pretty good money from a merchant banker, who took me on as a partner, especially in those early post-war years, so that I was able to retire from formal work at the age of fifty-three, a year after you were born. I never regretted it. I could have swum in money and become really rich, but what would have been the point? My reserves I didn't make at work, my boy, but at the New York Stock Exchange. I had a client, a German anti-Nazi of exactly my own age, who was a close friend of the then-President of Shell Oil. Gambling on the stock exchange is for mugs. The only point in putting money on it is if you have inside information. And I was lucky enough that I did. It all sounds like a dream to me now. But now you tell me something about your life. I know hardly anything about you. You write to me far too infrequently, two, three letters a year, that's hardly a very rich harvest! Six years have passed since our last meeting in Meran. At that time you were in love with a girl you called the Indian. What became of her? How did you meet Valeria, where, when, that must have begun four years ago already, your life with her? And how did it happen that you set aside the idea of becoming pious, as you still wanted to be in Meran, if I remember correctly? Those occasional letters of yours aren't enough for me to be able to picture your life. You promised you would come to visit me in Caracas. And you still haven't come, though we agreed on it six years ago."

The nephew talked about the little house that he and Valeria had recently moved into and whose rent was more affordable than that on their previous, bigger, grander apartment, whose monthly rate they were unable to pay. "An émigrée from Vienna, living in London since the nineteen-thirties, a vehement anti-Zionist by the way, gives us the top two floors of her house on the most favourable conditions imaginable. She asks us—out of Marxist conviction—for an absolute minimum, basically no more than the upkeep of the house. It's a great stroke of fortune, because low rents are very uncommon in London."

"What an idea, to live there, my dear fellow. London is said to be the most expensive city in Europe, were you aware of that? When Heine wanted to go to London, his rich uncle warned him: 'Life in England is very expensive. London's an expensive city, everyone knows that, even those of us who don't write travel pieces!'"

"I … yes, I am aware of it. And a book I spend two or three years working on," said Loew, "brings me an advance, but as soon as I've given it in, I don't see another penny."

He assumed Stecher would fall asleep while he spoke, but the more he revealed about himself, the more alert Alexander seemed to become: "How can a Jewish girl have a name like Valeria? And what exactly is it she does, I've never quite understood, to be honest."

She was the daughter of a Polish woman and a teacher in the Grisons canton of Switzerland, who in the early fifties lost his job as a headmaster in Chur, once it became known that he was deceiving his wife from an old Grisons family with a Jewess from Cracow. "Valeria's mother had somehow got to Switzerland after the war, and was living there without a residence permit. And her father got divorced from his first wife, was transferred to a village school in the mountains, and slowly fell into poverty. The family lived from hand to mouth." She used her mother's family name, Zajdmann, but her father had had his way with the Romansh first name. "As a little girl she spent every evening sitting with her father and mother, while they all told each other stories. Only true things, nothing invented. And you had to recount the events of the days and nights so vividly, and so excitingly, that you could be sure the other was listening in fascination."

"And what is it she does again, to earn money?"

"She creates coats, dresses, skirts, jackets. Every piece tells its own story. Every one is unique. Sometimes, the garments have sentences sewn into them. There is one work of hers that has a poem of mine woven into it, something else might have a candy, and a third has laces and ribbons. She made a coat that was called '*What happens when you see Swansea for the very first time?*'"

"And these things, they sell? People buy them? I don't understand! … "

"A dress mustn't look like a dress too much, a skirt mustn't be too skirt-like, and above all a coat mustn't be too much of a coat. And garments that leave her sewing table mustn't exhibit the body of a woman, not show the figure at all. That disgusts her, she says."

"How did you meet?"

"In the lobby of the Palace Hotel in St Moritz. I was visiting a publisher, who was hoping to start a relationship with Valeria."

"So you stole her from him, is that right?" Stecher was grinning all over his face.

Daniel nodded shyly.

" … Are you planning to have children?"

"My last volume that appeared four years ago still hasn't earned back its advance from the publisher, even though *Remote Control* is my most successful publication to date, with translations into four languages. And in spite of all the miraculous reviews I've written to you about … "

"You can't live off good reviews."

"But imagine, a while ago I had a letter from New Haven, from Yale University. A certain Howard Farrell, Professor of Comparative Literature asked me whether I would agree to leave my literary remains to the University Library. Perhaps they think I'm ninety, or something."

"Or they're trying to get in ahead of time, and make sure they really will one day have your papers."

"But what do you think? Isn't it incredible?"

"That reminds me—I have a confession to make to you."

"Confession?"

"Your poetry does nothing for me. I've read and reread your slim volumes, and I'm sorry to have to say—they leave me cold. Your poetry gives me no pleasure or satisfaction. It remains dark and murky, things seem contrived, if not downright off-the-wall. It's not just the rhymes I miss in your work, it's iambs and hexameters and trochees and sonnets in alexandrines! You know, poetry has to be lithe and rhythmic, it can't be chopped up and mournful, like your outpourings. I happen to think that poetry is one branch of writing where people get away with murder. And you, I have to say, were always a particularly gifted con artist. Even so, it's glaringly obvious that you're never going to live from poetry. Just think of the number of people who like poetry. And of that tiny number think of the tiny fraction who are going to want to read *your* poetry, and no one else's. I'm eighty-four years old, I'm not going to be impressed by your crying over your financial woes. It's your responsibility. I can't even give you any advice. But there must be jobs, for you or your wife, positions that come with a monthly pay cheque? Even if you lose a little of your independence. You're going to have to look for a post of some kind, otherwise you'll never live up to what's required of the head of a family. *Bueno*, you're not used to regular, hard work. Until you start to work day after day with the utmost diligence and application, you will never feel the fruits of your labour in your pockets. Whoever works as little as you do really can't be surprised to find himself with the wolf at the door. A little poem here, a few lines there, and in between a lot of thumb twiddling and breathing in London smog. Real labour is something you know nothing about, my unworldly friend! Well, and now it's time I had some sleep … "

He left his uncle, in a turmoil of rage and grief, but still firmly resolved not to pay him back in the same coin—to reproach Stecher for instance that he had been living the life of a retiree for decades, without lifting a finger, and had got together his fortune by blind chance. That sort of reply would have struck him as unworthy. "Revenge is a dish best served cold," his father had used to say.

On the way to his room, Daniel felt pain in his chest, which over minutes became ever sharper. His heart began to beat violently, and it occurred to him that it was now his turn to have to call for an ambulance. But then, no sooner had he closed the door behind him, than the pain and palpitations went away.

So that he didn't lose his charter flight, and counter to Dr Stallbohm's urgings, the convalescent proposed to fly back to Venezuela only days after leaving hospital. (The flight was anything but direct, with stopovers in Frankfurt, Madrid and Barbados.) The doctor decreed a compromise solution—till his departure, Stecher Bravo was to have strict bed rest.

"I don't know whether I have weeks or months or years to live, and so I need to keep something in reserve," Stecher began as they sat over breakfast with the balcony door open. There was a view of a narrow, lovingly tended strip of garden. "Even if I do have a couple of friends in Caracas, a father and son, who would do absolutely anything for me. They offer me help quite naturally, without repayment being an issue, or 'Why? What for?' When they come and see me, the first question is always: 'D'you need money?' It's nice to know, anyway ... "

One by one, an eggcup, a cup, a piece of toast, a pat of butter and a jammy knife slid off the round glass table.

"I was lying awake last night, thinking about you. *Bueno*—it's said one should give with warm hands, and not just in one's last will and testament. And so on this day of my departure I will present you with a cheque for twenty thousand marks, drawn on my giro account here in Hamburg with the German Bank of Latin America. For the equivalent, I might tell you, I could live for three years in Caracas, in spite of the idiotic inflation ... "

Daniel went around the little table, kissed his uncle on the forehead, sat down again, and upset the coffee pot. Fetched a towel from the bathroom, laid it on the glass plate, where it absorbed the black liquid. Called reception, and ordered a fresh pot.

"Thank you so much," he then said. "You've saved our lives."

"You'll have to speak up!"

"You say it would keep you for three years?! ... "

Stecher nodded.

129

"We'll get through it ... in four months ... "

"Now don't you start your moping and wailing again, my boy! Sometimes I get the impression you know as much about the realities of life as I do about the Provençal lyric. Have you ever given any thought to banks, interest rates, shares, dividends, Lombard rate, currency exchange? Or the organisation of the economy? You must have grown up in a cocoon, without any idea of the wider world! You know at best I feel pity for your father. A fool who doesn't know the first thing about money. How much I looked down on him, when he was young I prophesied he would always remain poor, without guessing how right I was! What did your good father manage to teach you? Money isn't dirty, my dear fellow, money's a necessity. The association between value and dirt is Christian—the way those Catholics turn up their noses when there's any talk of money! Coins don't carry germs. Metal doesn't communicate disease!"

The nephew did now speak, counter to his previous resolution, of the fortunate circumstances that had enabled the uncle to retire early from professional life.

"You're wrong about that as well, I'm by no means as idle as you like to think. There can be no question of a withdrawal or retirement from active life. I am always busy with what I own, I'm acquiring, I'm investing my capital. Do you know what a share is? Do you understand what governs the ways a bank pays interest? Do you understand that, the moment you're overdrawn with your bank, you start to pay interest on what you owe? Do you ever ask how much interest you're charged, say in this current quarter, or last? Do you even care about all these things?"

"To me your life looks lonely ... " Daniel sounded uncertain. "The way you've taken ... doesn't look ... ideal to me, if I might say ... "

"You may, you may. You're my nephew. I don't have any other, I don't have any nieces, any children or grandchildren. It's true, I have no one but you."

"And perhaps you too ... " Daniel felt emboldened, "made mistakes in your life? ... "

"Could be. Could well be. I don't have a clean conscience. Now

I have to lie down, come and sit with me. What are you going to do today? Shopping? A trip round the harbour? I envy you! To see the Blohm & Voss shipyards again! No, that's not your thing, you like paintings. The Kunsthalle on the Glockengiesserwall has a particularly good collection. Or would you feel more like heading up to St Pauli, to visit the whores? One of Cassuto's granddaughters, I should tell you, was a whore on the Hamburg docks, I've seen a picture of her from 1923, there's a woman who'd bring the dead back to life, let me tell you!"

The nephew cleared away the breakfast things, set the tray outside in the corridor.

"Another thing I notice about you is your dreadful posture," now lying under the covers again. "Slope-shoulders on both sides, no posture, no backbone, you have to do something about that, you can't go around looking like that. Apart from anything else, you'll feel it when you're old!"

And then he was asleep.

Twenty thousand marks! What a relief! A weight dropped from his mind. My uncle, I love you, I love you and hate you and love you. His eyes brushed over a little camera, a Leica from the nineteen-thirties. And the soft leather bag that Stecher always carried around with him, where he kept his papers and tickets. Daniel opened the zip. And encountered Alexander's Venezuelan passport, which he scrutinised as closely as an immigration official on the border between two worlds. Found his tickets, and a sheaf of hundred mark bills. Picked up a thick piece of cardboard, the size of a credit card, Alexander's mother Luna Bravo, at age nineteen. On the back of the bleached photograph, the year 1885 and the words: "Carl Stemsen & Son, Court Photographers, Hamburg, Steindamm 52". There were also other photographs, very different, he pulled them out, colour snapshots, girls in bikinis, half-lying, half-propped-up, fourteen, fifteen. One had her legs wide apart. One, with fair curls, was topless, the soft swelling of her pubescent breasts. On the back of the photographs, the names were scribbled, Fernanda, Manuela, Silvia, Mariella, Terese, and underneath, a heart with an arrow. In the middle of every heart the initials

ASB.

There was a knock on the door. Hurriedly he pushed the pictures back between the passport and the tickets, set the pouch down on the bedside table. Opened the door to a blushing chambermaid apologising for having taken so long to bring the coffee.

He had forgotten having ordered it.

Stecher Bravo left Hamburg on a cool, grey October morning. Daniel had been given special dispensation to accompany his uncle to the departure gate. And there, at the very last moment, Alexander gave him the promised cheque.

The farewell passed off without any particular show of emotion—both men were restrained, more even than was usual between them. They weren't to know that it was their last meeting.

16

FORTY DEGREES IN THE SHADE

"THAT'S ENOUGH SWIMMING NOW, YOU UNLUCKY FELLOW!"
The lawyer stands by the edge of the swimming pool in his dusty street shoes. "There are developments … "

Loew wraps himself in a couple of bath towels.

"There is only one entry under Eva Singer in Miami. My researches have yielded the information that she works for the US Coastguard. Strange, no? Originally from Poland, her parents survived Treblinka and emigrated to Venezuela in 1945. She was born in 1946 in Caracas."

"That was all more or less what she told me … "

"It's possible she might know Kirshman. From the time when he was at the Military Academy."

"Oh, Dr Johannes, please not!" Daniel accuses the lawyer of suffering from paranoia and persecution complex.

Dr Johannes remains adamant—Esther Moreno was a cover name for Eva Singer.

"If that's the case, then why would she have registered at the hotel under her real name?" the heir pondered.

"A fair point. I wonder too. But it could be that Kirshman only got in touch with her once she was already at the hotel."

"You're some logician … but I think it's unlikely. No one … no one can be so deceitful as that."

Friedrich Johannes ignores his client's last remark. "Get dressed," he says, "it's almost four o'clock. Time to get to work!"

The lawyer's office is not far from the seat of the Kiba-Nova Company, on Avenida Urdaneta, the part of the city that witnessed the most violent disturbances during the coup. The pavement is still littered with burnt tires, nailed together shelters, uprooted traffic signs and billboards.

The dark, wood-panelled rooms on the third floor of an office block are decorated with paintings and prints—sailing boats, ocean steamers, freighters, some at port, and others on the high seas. The heat is almost unbearable—a ricochet in the course of the recent disturbances damaged the air conditioning. A new unit could not be delivered before the end of next week.

"And that's the only thing that came to harm in your office? Just the air conditioning?"

"The bullet plugged in the machinery, otherwise there would have been further damage, clearly. Here, sit in the leather armchair … it's a piece from Evita Peron's private collection, I'm not kidding. Now, here's what I propose—we both of us act absolutely innocent with Kirshman. Not a word about Esther Moreno, or that we were at court this morning, or what we know about Panama. The fact that you mentioned Panama to him at all, well, an absolute catastrophe. We sell him the apartment. And for seventy-five thousand, since that's what you asked for. And as soon as he agrees, you say … "

"Only on condition that you give me what you took out of the Hamburg account after my uncle's death."

"Well, he seems almost to have given his verbal agreement to that, if what you say is correct? What do you think of that as a way to proceed?"

"We still have to bring up the question of what he's done with the Panamanian money," insisted the heir. "I can't just pretend it never existed … "

"You want to raise that with him? I'll tell you what'll happen with Panama. There's only one option open to you. You fly there tomorrow, and take it up on the spot, and in person."

"I can't do that … I have to work, I have to get back … I need to go home."

"And forget about your million dollars?"

"But they won't be there any more!"

"You fly to Panama tomorrow. In the first place, I'm by no means certain that the money will have gone. Who knows how long it might take the bank to carry out Kirshman's instructions. And secondly, once you're there, it'll be much easier for you to find out where the money's gone, if it has indeed already left. That's not so easy from here, in spite of Emil Gotthard's good offices. It's worth a little side-trip, I'd say. And now we're going to call Kirshman, and tell him we want to see him, and we're on our way over." He dialled the number of the import-export firm. "Or better yet, we ask him to come here, to the office!"

"He won't do that," Daniel objects, "we'll just annoy him if we ask him to do that! … "

"Of course—Kirshman doesn't seem at all surprised to learn that you've instructed me in your affair," Dr Johannes puts the receiver back. "What is surprising though is that he straight away agreed to come over. He'll be here in half-an-hour. Good God, it's hot! My handkerchiefs—all soaking wet! Will you manage to keep quiet about Esther Moreno? Do you know what? Why not let me talk to him. You can just keep out of it."

"She didn't keep up her strange game with us to the very end. That's what really surprises me," remarks Loew.

"A guilty conscience. Because she fell in love with me."

"Or me?"

"I'm afraid I have to disappoint you there, she didn't like you at all, she said to me. She thought you were too much of an airhead. Sorry about that."

The doorbell rings. Julio Kirshman, accompanied by his father and his two lawyers, Monica da Silva and Gabriel Miranda, strides into the conference room. They all sit around a rectangular glass table. A secretary serves iced water. And shuts the connecting door to her office.

The executor will not look the heir in the eye. Konrad Kirshman, however, keeps his gaze levelled at the nephew of his closest friend throughout.

The proceedings begin in Spanish, until Loew motions to Dr Johannes that he is unable to follow. The lawyer tells Kirshman and son that since he himself and both principals are equally happy in German, they should perhaps switch to that language.

"Fine by me!" growls Konrad Kirshman. "What's the matter with your air conditioning? It's beastly hot in here. Is it broken?"

From this point Julio translates for his legal team, sometimes simultaneously, sometimes afterwards. "I'm buying the apartment for seventy-five thousand dollars," he opens the meeting.

The heir counters by saying that he had since been advised that he shouldn't sell for anything under a hundred. Dr Johannes, unprepared for this intervention from his client, sighs quietly.

"You're a rotten bastard, Loew," Konrad Kirshman sinks lower in the cushions of his chair, "You know that?"

"That's not going to get us anywhere, Herr Kirshman," Dr Johannes radiates certainty and severity. "If I hear my client spoken to in those terms once more, I'm going to have you for defamation."

"Papa, I asked you, please leave this to me!"

"Shut up, boy," a smoker's cough fills the room, "I know what I'm doing."

"We are prepared to sell the apartment of the testator, which has been deeded to my client, to you, for seventy-five thousand dollars."

"That's OK." replies Julio.

"On one condition," the lawyer continues.

"You see! Here they come with their conditions! Didn't I tell you!"

"Papa, that's enough now!" And, turning to Dr Johannes: "And what's your condition?"

"That you pay back the sum of one hundred and five thousand, two hundred and fifty-five Deutschmarks, which you withdrew from the Hamburg account, and which is rightfully my client's. We are prepared to forego any accrued interest."

Konrad Kirshman's wheezing sounds like the crunching of a fistful of straw. "They're trying it on, absolutely not!" The coins are jingling in his pocket.

Julio turns to his team. They confer quietly. After a minute, he takes a piece of paper out of the breast pocket of his shirt. "Well, we were always going to do that. I agreed that with Herr Loew this morning—he gets two banker's orders from me. One man,

136

one word."

"Sonny, you've gone crazy! What are you saying?"

"Be quiet, Papa, or go outside! I only cashed the Hamburg account for one reason, gentlemen, and that was to help Loew to get around the German taxes. Anyway, there's no mention of Hamburg in the will. This here, admittedly, will have to be deducted," and he hands Dr Johannes a folded piece of paper that he holds between finger and thumb, "a little something that the late lamented Sascha gave me on his ninetieth birthday. I never cashed it."

A cheque drawn on the German Bank of Latin America for twenty thousand marks, written eight weeks before Alexander's death, the very same amount that Daniel received from his uncle six years before, on the day they saw each other for the last time.

The heir returns the cheque to Dr Johannes, who gives it back to Kirshman in turn. How strange that my opponent got exactly the same sum as I did once; I wonder what possessed Alexander to give money to Julio, the multi-millionaire, on his own ninetieth birthday? And why did he never tell me about Kirshman and son? "I just don't get it," he whispers to himself.

"What's that?" says Julio. "If you've got something to say, say it so everyone can hear it!"

"Nothing." And all at once he thinks: maybe Kirshman controlled all the letters that Stecher wrote to me in the last years of his life? Quite deliberately kept him from saying anything about the father and son? If only I'd travelled here while my uncle was alive—if I'd come, even once, I might have seen through everything, understood what was afoot! My indifference about money and material wealth is coming back to haunt me. I will never allow myself to be treated like that in future—" ... to be treated like that in future!" he suddenly says loud and clear.

"What d'you mean by that?"

Loew doesn't say anything. Promises himself: you will never be a victim again! Never!

Julio instructs his lawyers to draw up a document—the final settlement of the executor of the will. Sweat runs down the faces of those present, drains into their shirts. Monica da Silva's white blouse sticks to her pink brassiere.

Daniel calculates how much money he'll be left with after the deduction of the twenty thousand marks. Seventy-five thousand dollars for the apartment. Eighty-five thousand marks from Hamburg. He will have more money than at any time in his life.

"Finally satisfied?"

"Leave him alone, Papa, please!"

"No. I'm not satisfied." He hears his own voice, coming from far away, from a stranger.

Dr Johannes gets up, places both his hands on his client's shoulders. "While the lady and gentlemen are drawing up their document, you come with me for a moment." Pulls Daniel to his feet, walks him back to his office, the leather armchair, the pictures of boats.

"You know, you're really not doing yourself any favours with these outbursts of candour. What's the point of shaming and accusing Kirshman and son in front of me and their little toy lawyers? What you need to do is give them a sense of security, suggest you're completely happy with Hamburg and the money for the apartment. It's not so bad—it's the first step, which, with my modest help, we've managed to take. So now, when Julio asks you again—Is that everything, what do you say?"

Daniel stares at the pattern of rhombuses in the waxed parquet floor.

" … And then he'll believe," the lawyer resumes, "or maybe he won't believe—but there's at least the chance that he will—that you've given up on Panama. Why do you think he gave in to you over Hamburg, to his father's utter amazement? Out of decency? Why was he prepared to walk over here, and pay out so much money? Because he has high ethical standards? No, it's because he's got the Panama money, and he wants to hang on to it. That's all. Whereas you just stumble from one mistake to the next. We're going to pretend that's it, enough. What's the big mystery there? Let him think we're giving up. And now we're going back in. And when he asks you whether that's everything, you answer with one little word. And what's that little word?"

"Yes."

"You really drive me demented, you know that?"

Julio presents the document his lawyers have drawn up in the meantime, relating to the sale of the apartment in San Bernardino, and the money transferred out of Germany, with the deduction of the twenty thousand marks. A further paragraph declares that Daniel would in future relinquish any further claims arising from the Hamburg account or the Stecher Bravo apartment. Dr Johannes proposes slight alterations to the text, a word or two here and there. Insists on a clause that the agreement will only have legal force once the moneys had been paid into his client's account.

His father nudges him in the ribs at various times, but Julio allows all the changes and additions. The lawyer takes the draft with additional clauses through to his secretary to type up.

The document needs to be witnessed, without a notary's seal it would have no legal standing. In Caracas, it can take a week and sometimes much longer to get an appointment with a notary, in particular in the wake of a military coup. "But you want to get back to Europe today, tomorrow at the latest," says Dr Johannes, "so we'll have to call William Lopez's office to do the needful today, this afternoon. That'll cost you a thousand dollars in priority fees, is that clear to you?"

Kirshman and son smile—certain that Daniel will refuse.

"I suppose I have no choice," replies the heir.

Dr Johannes calls the notary William Lopez to come to his office. "He'll be here in a few minutes."

"Look at the shit you've got us into." No one reacts to Konrad Kirshman's remark.

"There's one other thing I want in the document!" cries Julio. "What about the monthly expenses on the late Sasha's apartment? Who's paying those? They've got to be met by the heir until I've managed to flog the apartment!"

"Herr Loew has just sold you the apartment, Herr Kirshman. Of course, the monthly expenses are entirely your responsibility."

139

"You idiot!" his father hisses at him.

Papageno's theme sounds—the doorbell of the office.

Señor Marin, the senior assistant of the notary Lopez is introduced. He asks to see the passports of Julio Kirshman and Daniel Loew, sets down the date, the thirtieth of November, and his own signature to the document, and then asks the principals to append their signatures.

Counting aloud, Dr Johannes pays down eight hundred-dollar bills and ten twenties on to the glass tabletop.

Señor Marin takes the money, and leaves the office.

Julio writes out two banker's drafts, one for the price of the apartment, one for the Hamburg money. From a folder he produces Alexander Stecher Bravo's certificate of inheritance and the original of the will, and hands both documents to Dr Johannes.

Kirshman and son, Monica da Silva and Gabriel Miranda all get to their feet.

"That's it. Now we're quits!"

"Of course. Thank you."

"You've got a lot to learn in life, you piece of shit," Konrad Kirshman whispers to his best friend's nephew as he leaves.

It's got cooler. Swarms of birds circle over the city at dusk. In the summerhouse on Dr Johannes' property, the lawyer and his client are celebrating the successful conclusion of the first phase of the case of Loew versus Kirshman.

Daniel paid his bill at the El Presidente, and then brought his suitcase along to Dr Johannes, who had invited him to stay the night.

Otto stands straddle-legged outside the glass door of the summerhouse. He barks without let-up. Otto, the lawyer explains, is an unusually nervous bulldog. He has opened a bottle of 1977 Chilean Tarapaca, and put on a record—*Charlie Parker Live in Boston*. "At last! A bit of peace! Otto! Quiet! My wife is busy in the main house, making us something delicious to eat, your last meal before you leave us … I think you'll be impressed by the

140

main house!"

Daniel hasn't asked about flights to Panama. He is not contemplating going on the journey he has been urged to take: "I want to go home tomorrow."

"We know the money was in Panama City. It may still be there. You will need to choose a local lawyer, I'll be happy to give you a couple of names. Don't forget the certificate and the will! ... Stay at a Holiday Inn, they always have vacancies, you won't need a reservation. And it's inexpensive too."

"First, I want to wait for the birth of my firstborn. Then we'll see. I have to settle down, Doctor, I have to collect myself."

"Do you want to know what's so maddening about you? It's your pathos, my dear man, your pathos ... "

"I'm very pleased we got the money from Kirshman that I asked for. It's a first step ... "

"All right. We'll leave it alone. No more talk. After your child is born! You must like your little jokes. In money matters, every day counts. Every hour. Of course it's your decision, yours alone, whether you want to turn your back on a million dollars. To me it's blue or green, as they say in Chile, I've got more than I can ever spend. My dream is what it always was—peace and quiet. I want to live out my days on a ranch in Patagonia—goats, chickens, horses maybe, but I don't want to breed animals for the table, God forbid. I want to live in peace with animals. Slowly but surely become vegetarian. No more fondue bourguignon. Until it's time for my ranch, I'll make do with my large garden and this little sanctum without a telephone—I only ever telephone in the main house. Here, my jazz collection, which I appreciate so much. And there, outside, where Otto's standing. Otto! Quiet now! Where it goes steeply uphill. Up there I want to build myself a tiny cabin, a tree house at the top of a long ladder, without any amenities, any luxuries. Neither my wife nor my son will be allowed to see me up there ... No one will be allowed there, not even my sick son. Don't look so shocked, I have one child, he's terribly ill, *immuno-deficiency* ... if you know what I mean. The day after tomorrow, we're celebrating his twenty-fifth birthday ... I'll even sleep in my tree house, sometimes. What do you think? Spending the night under the stars! What could be finer?"

He turns over the record, producing a crackle of static, lights a cigar with a gilt cigarette lighter, sits down again. "What a shame, felling trees for matches! I never use matches! You don't smoke, do you? Or may I offer you a cigar?"

"I didn't even get to … visit his grave. I cannot leave without going to the cemetery … "

"You need to set priorities in life, my dear fellow. Your uncle has left you nothing but trouble. If he gets wind of the fact that you left without visiting his mortal remains, he will quite understand that you flew to Panama City instead of scrambling up Santa Clara hill, at forty in the shade, fifty in the sun, to look for a mound of earth in a Sephardic graveyard, with no headstone on it yet. Ashkenazim and Sephardim alike only add the stone after a year, right?"

Daniel feels dread and heaviness in his belly, as if he had molten lead there. Has he already forgotten his resolutions of the afternoon? His promise never to be a victim again? Ever!

Otto stops barking.

"I can imagine why you're looking so gloomy, in spite of those two banker's drafts in your pocket. Because we're going to have to take away a bit of your new-won wealth. Easy come, easy go, huh? A thousand dollars went down the hotel's throat for five nights, plus my own modest night there, another two hundred, plus two hundred more for our fine for disregarding the curfew, a thousand dollars for Lopez the notary, two thousand for Señora Collado, six spanking perfumes for Señora Collado's pretty assistants, a flight, tomorrow morning to Panama City, and," his voice rising considerably, "the fee for your lawyer, Dr Friedrich Johannes, born in Santiago de Chile on the sixth of June 1944, the date of the Allied invasion in Normandy—six thousand dollars, all in, for services thus far rendered."

17

PANAMA CITY

A T SIX IN THE MORNING, after his guest has had a couple of hours'
sleep on the summer-house couch, Dr Johannes drives Daniel
to the Aeropuerto Maiquetia. On the way to the airport, they
pass the central prison of Catia—following the suppression of the
revolt two days ago, some eighty prisoners were shot here. When
Loew asked the lawyer to stop outside the prison, Dr Johannes'
first thought was that his client needed to vomit, after their con-
sumption of wine and tequila the night before. But in fact, all he did
was to pick up a couple of pigeon's-egg-sized pebbles for his friend
Barton, the blind author and photographer, who had asked him
to bring back some 'interesting pieces' from South America for his
extensive collection of stones.

The Friday morning flight to Panama City was booked up.

"I'll need to borrow another hundred dollars from you,"
Dr Johannes slipped the bill, which Daniel most unwillingly gave
him, into the breast pocket of a chief stewardess of the state airline.
Thereupon, a business class seat immediately became vacant—
at an economy class price. Out of the corner of his eye, Daniel
watched the protests of a British businessman who had arrived late
for the check-in, only to be told that there were no more seats
available on the overbooked flight to Panama City. "Are you out
of your mind?" he kept calling out. "Are you out of your mind?"

"I wish you luck, strength and success!" said the lawyer, and
asked to be kept informed of developments. "I must say, I've very
much enjoyed meeting you ... I haven't run across anyone like you
in twenty-two years of practice. So I cross my fingers for you and
for me—may victory be sweet!"

From the window, the view of the Caribbean islands of Bonaire, Curaçao, Aruba. The weather in Panama City is thirty-two degrees and slightly cloudy, the co-pilot informs them. The duration of the flight will be one-and-a-half hours. He wishes his passengers a comfortable flight.

The traveller closes his eyes.

The request from a young woman to the stewardess for a glass of still mineral water rouses him from his brief sleep. The voice seems familiar—it streamed out from behind the rhododendron bush, as Francisco Shatil was unlocking the gate to his garden. Is the daughter of the arbitrator of the Jewish community of Caracas sitting immediately behind him? How did Shatil know the heir would be on this flight to Panama? Has Esther Moreno been watching him, even after vanishing? Has Dr Johannes switched sides, and is he now with Kirshman?

He turns round. "Are you Mairah by any chance?"

"Yes, I am!" She is pleased to be recognised.

"Mairah Shatil?"

"How come you know my name?"

Through the narrow gap between the seats, he introduces himself—it was to him and his business that her father had given an hour of his time on the morning of the second day of the coup.

"Of course!" Father had told her and her mother about it.

He is kneeling now on the yielding seat cushion. Mairah has little red pustules all over her face. He applies his charm to his new acquaintance, gives the girl hope that he finds her attractive. What a coincidence, they say, a meeting like this. Mairah says that over the Internet server '*I Seek You*' (ICQ) she has entered into correspondence with a Sephardic Jew originally from Lebanon, who has recently by email made her a barely disguised offer of marriage. Now (lovingly supported in this by her father) she is flying to Panama for the weekend, and staying with cousins. "I am going to surprise my fiancé, call him up as soon as I get in, and ask him where he'd like to take me to lunch. 'How do you mean?' he will say. And I'll reply, 'What about a little intimate lunch somewhere … !'—I can hardly wait!"

He calms down—Mairah Shatil at least isn't part of any

144

elaborate conspiracy. And then he tries to make himself even more secure: "Did your father tell you what I came to him about?"

"Papa and I always discuss everything. He couldn't help in the matter of an inheritance, because he is on good terms with the other party, isn't that right?"

"Did he say there was ... apart from me, there was anyone else present?"

"Not that I remember. Who was it?"

"Oh, someone I know. Never mind."

"Can you keep a secret? I think those people are really scummy, and so does Mama, but Daddy ... I don't know what brings you to Panama, but I know some people who can maybe help you in one way or another. The Roccamoras are Syrian Jews who fled to Panama in the early 'fifties. Very rich people, with a lot of influence. I went to boarding school with the youngest of them, Uriel, for six years, in this place near Rochester, New York. Call him up when we get in, give him my regards, maybe he can advise you. I'll give you his number."

He thanks the girl with the velvet voice.

He puts the number in his pocket, and turns round. And doesn't speak to Mairah Shatil again.

The plane begins its descent. No house or settlement anywhere to be seen in the dark-green interior of Panama. Only the occasional mountain track, going nowhere.

The lobby of the Holiday Inn on the Via Italia is full of bearded, long-haired fifty-year-olds, who uncannily resemble one another. A conference of Central and Latin American sculptors is in progress. Loew manages to get a room for one night. The following day, as the girl on reception tells him, they are expecting a one hundred and eighty-strong trade delegation from Red China, and he would have to look for alternative accommodation. American Air Force pilots stroll past, waving to each other, forming little grinning bunches of friends. The Holiday Inn is where they are staying for their months of training.

In the lift, a young woman pilot is combing out her long

black hair with a wire brush, her elbow rhythmically striking against Loew's shoulder. Tucked under her left arm is her extraterrestrial-looking flying helmet—complete with tubes for the oxygen required for survival in the upper reaches of the earth's atmosphere.

It's ten am in Panama City, an hour earlier than in Caracas. A skyline of tower blocks is etched against the window of room 1992. Freighters lie at anchor nearby. A cruise ship, twelve gleaming stories high, approaches the passenger docks at a snail's crawl. Beyond, Daniel sees the open sea. Suddenly, a broad rainbow, more vivid than any he has ever seen, loops over the entire bay.

Following one of Dr Johannes' recommendations, he calls the office of the lawyer Isabella Eisenmann. She suggests a meeting at four o'clock, and tells him right away she wants seven per cent of the money at stake. Going on the assumption of a million dollars, her fee would be seventy thousand. Half of it up front.

Out of his trouser-pocket he fishes the piece of paper on which Mairah Shatil wrote down the number of her friend. The import-export division of the Roccamora family business also owns a whole portfolio of other businesses, among them property and construction firms, a bank, a travel agency and Jolly, a supermarket chain with branches all over Central America.

The junior boss wasn't in the office just now, the caller is informed, but he could try again in the afternoon at a different number.

He starts to unpack.

"You're a hero!" He's never heard that from Valeria before. "You overcame Julio!" She has been suffering from severe abdominal pain and nausea in the last couple of days, she adds.

"I'll be with you very soon."

"But why do you have to go to Panama? Be happy with what you've got already. Come home, please, hurry."

He has until four o'clock. He hasn't made any particular plans for the day. And he decides to pay a call on the German Bank of Latin America, without announcing himself in advance.

The taxi, a Lada, wheezes at every gear change. A hot draft blows through the back. He licks drops of sweat from his upper lip. Palm trees nod in the breeze like pious Jews at prayer. Tropical flowers with large brilliant yellow blossoms grow like weeds here. Indian, Spanish, American pedestrians, and Chinese, Africans, French, and they're all smiling—without exception. The municipal buses are festooned with waving popes, and with dragons, angels, devils. Like moving rainbows, they honk and wriggle their way through the congested main and side streets, past North American coffee shops and flagged lots for used cars and swimming pool machinery, past identical single-storey structures reminiscent of the endless suburban sprawl of the USA—pet shops, dry-cleaning businesses, eye clinics, strawberry-pink milk bars.

Outside the main entrance of the Torre Banco Germanico are a couple of security guards walking up and down, their sub-machine guns casually on their shoulders. The visitor is requested to identify himself. The branch of the German Bank of Latin America is on the ground floor of the high-rise. He would like to speak to the manager, he explains to a female employee.

"Señor Valdez is currently abroad. Did you have an appointment?"

He says no.

She could call the deputy manager. What was it about?

"I want to open an account at the bank."

She shows him into a room with a view of hibiscus bushes, and asks him to wait a moment.

"What was your name again please?" asks a short man in his late fifties, with thick bifocal spectacles and rather worn brown shoes. "Mr Valdez won't be back from the States until next week. Wiegand, Wilhelm Wiegand, how can I be of assistance?"

"I am the sole heir of a client of yours who passed away five months ago by the name of Alexander Stecher Bravo."

"Loew," murmurs Wiegand, and flicks through the passport. "Daniel Loew." His accent has a tinge of Bavaria. The hum

147

of air-conditioning. Creak of a chair leg. "Well, yes. And what else?" asks Wiegand.

"This is the will and the certificate, both original documents."

"What do you want me to do with them?"

"I would like you to transfer the sums owing to me to a new account, which I want to open now."

"I'm afraid that … that won't be possible. One moment, please." He leaves the conference room, and comes back carrying a folder. "Now, my dear Mr Loew … there we are. Let's see … your late relative did indeed hold several numbered accounts at this branch. Handsome sums … I see from the file that someone with power of attorney has closed these accounts … "

"There's surely a mistake there, Mr Weigand … "

"Wiegand … Doesn't matter. A mistake a lot of people make."

"What mistake are you talking about?"

"Weigand, Wiegand … "

"Mr Wiegand—here it is, in black and white, I am Stecher Bravo's only nephew, and his sole heir."

"Your esteemed uncle, a good customer of the bank, I should like to say, has given someone power of attorney. I'm certain a transfer of the moneys you claim will not be possible."

"On what date were my uncle's accounts closed or moved?"

"I'm afraid I am unable to give you any information about that."

"Who was the party with power of attorney? I should surely have been informed!"

"Mr Loew—Panama has a very strict law of banking confidentiality, especially where numbered accounts are involved. There are severe punishments for anyone who breaks this law, punishments up to and including the withdrawal of a bank's licence to operate. There is one exception, and only one—and that is the giving of information to the holder of the account, and his or her legal representative. In the case of an inheritance— why didn't you announce you were coming, I would have been only too glad for you to make the acquaintance of our legal adviser, Heinrich Fischer, at present in Guatemala on a well-earned short break, he would have explained everything to you much better than I am able to do … In the case of an inheritance, what this means is that the heir or heirs will have to prove their case and their entitlement to the estate through the Panamanian courts. Otherwise, we would run the risk of making payments to the wrong claimant, or even to someone with no real claim at all … "

The bank official's brow is running with sweat.

Daniel is perfectly calm. Lack of sleep, he thinks, is good for me. "In other words, the law concerning numbered accounts makes all kinds of shady deals possible. Down to the laundering of money. Even blood money. And you turn a blind eye … "

"Mr Loew, I must warn you not to repeat such a slur."

"I appeal to you, I appeal to you directly, Herr Weigand, please help me. I will naturally be most appreciative … "

"I would be in prison if I took so much as half a pace towards you! Ten years behind bars! In eleven months, on my sixtieth birthday, I'm retiring. And I'm going home! Back to Nuremberg. I wouldn't be so stupid as to jeopardise my entire future with a false step like that. To repeat—if, as you claim, you have right on your side, then let the state of Panama decide—if the case is settled in your favour, our branch will pay whatever is owing to you, every last cent. And may I tell you furthermore, that we have no shady customers among our clientele. Do you have any idea how often I go trekking off into tiny backwoods villages, to look at prospective customers under the proverbial microscope? Only last week, a businessman in Colon transfers four million dollars to the bank. I take a plane to go and see him, and I don't like what I see. I tell him his money is being transferred back to him. He threatens me! And now? We don't have any of his money at the bank. I'm forever having to take tiny propeller planes. Only recently, one crashed. A colleague of ours lost his life. Since then, I've been most reluctant to fly. Instead I go crawling along little country roads—"

"Anyone the Shatils send me is like family to me. Come over

149

right away," says Uriel Roccamora, no sooner has Daniel mentioned on the phone from whom he got his name, and in what connection he needs advice. How is it possible that this stranger asks him to his office so promptly? Is it possible the Roccamoras are also in cahoots with his enemies? Did Mairah, acting for her father, after all ensure that the traveller took no unobserved steps?

On the fourth floor of the synthetic-carpet-smelling head-quarters of the Roccamora Calidad Company, the stranger rushes towards him, no sooner has he stepped out of the elevator. "Welcome! Please make yourself at home here. How is Mairah?" The young man's receding hair and the dark rings under his eyes make him appear many years older. He is wearing a short-sleeved shirt with a red-and-blue Liberty pattern. A silver star of David glints in his chest-hair. On the walls of his office are sketches and photographs of scale-models of two high-rise blocks. "Thirty-nine stories each, side by side, like twins!" Roccamora says proudly, "they'll be the biggest constructions in our country's history. The cornerstone is being laid in February."

Daniel considers mentioning Jacob Loew's big projects, very few of which ever got beyond the planning stage—generally he would have an almighty argument with his employers immediately before the first sod was cut. Then Uriel suddenly leaps up—his father has stepped into the room. The son introduces the visitor, almost with a heel-click, repeats what he was told on the telephone " ... and even if he doesn't look like it," he adds softly, "he is one of us."

"What's the name of the other party?" is Leon Roccamora's first question.

" ... I'd rather not say."

"Then I'm afraid we won't be able to help."

"Father! Please! ... Mairah Shatil sent him ... "

"And what if the family in question are business partners of ours?"

"Kirshman and son," says the heir.

"And their company?" Roccamora doesn't give up.

"Kiba-Nova in Caracas, Venezuela ... "

"Never heard of them. No partners of ours." The father gives a signal to his son that allows him to devote his attention to the case. " … And if you're not doing anything else," he adds on his way out, "why not come and have dinner with us at home tonight?"

After Roccamora senior has left the room, Uriel tells his visitor that he is inclined to take the injustice Daniel Loew has experienced as an injustice against himself: "What a dreadful thing has happened to you. Those criminals! I can hardly believe they are Jews. What a disgrace for our people."

"We have as much right to bad people, Uriel, as any other race in the world."

"No one has ever put it to me like that before." The young executive shakes his head and smiles.

"My uncle always used to say—there are terrible rogues among our people, but no more and no fewer than with any others. A cousin of his mother's pretended to be an emigration agent, and made thousands and thousands from people trying to emigrate, ostensibly while trying to help them … till they were bankrupt. And then he dropped them. In the end, he too wound up in a concentration camp, where he was murdered by his fellow Jewish inmates."

"Most Sephardim have never heard stories like that … To us, the Shoah seems remote, as incomprehensible as for instance the Armenian genocide by the Turks. Only, they were *Jews* who were pushed into the gas chambers!"

Roccamora reminds Loew of a school friend he was especially fond of, he hasn't seen him now for a quarter-century, Arthur, who asked him once: "Are you really Jewish?" Arthur Weininger, who took him along to the gloomy synagogue, and invited him home to his parents, where for the first time in his life Daniel participated at the feast of Passover, at the festive table, with the unleavened matzos bread.

"Strange thing, isn't it?" says Uriel, as though he's read his visitor's mind. "This morning we didn't know each other. Now it feels to me as though we've been friends for years."

They climb up a rusty fire escape to the second floor of the

151

Calidad building. That's the den of Dr Hernan Garcia Aparicio, one of just ten state notaries in all of Panama. In the anteroom, several people are waiting. Uriel and the visitor walk past them, enter the office without knocking. Roccamora and the Notario Primero del Circuito de Panama embrace. Dr Garcia quickly dispatches the client who is sitting opposite him. There is a five-foot milk churn standing in the middle of the room. The notary hands Roccamora a photo album. It is full of pictures of cows.

"He has a cattle-breeding farm on the shore of the canal that he's terribly proud of," Uriel whispers to Daniel. "He always tells me all about their latest acquisitions and calvings ... " He gives the cows five minutes. But then he summarises the case of the man he is pleased to call "My friend of many years, Loew."

The notary looks at the certificate and the will. "Very good indeed, you have everything you need! Our senior court will confirm the validity of these documents. And then you can go back to the bank to take the next few steps, as sure as Uriel is my friend!"

A sensation of triumph, of a kind never experienced before, takes over the heir. "I thank you!" he blurts out. "At last I'm in the hands of the right people ... "

"We'll get everything seen to!" Roccamora says happily, as they leave the notary's office. "In a couple of weeks all that's rightfully yours will be in your possession. I'll help you find the right lawyer. And as soon as we've won, I'll tell you where to bank your small fortune. A million is not so much. But then ... it is not so little either ... "

Daniel explains that he won't be in the position to offer his lawyer payment in advance.

"Not to worry. I'll find you someone who will only put in his bill once the thing has happened. I've got someone in mind already."

That evening outside the revolving door of the company head-quarters there is a black limousine waiting for young Roccamora and his visitor. At the wheel is a frail-looking lady in a colourless dress. She seems quite exhausted. Daniel assumes she is an employee. The car slowly moves off.

"Daniel? Meet my mother, Lilith. Mother, this is Daniel Loew, a friend of Mairah's … "

Lilith is presented to him as the owner of the El Mundo Libre travel agency, which is part of the multifarious business empire of Roccamora-Calidad. She asks her astonished passenger where he was born, where he grew up, when he moved to London? Why London? The origins and jobs of his parents? Any brothers and sisters? Married? Children? And his own occupation? "Poet? And you can live off that? … And what brings you to Panama?"

She stops in front of a villa nestled in tropical grounds, hoots three times. Two old ladies, way past eighty, step nimbly up to the car. Lilith's mother Gilah, and Gilah's best friend Sarah sit either side of Uriel. They ask Daniel—where was he born, where did he grow up, when did he move back to Europe, why Vienna, why London? His parents' jobs? Any siblings? Poet! Surely no one can live off that! " … And what brings you to Panama?"

He is freezing in a gale of refrigerated air.

"We are one heart and one soul, Sarah and I," Gilah tells the stranger, "from the moment of our flight from Syria in 1951. But we've known each other much longer than that, we used to play together as children … "

They leave the limousine on the Avenida Cuba, outside a mighty, cube-shaped synagogue. The sky is purple and orange, but oddly milky as well. To Daniel the hot light and the fragrance of the air take him back to his dreams. On his return, he promises himself, he will write something about dusk in Panama.

Friday service in the lofty *snoga* hall. "What, you haven't come across the word *snoga* before?" Uriel had asked him that afternoon, in his astonishment. "That's what we Sephardim call the synagogue, didn't your uncle ever teach you that?" The Roccamoras take the visitor in their midst. Leon arrives a little later. His firstborn, Aron, is introduced to Daniel, with wife and child. "Do you like the coloured glass in the synagogue windows? The twelve tribes of Israel. Commissioned by Gilah and my late grandfather," whispers Uriel. "Four years after their successful flight from Aleppo—as a token of their gratitude … "

153

Is it true you are now directing my steps, after all, Alexander Stecher Bravo?

The nephew speaks to his dead uncle, while the cantor declaims "*Lechah dodi likrat kalah*," let us receive the Sabbath happily.

Alexander, are you watching over me?

Everything will turn out right, my boy, I just wanted to give you a little fright, that's all. Just as God sometimes sends us signs as a way of admonishing us.

You wanted to be like God?

I wanted to be like God. Even God isn't infallible, my boy, you know? Sometimes his intentions overreach and go bad.

You gave Kirshman and son power of attorney and not me, because you wanted to give me a fright? If that's true—then I curse you, Alexander Stecher Bravo.

The Villa Pacifico is in the Paitilla district, hidden behind high bougainvillea shrubs. A modern construction, of pleasing design, single-storey, all glass and marble. (Daniel's father also designed houses of this type, though they rarely got beyond the paper stage.) Serving, cleaning, and cooking personnel flutter through the airy rooms, open French windows, water the garden, lay the table, serve food, and arrange flowers in quadrangular vases.

The lady of the house disappeared from the *snoga* towards the end of the evening prayer, now the stresses of the week just ending have gone from her features. Lilith greets the guest in a seemingly reserved fashion, yet the kindly inclination of her head tells Daniel how happy she is to have him visit, how well she is beginning to feel in his presence.

Aron, of quiet, noble manner, asks after Loew's history, volunteers that, for his part, he is a devotee of the poetry of Rainer Maria Rilke, whose works he was only able to read in English and Spanish translation.

Leon grips Daniel by the shoulder. They stride towards the dining table glittering with Sabbath candles, silver cutlery and crystal glassware. "Are you happy here? Do you like the house?

Uriel will inherit it one day. Aron will get the villa in Colon, my sons are to own everything I now own, from the villas and the high-rise blocks down to the last jar of pickled gherkins which we import from Poland to distribute all through Central America." They are standing on soft, pastel-coloured carpet. "Persian. Isfahan—does that mean anything to you? I bought it at an auction in New York, five months ago. Guess how much?"

"I don't know ... twenty thousand dollars?" Daniel thinks he must have guessed wrong, far too high.

"Papa, please," Aron begs him. "What is our guest to think of us! Besides, we don't speak of money on the Sabbath!"

Leon is splitting his sides with laughter: "One million three hundred and eighty thousand dollars!"

Loew doesn't believe him.

"You're thinking I'm telling stories, I can tell from the tip of your nose. But it's the truth, I swear. By the lives of my sons."

"One shouldn't swear, even if it's the truth!" Rabbi Eli Mandel speaks up, the vice-president of an ambitious mobile telephone company, from Ramat Gan near Tel Aviv. Leon is planning to form a business partnership with him. Rav Eli is wearing a caftan that reaches down to the backs of his knees, and a fur-trimmed *streimel*, the Hasid's Sabbath and feast day hat.

Loew is offered the place of honour beside Leon, at the head of the table. The master of the house speaks the Kiddush, the blessing over the wine, and he blesses the bread, tears one of the two braided Sabbath loaves in ten pieces, and, this is the Sephardic custom, throws all those present a piece of bread in a high arc. His aim is good even over twelve feet or more, down to the other end of the table, where Lilith sits.

Eli doffs his hat, wipes his brow and beard with the cloth napkin. A black cap is on the back of his head, slightly askew. "So, grown up in Vienna and living in London!" Did Daniel know the Viennese synagogue in the Seitenstettengasse? "And what about the big wheel in the Prater? Do you know the big Ferris wheel?" His grandfather who was born under the old Monarchy and fled from Vienna in 1938, had taught him a few scraps of German, and told him often about the sights of the

155

capital. He himself had never set foot on Austrian soil.

"I don't suppose, Mr Eli, there is anyone in Vienna who isn't familiar with the big wheel ... " Loew tells him.

"On the beautiful blue Danube! ... There will be wine, and we will not be!"

Mandel hums to himself.

"Cette vie est un songe," says Sarah, *"et la mort est un réveil ... "*

"Pardon me, but that's French," the rabbi puts in.

"I know it's French!" says Sarah crossly. "What do you think I am?"

"Do you like the food here?" asks Lilith.

Without a word, Daniel gulps down smoked salmon and roast duck, sweet corn, potato croquettes and courgette flowers. "Mmm, it's all ... lovely!" He eats as though he hadn't had a full meal for days. For dessert there is fresh tropical fruit. "I have a Roccamora ancestor," he says, after dinner is finished. "Isaac Roccamora. He lived, my uncle told me, in Hamburg, and was a lottery agent, with, apparently, an extraordinary memory for figures. The poet Heinrich Heine immortalised him in one of his works ... "

"Heine? I know Heine. Admittedly only in translation, more's the pity!" observes Aron. *"Atta Troll! The Rabbi of Bacharach!* Didn't Heine convert to Catholicism?"

"In the middle of the jungle, among the savages," says the lady of the house, "you've managed to find an island of Jewish tradition. True, isn't it?"

"What do you say to this, Papa? Daniel thinks we Jews have as much right to bad people as any other race in the world," Uriel speaks up, it's the first thing he's said all evening.

In place of Leon, it is Eli Mandel who replies, "There are no bad people among us, no crime, and no wrong ... "

Lilith laughs: "You can't mean that, can you?"

"It hurts God when bad things are said about Jews. There is nothing more poisonous than slander. It's deadlier than a sword. A sword kills whoever stands next to you, *'loshon hora'* however, slander, can kill someone at the other end of the world!"

There is silence at table.

Until Lucas, Aron's three-year-old son, upsets the silver beaker of Sabbath wine, and starts wailing piteously.

"Recite one of your poems to us, won't you please!" Lilith begs him, over the cries of her grandson.

"At least one!" her mother backs her up.

"Yes, a poem!" calls Aron.

"My work is almost entirely composed in German … I don't feel best able to recite my verse here and now … "

"Why not?" calls Sarah.

" … sorry though I am."

"A little later on, perhaps?" asks Leon.

"He has had a trying day," Uriel puts in.

"It's true; I've been on the go since six in the morning," the guest adds.

"I get up at six every day," says Aron.

"Maybe I'll feel better tomorrow … "

That night, alone in his hotel room, he writes down what has happened to him in the course of the last seven days. "I am no longer the same person I was just a week ago," was the final sentence, at the end of ten pages of diary, written in savage exhaustion. "I have stopped begging, and started cursing."

The following day, he is once more a guest at the Villa Pacifico. After lunch, Uriel walks him back to the hotel, and effortlessly secures permission for Loew to keep his room, and stay in it as long as he wants. Roccamora takes his leave: "Sabbath afternoon, the only time in the week I can rest. What a luxury—two or three hours of siesta!"

In the evening, they're sitting together on the broad window seat in room 1992. "Father and I," says Uriel, "have been thinking after sunset, whom we might recommend for your case. I think we've found the right person. I know him well, we went to Hebrew school together. There are not many men in Panama who are so well connected. His father makes the most beautiful bridal gowns in the country, is close to the Senior Judge and has personal access to the President himself. Papa

157

and I are agreed that Amadeo Spadafora Bonett would be the best man for you. He'll come to you in the hotel tomorrow morning. I need to accompany Father to Colon, to inspect our warehouses, at the other end of the canal. We are expecting a consignment of microwave ovens from Taiwan tomorrow. I'll be back on Monday. Why are you so quiet? … "

How much time it takes me to come to decisions, to settle issues, Daniel thinks. How quickly businesspeople, executives, make up their minds, compared to my profession, compared to my sluggish pace—two lines can take me all day.

They are cruising through the old city in Roccamora's cabriolet. The canvas hood is down. On the coast road, there's a stink of petroleum and dead fish. Between the buttresses of a couple of churches, he spots the green emblem of the German Bank of Latin America, set high on the roof of the Torre Banco Germanico. The heir does all he can not to be affected by the flashing sign. But on every crossing, there is a view of the top of the building where Stecher Bravo's fortune was held in the last few years before his death. His painful yearning for Alexander's estate, he admits it to himself now, has accompanied every one of his steps, all his feeling and thought, for the past five months.

"What are you thinking about, Daniel?"

"Oh, about my wife, about home, about everything … And the chance that brought us together … "

"Mairah always used to call me a frog, when we were together at school in Rochester," Uriel tells him. "Frog. That's not the sort of thing people do if they're in love. I know I'm not a good-looking man, but I have other advantages, or maybe not? Will I ever marry? I doubt it. That depth of feeling that you have at sixteen or seventeen! That won't come back. But without that trembling in your belly … love is meaningless."

In a side street, an archway with red flickering lights, the entrance to a ramshackle two-storey building. "Do you fancy it?" This here was the site of his most intoxicating escapades. "The girls are the prettiest you've ever seen, I'll bet you anything you like, you won't have had such an exciting time anywhere."

" … Cut a swathe through the whorehouses, your uncle and me, when I arrived in Caracas, in December 'thirty nine!" Konrad Kirshman had said to him, when they first telephoned, a few weeks after Stecher Bravo's death: "That's something you don't forget!"

Daniel doesn't know what to say. He has only twice consorted with prostitutes in his life, the first time was a complete fiasco, a few weeks after his final school exams, and the second, oddly enough, only a few days before that first conversation with Julio's father. Held her large, firm breasts in his hands, while thrusting into her from behind, '*á l'audriette*', as she laughingly called it, he didn't understand the term, couldn't find it in any dictionary, assumed it was some kind of cart, she was the draft mare, and he the cart. They were only a few minutes he spent with Sonia, but they had been quite unforgettable.

"I'll treat you," insists Uriel Roccamora. "Commercial love, I'm afraid, is the best you can get in life. For twenty dollars, you can do anything you want here. Really, anything! So, are you coming or not?"

"I don't feel like it. At least not today."

"Why not? Tell me! What's wrong?" Uriel drives the car down gloomy streets, where the humidity of the day was trapped between the walls. "You disappoint me. Or do you have some problem … with women?"

"I'm not up to it at the moment, Uriel. I find it very hard to switch from one mood or state of being into another, just like that. I envy you that, I must say … I'm afraid I can't do it."

"You're short of lightness and humour, my friend, and those are the most important ingredients of a successful life. Shame. You really don't know what you're missing … "

I cannot escape from my own skin, thinks Loew, much as I would like to.

Only after a long silence does Roccamora next address Daniel. Amadeo Spadafora Bonett, he emphasises, brought an extraordinary commitment to his work. He wished he himself had anything like the same passion Spadafora Bonett did. He only ever worked, it seemed to him, at half-throttle. He was twenty-eight years old, and couldn't lose the sense of already being past halfway. "Things won't get any better. They will only go downhill from here. Everything seems to rush past me in the strangest way, without leaving any impression. I don't really seem to exist in my life. Soon I will be old. And then I'll be under the ground."

"Please forgive me if what I say is intrusive," replies Daniel, "but it seems to me you are something like an employee of your father's. The business has not become what it is through your determination and your ideas. Leon Roccamora has set the course, and given the direction … "

"Ever since I was a child, the world and the universe seem to have just fallen into my lap, I think there's some truth in what you say, Daniel, everything just fell into my lap, pampered as I was and still am. I have never made anything blossom or grow by my own effort. Aron neither. Papa's the boss. We're both little fish."

He stops outside a nightclub. "Don't look at me with that horrified expression, the Elite isn't a brothel! Come on, you'll like it! For five bucks, the sweetest little thing will sit on your lap, completely naked. It's dark inside, almost pitch-black, and for five minutes, she'll ride up and down on you, stretch and twist, and rub her hard nipples over your face. And if you give her ten dollars, then you're allowed to touch her anywhere you like, and she'll rub herself against you, and stretch and tease, till you're half crazy. And then you don't have to do anything … you can just go home to your hotel room, all alone, and dream about her afterwards … I expect that's the way you like it?"

At three dozen tables, girls are swarming around customers, to driving rock music. Daniel sees an immaculate beauty riding up and down on the lap of a man dressed in a suit and tie quite near him. She rubs herself against him. She slides her tongue along her upper lip. He sees the tender grip with which the man holds her waist, and strokes her back, her bottom, her thighs.

"Be my guest!" yells Roccamora, and propositions a girl on his behalf. But already Daniel is in the doorway, and wants to get as far away from the place as he can.

18

ELDORADO

H E ASSUMES THE YOUTH who walks up to him on Sunday morning in the lobby of the Holiday Inn is some assistant of Spadafora Bonett's, under instructions to drive him to the lawyer's office. Instead, the fellow in tracksuit pants, tennis shirt and shoes whispers: "Spadafora."

When Uriel claimed to have found the perfect man for the task, Loew was imagining a man in his middle years, with decades of experience behind him. Amadeo's palms are damp. He is lanky, a good head taller than Daniel.

"I was at kindergarten and elementary school with Daniel, didn't he mention that? We are almost exactly the same age." His manner is rather jumpy. "A friend of mine is expecting us, at the edge of town." He stutters slightly, the words come out choppy. At the end of even the shortest sentence, he clears his throat nervously. "My friend owns a very powerful computer."

On the potholed side roads he drives into every one of the hollows, avoids oncoming traffic with exaggerated movements. The passenger is several times thrown against the right hand door.

"Uriel just told me a few basic points yesterday," says the lawyer, "so I'd be very grateful if you would tell me a little more yourself."

Daniel summarises his case with a certain routine that he has acquired in the course of the past week, and adds on all the experiences he has had since his first arrival in Caracas. He mentions the names of Kirshman, of Esther Moreno, Friedrich Johannes, Francisco Shatil.

163

The case would bring "enormous prestige" to him and his firm, says Amadeo, and his rasping voice seems to tremble with worry lest the stranger take the probate case to any of his numerous rivals, with which the canal state was teeming. Tells him about his studies in New York and Panama City, of his earliest successes, of a case won: "A Honduran jeans manufacturer copies the designs of a Panamanian jeans manufacturer. I made the Hondurans pay heavily for their crime!" He refers to his connections in the country, many of them going back to an uncle on his father's side, who, seven years ago, had fallen victim to an assassination perpetrated by the then all-powerful military. The headless corpse of the nationally famous advocate of human rights had been found in the jungle, not many days after Dr Hugo Spadafora had published a study documenting the extent of corruption in the army. "I have opportunities everywhere! If you place your trust in me, I will never ever let you down!" (Clearing of throat.)

"Who is this friend of yours we are on our way to see?"

Amadeo ploughs through a red light at a crossroads. "Who? My friend? He works for the German Bank of Latin America. We are relatives by marriage, but that's already telling you too much, kindly forget that right away … If anyone gets to hear that he's seeing us, he'll go straight to prison. Or he'll be shot. Wouldn't be the first time in the case of someone betraying a bank secret … "

A cat trots from left to right across the steep lane they are driving down. Spadafora Bonett sees the dark-brown creature. He doesn't brake. They feel the soft impact of the left front wheel against the animal's head. The car runs over the scrawny body, they hear the crunch of the bones. In its death agonies, the two hind legs kick out in frenzy, while the front half of the body is motionless, as though glued to the asphalt.

"She's past help," mutters the driver, looks up in the rear view mirror.

" … We still ought to stop for it!"

"I can't stop here, and if I do, there's someone else coming behind me who will hit her!"

164

The following car runs over the cat's body.

No more is said about the incident.

Spadafora's mobile phone goes off. He carries on driving with one hand.

"*No! Sí! Naturalmente!* Fish and chips?! *No!* (Throat clearing.) "*Exacto! No!*"

The conversation is over. Amadeo, deathly pale, groans. His spectacles are covered with moisture.

"What's the problem?"

"No problem. My friend was scared. That's all … "

"And what does that mean? … "

"It just means we have to nurse him through his panic a bit. He asked me if you were coming. Because he was worried about someone listening in, he said: 'Are you bringing fish and chips?' He thinks because you live in London, you must be English, and so he screams: 'I don't want any fish and chips! I'll die if I have to eat fish and chips!' I lie to him, and say, no for sure I don't bring you. Last night he seemed to agree to you coming, now he seems to think differently. I'll have to drop you. I'll pick you up here in half-an-hour. No, better go back to the hotel, I'll call you a taxi. In an hour at the latest I'll be back with you. I'm sorry, Señor Loew."

The heavy car kicks up gravel. Amadeo comes to a stop next to a wooden pier, jutting out into brackish, oil-smeared water. "*Peligro! Colera!*" announces a metal sign. The lawyer calls a taxi driver he likes to use, and describes the place where a *turista* will be waiting for him.

Daniel slips into the swimming pool on the edge of the hotel grounds. He listens to the creaking of the palms, and the wash of the sea nearby. Do you hear my soft fiddle playing, my boy? he hears Alexander's voice echo back to him. In kindergarten I played the triangle. A year before I went to school, I started taking violin lessons—a brother of my father's was a violinist, he came to us at home. He gave me lessons. Mama hated it when I played violin, I even had to hide when I was practising. And do you know where I used to hide? In the empty swimming pool. Between mid-October and late March, the pool in our garden was empty. It was such a pleasure to climb down into the dry pool, and practise my violin down there!

A hotel employee comes running up to the swimming pool with a cordless phone, calling out Daniel's name. Loew waves his hand, swims to the side of the pool, takes the phone.

" … Be at the gate in ten minutes, I'll pick you up." Amadeo doesn't even wait for his reply.

More than three hours have elapsed since the lawyer dropped him at the crumbly pier. In the meantime, Daniel has tried vainly to get in touch with Uriel. He knew Roccamora and son were in Colon, hoped Lilith might have a number where he could get hold of her son. He wanted to tell him that, in his view, Spadafora Bonett was not the ideal choice.

"Where have you been? What took you so long?" asks Loew, once he's back in the car, next to Amadeo. "You told me—half-an-hour!? Why didn't you tell me you'd be late?"

"We're going back to my house," mutters the lawyer.

"Were you able to get any information?"

Amadeo is concentrating on the traffic lights. He is intent on cars coming the other way, those overtaking him, and masters the steep, narrow descent into his underground garage.

They enter an apartment on the twenty-fourth floor of a condo block. "Welcome," he says. "Are you thirsty? I live here with my father. Mama has lived apart from us since I was twelve."

The apartment is decorated with plastic flowers, and stuffed full of tinted Perspex furniture. In the drawing room there are five brilliant white models of bridal gowns exhibited in glass display cases, the latest products from his father's factory.

The lawyer conducts his guest on to the wide, sunny terrace. Steamships and oil tankers are caught in a kilometre-long line of ships waiting to enter the canal. Halfway between Panama City and the horizon there is a large sailing ship looking like a pirate clipper. Its trapezoidal canvas sheets sparkle in the sun.

An old woman serves them ice-cooled lemonade. They are sitting on a swing seat. Amadeo sets them gently in motion. "This Sunday

166

will be the most important moment, the most dramatic day of your entire life to date," he suddenly opens. "My friend gave us all the data we could dream of acquiring. The whole thing will cost you just three thousand dollars, which I've advanced on your behalf to my informant. He is afraid you may one day discover his identity. That would be the end of his professional life. I swore on the life of my father that you were ignorant, and would remain so. We now know everything. Much more than that bank woman in Hamburg could ever have found out for you, because this sort of information is not easily available abroad, even to senior employees. At the beginning of July, not many days after your uncle's death, equipped with his power of attorney, Kirshman transferred all of Señor Stecher Bravo's holdings to secret numbered accounts belonging to his father and himself. You see, I've got printouts of everything, you can have a look at it all later before we destroy it. Up until the day of his death, your uncle kept in all six accounts in Panama. And the total of his holdings was not, as you thought, and as your lawyer in Caracas believed, one million dollars, my dear Señor Loew. Your uncle's net worth on the day of his death was one point eight million dollars. With the accrued interest, the value today is: one million, nine hundred and ninety-seven thousand, eight hundred and forty-four dollars. And nineteen cents. Just a tad under—"

A US Air Force plane overflies the Paitilla district. The low-flying AWACS jet drowns out the syllables, " ... two million dollars".

He has lip-read the words of his lawyer.

He struggles to breathe.

It is only in his dreams that breathing has sometimes seemed as difficult. (Don't forget what you dream, he calls out to himself every night. And in the morning, it's all lost and forgotten.)

He breathes inheritance.

"Here," gasps Spadafora Bonett, "those red-ringed numbers marked *secreto*, those are the numbers of the accounts to which Julio Kirshman transferred the money five months ago, see?"

Daniel drifts over to the balustrade of the terrace, looks into the depths, which are tugging at him like a tide of water.

"You are wondering," Amadeo has come after him: "How is it possible that Julio has left everything here, at this branch of the German Bank of Latin America." He isn't clearing his throat so much any more. "A riddle. A couple of days ago, admittedly, he transferred everything to a different set of numbered accounts, still here, but new accounts, certainly a step that was prompted by your visit to Caracas. Here, on the second sheet of paper I've brought are the secret numbers of the new accounts—do you see them? Here!"

"But why didn't he try to make everything disappear? Send the money round the houses, to different banks in different countries? ... " Every word demands a great exertion.

"Good question, Señor Daniel, good question! I'll tell you why. Because he thinks it's safe in Panama, because of our banking confidentiality laws. He thinks he's protected here. Even though you got on the scent. Plus, switching money from bank to bank is expensive. He might have been asked questions by the other banks he would prefer not to answer. So it's easier to keep everything here. With the modest extra precaution of creating new numbered accounts for the money."

Daniel grips the balustrade, forces himself to look up at the sky, to put an end to the feeling of vertigo, the lure of the deep that he feels the moment his eyes light on streets, port, waterfront.

"Send me all the documents you have from Europe," Amadeo carries on, "that will prove to a court of law that you are Señor Stecher Bravo's only close relation, apart from your father, I need everything you have, including family tree, going back to your uncle's grandparents, and get a legalization *apostille* from the Panamanian Consulate in London. The same day I get the documentation, I will freeze Julio Kirshman's accounts, so help me God. An embargo not only on those accounts where he has what he stole from you, but also a freeze on all his legal accounts as well, you see, there's the inventory of everything on the third piece of paper, the accounts that he and his father have kept here for over twenty years. In other words, by state decree, we will freeze not only your two million dollars, but also the two point eight million he had in Panama before he turned his attention to you, a total of four point eight million dollars. You may be sure of one thing—

within an hour of learning of the freeze, he'll give in. Forgive the expression, but if we succeed with the embargo, we'll have him by the *cojones*!"

And with a jerk that he feels through his ribcage to his throat and thence to his eyes, forcing him to laugh for the first time in many days, Daniel now believes his uncle is pulling the strings for him—the name Alexander Stecher Bravo, he abruptly realises, shares the same set of initials with the man chosen to be his lawyer—Amadeo Spadafora Bonett. The shy man smiles, once Loew points out his discovery, disappears into the sitting room, comes back with a book, so much read that it is falling out of its binding. "My favourite book—*Many Lives, Many Masters*. It's like a second Bible to me. The proof that each man is incarnated many times. In each new life, everyone subconsciously looks for those people and those souls he knew in his past lives. And so we too have found one another."

Amadeo takes off his spectacles and looks at Daniel. They hug, and pledge their future collaboration. Everything can be put down in writing the next day. And Loew sees that the way everything has happened is good.

On the Monday morning, he signs over a power of attorney to the lawyer, and concludes a contract with him, witnessed for two hundred dollars by Dr Hernan Garcia Aparicio, the Notario Primero del Circuito de Panama, affirming that in the event of the winning of his case, he will owe Amadeo Spadafora Bonett twenty per cent of the sum at issue, some four hundred thousand dollars.

And he writes out a cheque—reimbursement for the money for the informant that Amadeo paid the day before.

He says goodbye to Uriel, Leon, and Lilith, thanks them for their hospitality and their help. He does not keep from the Roccamora family the size of the sum, which Julio Kirshman has stolen from him. "Come to us as soon as you have your money," they tell him again. "We'll be only too happy to advise you, tell you how to go about making your capital work for you."

Panama, the poet thinks to himself, as the American Airlines plane lifts over Curaçao, Panama City, my Eldorado!

19

WE HAVE MADE HISTORY

FOUR MONTHS AFTER DANIEL'S RETURN, Valeria was delivered of a son. The father was barely aware of the first few months of the life of his child. Max was five weeks old, while Loew, the telephone pressed to his ear, strutted back and forth in front of the nursing mother, back and forth, over the creaking boards, for fully an hour. It was the day before the embargo was due to be slapped on Julio Kirshman's numbered accounts. Amadeo Spadafora Bonett had received all the necessary documents from his client, the birth certificates of his father and his paternal grandparents, Alexander's birth certificate and that of his mother Luna Bravo, and those of his maternal grandparents, together with sketches of the family tree, and expensive consular stamps.

If he ever walked up and down and yelled into the phone in front of her and the baby like that again, Valeria warned her husband, then she would leave him. Moreover, she didn't want to hear another word about Panama. She was convinced he was running into some sort of nightmare illusion, that, Sisyphus-like, he was trundling a stone up a hill, but each time he reached his objective the boulder would roll down to the bottom.

Amadeo succeeded in having all of Kirshman's accounts with the German Bank of Latin America frozen. "Four point eight million dollars have been sequestrated by the law," he roared. "He'll come crawling to you today, I bet!" The lawyer emitted a yelp of joy. "We have made history. Never since the founding of our state have numbered accounts been frozen, unless it was drug money involved. Señora Antonia Aragon Rodriguez, the judge who imposed the embargo, a very dynamic and progressive young lady, told me—'I want to put an end to this moral decay, on state and private level!'"

The heir could sense it more clearly than ever—the fight for Alexander Stecher Bravo's estate would very soon be brought to a positive conclusion. "I'm very grateful to you, Amadeo, for your impeccable work. Can I embrace you, via satellite?"

"Your optimism is absolutely justified, Señor Daniel, within a month or two, we shall have won. Then you will come here with your family, and we will have a party, the like of which none of us have ever seen. Uriel is already wondering which rock band he should invite. As soon as you are recognised as the legitimate heir, the judge will lift the embargo and allow us to take possession of our part of the Kirshman money. No one but Señora Aragon has the authority to reverse her disposition. That's what the law says—whichever judge imposes an embargo is the only one entitled to lift it again, and to decide what will be done with the unfrozen accounts.

A day passed. Two days passed.

Forty-eight hours later, Spadafora sounded just a little less bullish. Julio Kirshman had not as yet responded.

On the third day after the freezing of the accounts, Amadeo reported that he had called the Kiba-Nova Company an hour previously, and had spoken to Julio Kirshman directly. "I thought: perhaps word hasn't reached him about what's happened? But he knew. I urged him, told him we Jews should sort things out peaceably among ourselves, and that I was prepared to do anything to avoid a court hearing. Let's sit down together, and try and work something out, I said. I'm sure my client will agree to leave you a part of Bravo's money. Kirshman listened to me carefully. No, he said finally, he would fight the thing through. He wasn't in any way dependant on the money that was tied up in Panama. Señor Daniel, don't worry, I'm sure he's shaking, in fact I could even hear it in his voice. In a week, at the latest, he'll give up."

Months passed.

Loew worked less and less, kept hardly any of the few poems he did manage to write. There was only one piece that didn't land up in the bin immediately, which he called 'Panama', and dedicated to his newborn son. He worked on the translation of an American play. The publisher returned the manuscript to him, marked 'unusable', and entrusted the work to a young woman from the Tyrol instead. He was paid a kill fee. The money was enough to pay for about two weeks of their life in London. By and by, he completely stopped working. Day after day, he sat in a little attic room in the house on Agincourt Road, Hampstead, staring out of the tiny window. Counted the number of double-decker buses that wound their way every hour through the far too narrow lane. He took down books, opened them somewhere, started reading, without knowing what he was reading. It wasn't unusual for him to lie down on the floor in the middle of the day on top of the letters, bills, old newspapers and journals that had collected there, and fall into a dead sleep for an hour or two. Valeria wouldn't have pets in the house, so he bought himself a plush toy cat, took it up into his attic, stroked its back, scratched its throat. He stopped going out, hardly ever accompanied his wife to other people's houses, restaurants, theatres, or cinemas. Sat in the afternoon, lay at night in front of the television, channel hopping for hour after hour, from language to language, with his toy cat on his lap.

His father and mother had received news of the birth of their grandson, but the frail state of their health wouldn't allow them to give the baby more than a little vague attention. When Daniel suggested to his mother that he might come and visit so that he could introduce her to Max, she merely said: "You're lucky it's a boy! A girl would have been unbearable! But you know—after the birth of a child, love between two lovers is finished … " He never took that trip to Vienna.

They lived off the money he had brought back from Caracas, which he had paid into the Hamburg account of the German Bank of Latin America. Out of worry about her job, Simone von Oelffen was careful not to meet him—Julio had followed up his threat, and started an internal procedure to have her sacked. If Daniel tried to call her, she would have her assistant say she was away. Her new private number was unobtainable. He sent three registered letters, but they went unanswered.

Two or sometimes three times a week, he would speak to Spadafora Bonett, and discuss the latest developments in the case. Since these conversations usually took place at one am Central European time, six pm Panamanian time, the moment of Max's regular awaking and crying, the heir would not infrequently be holding his son in one arm while he spoke to the lawyer, pushing a bottle of hand-warm milk (Valeria was long asleep) between his son's lips.

The next higher court of appeal in Panama confirmed the lawfulness of the freezing of Kirshman's accounts. Half-a-year had passed since the imposition of the embargo, sixteen months since Stecher Bravo's death. Then Kirshman and son instructed one of the most successful lawyers in all Panama, famed far beyond the national boundaries, to take up the case on their behalf. Dr Juan Alvarez and his two closest aides tried with all the means at their disposal to block all further actions by Spadafora Bonett, in particular trying personally to persuade the judges that the sequestration of their client's assets had been utterly unlawful, and ought to be rescinded immediately.

"Don't worry, Señor Daniel! I'm fighting like a lion. Justice must prevail! *Many Lives, Many Masters*—we know one another from a previous incarnation! *Venceremos!*" A few days later, Amadeo said: "I'm now on first-name terms with a judge from the court of appeal, who has formed a most favourable view of your case, and takes Kirshman's lawyers for nationally renowned crooks. He came to visit my father's beach house last weekend, and we had a wonderful time." Only to say, a week later: "Unfortunately—the judge I was telling you about last week? He had to give up the case after Kirshman's lawyers threatened him. He was told that the lives of his two daughters would be at risk if he continued to show an interest in your case. Even so—everything will turn out for the best. Please wire me another two thousand dollars, otherwise I won't be able to oil the wheels, you understand what I am telling you … "

Innumerable long distance conversations, greater and greater sums for Amadeo's helpers and helpers' helpers, and the continuing expenses for rent and bills gnawed away at the modest savings like a swarm of ants at a piece of gingerbread.

From time to time, he would send brief reports to Dr Friedrich Johannes. Often he would have to trouble his neighbour, Misha Zilkha, the jazz correspondent of the *Herald Tribune*, living at eighteen Agincourt Road, to use his fax machine for his extensive correspondence with Latin America. His own, ancient appliance tended to break down, he would send it off to be repaired, or he would tinker with the big machine himself, promised himself on an almost daily basis that he would buy himself a new one, but kept putting off the investment. Until the old dreadnought suffered another breakdown, and he was forced to go round to his neighbour's again.

The unexpected doubling of the total moneys held in the numbered accounts was something Daniel had not passed on to his Venezuelan lawyer. If Loew should win, then, so the contract between them stated, Dr Johannes was due fifteen per cent of the fortune, even if he made no contribution to the recovery of the money. It seemed more prudent, therefore, to leave his lawyer in the dark.

"The appeal court judge, Señora Graciela Collado, you remember the present we gave her, and the perfumes for her secretaries, all that has done wonders," it said in one of Dr Johannes' numerous faxes. "I was told that the lower court decision that everything was legally unimpeachable is about to be reversed, and Julio Kirshman will be arraigned. So you have time still. The statute of limitations only kicks in after ten years here. But what good is that to us? The money's in Panama! Incidentally, he has so far been unable to sell on the apartment you sold him. Perpetua's now twenty-one-year-old granddaughter Manuela, the one you told me had conducted voodoo rites in her room, now claims before court to have been Stecher Bravo's concubine. According to the law here, that would mean fifty per cent of the value of the apartment would

175

be hers by right. I only pass this on for your amusement … "

A year had passed since his return from Latin America. Then one afternoon he decided to give Julio Kirshman a call, to urge him personally to give in. He stood with knees shaking in a corner of the apartment full of dust balls, and dialled the number of the Kiba-Nova Company.

"Julio? It's me, Daniel."

No response.

"I just wanted to tell you you've got no chance, all that will happen will be that—"

Silence at the other end.

"Give it up. You know I'm in the right. You'll end up paying your lawyers a fortune, but they won't be able to do anything for you. Now, out of gratitude for what you and your father have done for Alexander, I'm prepared to offer you a considerable portion … Does that meet with your consent?"

Kirshman didn't reply.

"Julio?"

"My lawyers are working on the case. They'll manage, never you worry," he heard Julio say.

"It won't bring you and your family any happiness! I swear to you—it won't bring any happiness to any of you!" Back against the wall, he slithered down to the ground, and remained sitting there, for an hour.

A few days later, Amadeo told his client that there had been some unforeseen changes in his life. "But don't worry, Señor Daniel, your case will remain in the very best of hands. I have been invited by the newly elected president of our country to join his government. He is looking for young, fresh, untainted individuals to take over the levers of power. As of next month, I will be responsible for the worldwide network of our consulates abroad. Also, our entire fleet of trading ships will be my responsibility. You must not call me any more; I have officially left my office, so as not to incur any conflicts of interest. I will try to support my new partner with advice whenever possible. Any questions you may have should be directed in future to Señor Simon Urosa Mateo. I have transferred to him the power of attorney you assigned to me. If you want more detailed information, I suggest you turn to our mutual friend, you know whom I mean."

"What do you say to that development?" He called Uriel, beside himself with anxiety and disappointment. "Surely it can only be a catastrophe for me, for my case?! ... "

"On the contrary," said Roccamora. "Our Amadeo will be a very important man in government, now all sorts of possibilities to influence judges and lawyers in the case will be open to him. Your cause has never looked brighter than it does now, believe me. Did he tell you about his new love?"

"No."

"A woman wormed her way into his life, a couple of months ago, Barbara, an ugly duckling, but very warm-hearted. She'll be good for him. She's tremendously ambitious."

From Dr Johannes came a brief missive: "If Spadafora is working for the government, who now will direct your case?"

After two years, the sums won in Caracas were used up. The freeze on the accounts remained in place. Daniel couldn't understand why there was absolutely no impetus in the case, no reconciliation, no decision. The Panamanian court had long since recognised him as Alexander Stecher Bravo's sole heir. Why was his rightful property not paid out to him? The situation reminded him of a game of chess, drawn out over many years, where one side has taken the other's queen, castles, bishops, but still can't deliver the deathblow.

Every three months, Amadeo called his erstwhile client. He got in touch each time he found himself abroad on an official visit for his government, when he thought himself unobserved, inspecting port facilities and merchant shipping in Japan, Finland, Brazil or Italy.

"Señor!" (this from a hotel room in Odessa) "Things are looking very good. Thanks to my new position, I have been able to have a detailed conversation with the Vice-President of Panama on your business, last week. I told him the whole story.

177

Thereupon, he met our senior judge, claiming to be a personal friend of *yours*, and asked him to bring all outstanding problems to a speedy and favourable resolution.

"Did you have to promise him anything in return?"

"I'll pretend I didn't hear that. I am working on the creation of a new Panama, a nation where such transgressions may not and must not exist."

Valeria never let a day pass, without haranguing her husband for his mistaken actions and negligence towards her and their son. Of late, the impression had been growing all the time that he was heading for a catastrophe. "The money you were given, or rather that your uncle left you ... is all used up. I'm sure you must have spent at least half of it on your case. You've done no work now for years. Four skinny books of poems in ten years, I ask you! You've got your head in the clouds, in the fog, like some rich aristocrat who sleeps half the day!" On the other hand, he struck her as becoming dangerously obsessive, since his return from Latin America, she hadn't been able to get through to him at all. "Do you hear me? You've stopped listening to me. I have the feeling I'm wasting my breath. People talk to you endlessly, and you reply in half-sentences, if at all. You're just not there." The only object he had any tenderness for was his toy cat, only rarely his son, and never ever her. "I really think you should see a shrink."

"From my thirteenth year, I've been completely conditioned to expect Stecher's inheritance. The day will come. I've never doubted that ... "

"I think you're going mad," Valeria replied. "Can't you feel how you've become a stranger to me?"

She was looking pale and had aged since Max's birth. He thought her anger with him was perfectly justified. In his despair and not inconsiderable guilt, he toyed with the idea of getting himself seduced by his neighbour, the jazz correspondent's wife. Whenever he went round to Zilkha's house in his absence, the young Welsh woman showed him signs of her affection. Apparently, the pair was about to move to America, the newspaperman had accepted an offer from the *Boston Globe* to edit their music page. The planned move kept stalling. The neighbour's wife spent her days without purpose, without content, as passively as Daniel. At first he couldn't muster the strength, the attentiveness, and most of all the courage to have a liaison with this other woman. But then the notion of making love to her on the rough floor of his attic room became the governing fantasy of his life. He gave her translations of his poetry, she didn't catch on to them, laughed at their subject-matter and style, told him his writing was unbearably old-fashioned, 'out of touch' with the time, the fashion, the changes of the past few years. "Why aren't you one single little bit *provocative?*" Evidently, the latest developments in the visual arts, in the cinema, in literature, had all passed him by, he seemed to have no knowledge of anything. He struck her thus, his neighbour, like someone stuck in the nineteen-fifties. Wearing trainers all the time, day in, day out, that wasn't enough in her view, to make him contemporary. She didn't mind it as a sort of *tic*, but it did nothing to change her overall objection to him. His elaborate, rather artificial speech, which also strikingly resembled his written style, struck her as dusty, the speech of an elderly gentleman. Plus: "You always seem like someone who's drowning but doesn't do anything about it."

He listened to what the young woman had to say. Didn't react. Remained, as so often, unmoved, seemingly unaffected.

"Show some fight! Tell me I'm wrong if you think I'm wrong," she taunted him.

He resolved, after the case of Loew versus Kirshman had been settled, to find some new tone for his work. "I will begin to resist," he promised her, "as soon as I'm able to breathe freely again … "

He invited her to a French restaurant on Fulham Road. They drank a couple of bottles of their best white wine. They exchanged kisses—also French—across the table. The waiter let them know that other diners in the restaurant were complaining about them. And then, over a period of several months, he experienced what he had only dared to imagine in his wildest daydreams.

'*Your account is overdrawn by DM 2280.81, for which we request prompt settlement,*' he read in a registered letter sent him from the German Bank of Latin America in Hamburg, '*further we would ask you in future to avoid incurring uncovered debts.*' Once again, he tried to get in touch with Simone von Oelffen. And once again, he was unsuccessful. He wrote back to the bank: '*Through the refusal of your branch in Panama to assist me in a cast-iron legal case, I have seen myself compelled to seek recourse through the courts, which expedient has to date cost me some eighty thousand marks. I have become impoverished. For which reason I am unable to transfer the funds you desire.*' Whereupon the bank (to Daniel's considerable surprise) made no more demands of him.

That same week, he received a letter from an unknown party in Frankfurt am Main: '*I turn to you as a fellow-writer in a confidential request for assistance,*' he read. '*I am another to whom writing means as much as life itself. I have neither a typewriter nor a desk. (I am typing this in a public library.) I am often forced to choose between eating and writing. I turn to you for a once-only subvention. I require, among other things, a new chair, since my present chair was broken two owners ago. A food parcel would also be of assistance. In the hope that you may answer, and with cordial greetings …*'

Simon Urosa Mateo, Amadeo's partner, whom the heir telephoned from time to time, remained very sanguine, even two-and-a-half years after the freezing of the Kirshman accounts. He, it seemed, was not surprised that even after thirty months Señora Antonia Aragon Rodriguez had not yet come to a final determination of the case. "Perfectly understandable, eminently excusable! Señora Aragon is anxious not to make a mistake. Do not lose from sight the fact that yours is a groundbreaking case in the history of our nation. She tells us she must study all the papers minutely, since she has not in all her career encountered a similar case. The files by now contain thousands of pages! She wants, if you will, to deepen her studies, in some areas to refresh her understanding—of probate law, international law, banking law, all these are now, thanks to your case, Señor Daniel, being studied anew!"

"If our judge carries on 'studying' in this way, and at our expense, then I'm afraid that in little time Kirshman will succeed in getting his assets unfrozen," responded the heir, fearfully.

"Out of the question. No one but Señora Aragon is entitled to order such a move. You worry too much, señor. She will decide in our favour, she has many times intimated as much. She is a very clever, and serious-minded woman, who one day may be elected President of our county. You need to relax a little. Take a trip to the mountains. Isn't Mont Blanc somewhere in Europe?"

"What do we do if Señora Aragon should for some reason be replaced by someone else, suddenly?"

"She will not be replaced." Simon Urosa laughed. "She will remain in office. Please, do not worry."

A fortune-teller, recommended to Loew by his French publisher, and who had also advised the President of Egypt and the House of Saud, confirmed the optimism of Amadeo and Urosa—the tarot cards she laid for him in her boudoir on the Île-Saint-Louis, while a snow-white lapdog eyed them sceptically, all pointed unambiguously to a positive outcome. "In not many weeks, your case will finally be settled!" the friendly lady prophesied for him. "Admittedly, you will have to pay out half of your winnings to various persons, you should be prepared for that, the cards told me that very clearly."

"You write a letter," thus the suggestion of a rabbi friend of his. "You tell the Rebbe what has happened to you so far. And you give me the letter." Menachem Mendel Schneerson, for many years the head of the Chabad Lubavitch Hasidim, had died not many months before, but revered by his supporters as a sort of Messiah, remained a spiritual leader even after his death. "When I go to New York the week after next, I will put your letter on his grave, along with a few lines from myself, and rest assured—your wish shall be fulfilled!"

Isaac Weiss left the missive on the grave of the Rebbe, covered to a depth of several feet by appeals and expressions of thanks from all over the world, in the old Montefiore Cemetery in the

New York borough of Queens.

Spadafora Bonett got in touch—once more; several months had passed without any change in the position—from the Norwegian harbour city of Bergen.

"These long intervals in which I can't talk to you, they're unbearable to me, Amadeo! I can't stand any more of it. We must talk more regularly. Your partner is no substitute, where I'm concerned."

"What is it you need to tell me so urgently, Señor Loew?"

" … Well, that I've come round to the view that we should help Señora Aragon a little in her quest for the truth."

"How am I to take that 'help', Señor Daniel?"

"We should give her to understand that we're willing to give her a handsome present. We should have tried that a long time ago, two years before … "

"And I thought you understood that I will never—do you hear me, *never*!—have recourse to such methods. It was with good reason that our new president invited me to join the government—because he knows I have an upright soul and a clean conscience. To hear you now proposing such expedients, well, I must say, that fills me … !"

And he hung up.

Mairah Shatil occasionally asked after Daniel's welfare, though admittedly she generally avoided asking questions about the progress of the case. Only once, three years after their brief meeting on the flight from Caracas to Panama, did she refer to events around his inheritance: "I happened to hear of something through my father that seems to have some bearing on your case. Just imagine—your former lawyer in Caracas, the man you told me about, Señor Johannes, or something was his name? Well, for the past twenty years, he's been the legal adviser for the local branch of the German Bank of Latin America. Did you know that? It's nothing to do with me, I know. I just thought it was strange. Excuse me for meddling. Sunny greetings from Venezuela … "

He called Dr Johannes the same day he got her letter, and put him on the spot.

The lawyer said nothing at first. He took a deep breath. "Now please, Mr Loew. Those are things from the past! Calm yourself.

Your opponent isn't the German Bank. It's who it always was, namely a certain Julio Kirshman. I undertook to represent you against him."

"But you should have made it clear to me from the outset," insists Daniel, beside himself with fury and bafflement, "that you represent the very bank I've been trying to proceed against for the past three years … !"

"Well, who was it," the attorney defended himself, "who was the first to tell you of the moneys that were hidden in Panama? It was I, of course! I concede I may have deceived the bank with my behaviour, but surely not you, Mr Loew!"

Just let Dr Johannes try to claim his percentage across the Atlantic, thought Daniel after the conversation was finished, one day soon, once my inheritance has been paid out to me.

Two days later, feeling very poorly with tachycardia, he had to undergo extensive cardiac examinations. The specialist at the Whittington on Highgate Hill insisted on keeping him in over a couple of nights. He discharged his patient with the remark in his medical notes: "Severe psychosomatic symptoms." The battery of tests could not provide a more conventional explanation for the patient's state.

20

THE HEARING

THREE YEARS AFTER the imposing of the embargo on his assets, the Panamanian Consulate in Caracas summonses Julio Kirshman. The questioning, decreed by an attorney in Panama City, cannot take place on Panamanian soil, since, at the same time as his accounts were frozen, Kirshman was also banned from entering the country.

The man with consular responsibilities, Roberto Jovane Lopez, has known the Kirshman family for many years. His elder brother, Carlos, an urologist, has been treating Julio's father for twenty years. Roberto, a cheerful man no longer in the first flush of youth, fond of good food and fine wine, leads the life of a retiree. Rarely does he give more than eight or nine hours of his week to work.

Jovane Lopez informs Julio that, following paragraph two thousand, one hundred and twelve of the Venezuelan constitution, he is not obliged to swear an oath. Further, he is told that in accordance with paragraph twenty-two, he is entitled to the assistance of a lawyer. Further, paragraph twenty-five of the constitution allows him to refuse to give evidence that would be injurious to himself, his wife and immediate relatives to the fourth degree.

"Would you like to avail yourself of your constitutional rights?" asks Roberto.

"I am innocent of the accusations that have been raised against me," replies the executor, "and therefore see no reason not to speak."

"Are you acquainted with one Daniel Loew, and if so, from when does your acquaintance date?"

"I met him after the decease of Señor Stecher."

"Are you in a familial, friendly or hostile relationship to him?"

"No, none of those."

"Were you acquainted with Señor Alexander Stecher Bravo, and if so, from when? Were you in a familial, friendly or hostile relationship to him? Would you like to say anything about the circumstances under which you met?"

"I knew Alexander Stecher Bravo from the moment I was born, he was my father's best friend. They met in 1939, at a time when many refugees from Germany emigrated here. My father always supported him. He even picked up some of the costs of getting his mother and brother over from France and naturalised in Venezuela. Beyond that, my father gave him money to buy his first house, on the Avenida San Felipe, in the Castellana suburb, which, later on, following the death of his mother, he sold at a hefty profit. Then he bought the apartment in which he lived till the time of his death. Señor Stecher was forever calling on us at home, and in the office. We were, I stress, the only people who were at all close to him. We looked after him whenever he needed anything, and we were there for him through all his numerous operations. In the days before he died, we stood by him."

"Is it true that you have accounts with the German Bank of Latin America, and if so, what accounts, with what numbers, and since when?"

"I have had a secret account at that bank for a long time. I don't know the number by heart."

"Did you know that Señor Stecher had accounts with that same bank, and if so, how did you come to learn of them?"

"Yes, I knew he had an account with that bank. He told me about it. Also, he gave my father power of attorney to access that account. Later he gave me free access to it as well. Again, it was a numbered account, I don't have the number by heart."

"When and where did you learn of the decease of Señor Stecher?"

"I already told you. We stood by him throughout his last days. My father and I took it upon us to organise the burial ceremonies in accordance with the requirements of our religion. In order to bury a Jew, ten Jews must be found to speak the prayers for the dead. We got those ten men together to pray at his graveside."

"Was Daniel Loew present at Señor Stecher's funeral?"

"We told Herr Loew on the day that Stecher died that his father's cousin was no more. Then it was some five months before he came to Caracas. Further, it was I who paid the costs for the funeral, and had the stone put up on the grave, which was something Herr Daniel Loew had promised, as a last honouring of the dead, but failed to do."

"Did you know that Señor Stecher designated Herr Loew as his sole and universal heir?"

"Señor Stecher Bravo specifically appointed Herr Daniel Loew as the universal heir to all his property in Venezuela. That's all I would like to say at this point."

"Did Señor Alexander Stecher Bravo name you as his executor, specifically with regard to his accounts in Panama with the German Bank of Latin America?"

"In his will, Señor Stecher named me as the administrator of his entire estate, admittedly only—I emphasise only—of his property in Venezuela. Not of the money he had invested with the German Bank of Latin American in Panama. There was no mention of that account in the will, seeing as it was held outside Venezuela. We knew very well that by Panamanian law, secret numbered accounts and the money held in them is usually exempted from probate ... "

"Forgive me for interrupting, Julio—how can you say that moneys deposited in Panamanian numbered accounts are excluded from probate?"

" ... except when the testator makes an explicit mention of them in his will, or, alternatively, has a second, secret will, in which the numbered accounts are listed."

"I'm terribly sorry, Julio, but that simply doesn't accord with the facts."

"Next question."

"You mentioned a second, secret will—was there any such will

187

in this instance?"

"No."

"Police enquiries from Panama have established that not many days after Señor Alexander Stecher Bravo's death, you moved the money that he had left on deposit in a secret account of the German Bank of Latin America in Panama to secret accounts of your own at the same branch. Explain to me if you will why you did this?"

"I put through that transfer because I was perfectly entitled and authorised to do so. By way of explanation I would stress that Señor Stecher had made the decision in his lifetime that these moneys were to go into my possession on his death, out of gratitude for the support my father had given him ever since his first arrival in Venezuela, fifty years ago."

"Is there any official paper on that disposition, among the dead man's effects?"

"No."

"In the absence of any such document, I'm afraid the court won't find it easy to recognise the validity of your claim … "

"Oh, I don't agree at all. Besides, Señor Stecher wanted by transferring the power of attorney to my name to indicate his gratitude to me. I always looked after his personal and financial business for him. For years he gave me unimpeded access to his account, and even relieved me of any obligation to keep him informed as to what I paid in or took out."

"Does that mean you ever deposited money in his account that did not belong to Alexander Stecher Bravo?"

"He gave me absolute freedom to do as I pleased, and to wind up the account when he died. At this point, I would like to record that three years ago I paid Herr Daniel Loew the sum of eighty-five thousand two hundred and fifty-five marks, which Señor Stecher had left on deposit in an account with the German Bank of Latin America in Hamburg."

"But according to what you told us a moment ago, the will included only assets within the confines of Venezuela?"

"I did so on the express wishes of Señor Stecher, shortly before he died. Allow me to add the original of the confirmation of payment to the files."

"How could you withdraw the money from Señor Alexander Stecher Bravo's account with the German Bank of Latin America, and transfer it to one of your own, without producing a piece of paper that established that Señor Stecher had actually died?!"

"Because I had that very same power of attorney that Señor Stecher had given me, that I mentioned to you earlier."

"Explain to us why you didn't repatriate Señor Stecher's money to his estate in Venezuela, but instead transferred it to your accounts in Panama?"

"Roberto! Come on! All right, I'll tell you again, because those moneys were not included in the will, as the account was outside the Republic of Venezuela!"

"How do you account for the fact that the last will of Alexander Stecher Bravo takes in only his property in the Republic of Venezuela?"

"Because that's the way it was expressed in the will. That's the reason! I must say, I find your questions baffling … "

"Calm yourself, there's no reason to get angry! I have to ask you these questions, Julio … What would the protocol look like otherwise? We're almost done. What occupation do you pursue? How do you make a living?"

"I'm a businessman."

"Are you responsible for anyone else, and if so, for whom?"

"I have a wife and three children."

"Do you suffer from any illness, are you taking any medication, or are you on any unlawful drugs?"

"I'm not ill, and I don't do drugs."

"Do you have anything you'd like to add?"

"No, that's all I have to say."

"Then, as the party responsible for consular affairs, I, Roberto Jovane Lopez, declare the questioning required by the third district of the court of Panama, of the witness Kirshman, Julio, is complete. That's it."

Late in the afternoon of the same day, the consular secretary types out a transcript of the taped questioning. Jovane Lopez edits the transcript, and has a clean copy made of the revised version. And then he submits it to the General Consul of the Panamanian Embassy in Venezuela, Dr Jorge Herrera Kattenburg, to be signed.

The following morning, the document together with a legalisation *apostille* is sent in the diplomatic bag to Panama City.

21

MADURODAM

"I'M IN AMSTERDAM. In two days I have to go on to Rotterdam—another port inspection," Amadeo Spadafora Bonett calls for the first time in three months. "We have a few things to talk about that I don't want to discuss on the phone. Bring your family, I'd like to meet them, and I'd also like to introduce you to my wife. Barbara and I got married two weeks ago. We're on our honeymoon."

They meet on a day of boiling sun and sultriness. In the lobby of the hotel in central Amsterdam, Amadeo throws his arms around his client, as if they were the best of friends. Barbara, twenty-two, is in Europe for the first time. She is in full make up. On her pointed chin is a puffy scar, heavily pancaked over. She kisses Daniel, Valeria and Max on both cheeks, leaves crimson lipstick marks.

Amadeo has reserved tickets for a sightseeing trip at the hotel reception. "A memory from my childhood that has never left me. I want to show Barbara the miniature city of Madurodam, just outside The Hague, which I saw when I was seven, on my own first visit to Europe, with my parents."

"We have to get the night train back ... Are you sure we'll have enough time for our conversation, Amadeo ... ?"

"Our conversation? We can have that on the bus! That way I'll feel least likely to be observed."

"He has sweaty palms," is Valeria's first reaction. The Spadafora Bonetts have gone off to pay for the bus tickets. "We haven't come to Amsterdam to take a drive through the Netherlands with a bunch of tourists! Tell them to take their trip tomorrow, please, without us!" Her view of people is simultaneously kindly and austere. Everyone meeting Valeria for the first time is awkward. She herself seems shy and awkward at first as well.

The bus doesn't go directly to Madurodam. The first destination is a porcelain factory in Delft. Max is crying. From birth he has disliked riding in cars and buses. Halfway between Amsterdam and Delft he goes to sleep, even though the loudspeaker on the bus is turned way up. The hoarse tourist guide, clutching a defective microphone, draws attention to the sights of her homeland in three languages.

"You can't hear yourself think!" exclaims Valeria.

While the tour group inspects the porcelain factory, the Loew family stays on the bus.

"Do you think it would be possible," Valeria passes through the rows of empty seats to the front of the bus, "to turn down the volume a little bit?"

The driver switches off the loudspeaker unit. A quarter-of-an-hour later, he switches it back on. The drive through Holland resumes. The noise, if anything, is greater than before.

Ten minutes' stop in The Hague, on the roundabout in front of the European Court of Justice—the two men grip the wrought-iron park gate. "For the first time ... our case ... doesn't look that good," the lawyer begins. "But we will still win, I don't doubt that for a moment. Especially in view of my decision to retire from my government post as soon as I can."

"The case isn't going well?"

"I can't get by on three thousand five hundred dollars a month, now that I want to start a family. It's not enough. And the only way a government employee can make money in Panama is if he's prepared to take presents from every Tom, Dick and Harry. So I've decided to go back to my law firm. This autumn some time. I've already tendered my resignation."

"But you said there was a change in our case? What is it that's happened?"

The tour guide is calling them.

"I'll tell you in a minute ... "

They are back in the midst of the noise.

And now Valeria has managed to fall asleep as well.

The bus stops in the Madurodam car park.

With hordes of sightseers from all over the world, they stroll past miniature airports, stations and port facilities, past tin windmills, palaces, concert halls, television masts, no higher or wider than Max. Amadeo and Barbara take photographs of each other against backdrops of Lilliputian monasteries and cathedrals; at the end of an avenue no thicker than a man's arm, hung with bunting, they bow down to peer at a military parade of hundreds of blue-uniformed tin soldiers. In front of the 1:30 scale model of the European Court of Justice, together with the surrounding park and wrought-iron gate where they had stood earlier, Daniel plucks the lawyer by the sleeve: "You wanted to tell me … the change in the circumstances of the case—"

"Not now, not here. I want to enjoy Madurodam, which as I say, I like very much, in peace and quiet, Señor Daniel. We'll have time enough, please!"

The newlyweds keep stopping to kiss.

Toy-sized container ships shuttle back and forth between two locks. In a brief lecture, Amadeo compares the qualities of Dutch canal locks with those of each of the three pairs of locks that regulate the traffic in the Panama Canal. And suddenly interrupts his discourse. He has to find a toilet.

"I don't believe it!" wails Barbara, "my poor baby must have diarrhoea again!" In the glassed-over souvenir shop, during her husband's absence, she picks up two pairs of wooden clogs and a foot-long papier mâché windmill.

Max is perched up on his father's shoulder.

"Don't you even notice what a pup you've been sold?" Valeria is close to tears. "Can't you tell? That poor sap hasn't got a hope of solving your case! You really thought that man could help you obtain justice?"

"Amadeo is very decent. I trust him. He could never have got such a senior government appointment if he was as unqualified as you would have him be. Uriel Roccamora also thinks very highly of him … "

"And how stupid to drag us along with them on a drive all round Holland! That surely must prove to you how pathetically limited this guy is … !"

Spadafora Bonett returns from the toilet. He looks wretched. "Our judge, who imposed the embargo three years ago, Señora Antonia Aragon Rodriguez, has recused herself from this case a week ago." He speaks so softly, it's almost impossible to hear him.

Daniel thinks he must have misheard Amadeo.

"She says," the lawyer continues, "she didn't in all conscience feel able to give a verdict. Neither for or against."

"And it's taken you till *now* to tell us that?" Valeria's voice cracks with indignation, "After so many hours spent together?"

A Brazilian tour group stops in front of them, as though they too were one of the sights.

"Well, better now than never. That's why I wanted you to come to see me in Amsterdam—so that I could give you this not terribly encouraging news in person."

"But for months I've been warning you and Urosa Mateo," Loew exclaims. "We have to do something so that Señora Aragon doesn't drop the case. I said we have to make it easier for her to come to a decision, and if a little money—" He struggles for breath, is beside himself. "Do you remember how furious you were, when I suggested it to you over the phone, you were in Norway, if I remember? Do you remember?"

On his father's shoulder, Max begins to cry.

"I remember very well, Daniel. Now please calm down."

" … Has the freeze been lifted?"

"Not yet. We will have to … get the Chief Justice of Panama involved!"

" … In what way?"

"I know him well, as you may imagine. He was one of my professors at university, I was one of his favourite students."

"What are we going to do?" Daniel is on the brink of despair. His voice sounds choked by tears.

"He will be prepared to help us and exert a positive influence on whoever the new judge in the case is, if we … "

"If we? … "

" … make it easier for him to intervene."

"Bribe him."

"Give him a present. We will have to offer him a certain sum, at least as much as you are going to give me. Perhaps even a little more … We have to go back to the bus, come, otherwise they'll go back to Amsterdam without us. Twenty per cent for me, twenty-five for the Chief Justice."

Daniel works out how much he is left with, following this latest development. Two million less forty per cent, if I manage to keep back Dr Johannes' share … that would still leave me with one million two hundred thousand dollars.

"Are you trying to work out how much you'd have left?" asks Spadafora Bonett. "Bear in mind the interest that will have accrued in the meantime. Also that we're asking for damages. But you mustn't give your man in Caracas anything, after all, what has he done towards rescuing your fortune?"

"Who said the Chief Justice of Panama would take our money, and not the far larger sum that Kirshman could offer," Valeria puts in. "Plus," she adds, while they're climbing aboard the tour bus, "he can pay *now*, *before* the judgment is made, and not just afterwards … "

"Good question. Good observation. You have a clever wife, Señor Daniel. The Chief Justice of Panama will listen to our offer, rather than a possible offer from the other side, because he wants to help justice get its way. He'd rather even take a bit less from you than a bit more from Kirshman … "

"I'm afraid I doubt that … " Valeria throws her head back against the grimy pillow on her seat. Her lids come down over large brown eyes.

At eight pm, the tour bus reaches Amsterdam. The baby is thought not to be up to going on the night train now. They take a room in a two-star hotel near the Leidseplein. In a twenty-four hour convenience store, Valeria buys a few items. Then she and the child withdraw.

In a gloomy Indonesian restaurant next to the Hotel Java, Daniel, Amadeo and Barbara meanwhile order a fire-hot vegetable rice-platter.

"I fear, or am I mistaken, your wife doesn't think much of me?" asks the lawyer.

"She was very tired today. It's nothing to do with you, Amadeo ... "

"I'm not so sure."

Barbara hasn't spoken for hours. Has she perhaps been asked to keep quiet?

"May I ask you a question, señor?" she speaks up, no sooner has Daniel begun to ponder her long silence. "Do you wear phylacteries when praying?"

Daniel shakes his head.

"Do it, my wife's right," Amadeo follows up, "I would even beg of you. Do it—*tefillin* work wonders, believe me! Start as soon as you can."

Shortly before midnight, in the large lobby of the Hotel Americana, the heir and his lawyer draw up a handwritten document: Daniel Loew hereby gives Amadeo Spadafora Bonett the right to forty-five per cent of the sum at issue, following any successful resolution of the case.

"Right. That'll give me a free hand to leave the Chief Justice twenty-five per cent at the end of the case. Or more, if need be. I hope to be able to persuade him to slap on some damages too. That way we'll end up with a total of much more than two million gross." He folds the piece of paper, and pops it into his jacket pocket. "Thank you for your confidence in me. I will not disappoint you."

As they say goodbye, Barbara kisses her husband's client on both cheeks. "Have faith in us," she whispers to him. "And start wearing phylacteries, right away."

22

PHYLACTERIES

BACK IN LONDON, Daniel began laying *tefillin* every morning. He did it secretly, up in his attic. He didn't want Valeria to see him with the two leather boxes painted black with leather straps, placed above the forehead and on his upper arm, tightening the leather band, and wrapping it seven times around his left arm, and then round his head, and then the left hand, the middle finger disappearing in a multitude of bands. Valeria wasn't to know; she would only have laughed at him.

A few weeks later, he read to an audience of twenty people in Warsaw. Asked by the director of the local Goethe Institute what his customary rate for a poetry reading was, he for once did not hesitate: "A thousand marks." It was much more than he had ever asked for previously.

Afterwards, Herr Jonas Sohn and his wife Hilde asked him to accompany them to one of the new gourmet restaurants on the banks of the Vistula that had opened after the fall of the Iron Curtain: "There's a snug little place with a garden near the Syreny Bridge … " Three elderly German-speaking Polish ladies of aristocratic background shyly asked whether they might come too. Janina Wirpsa, the translator of a clutch of Loew's poems that had appeared a few years earlier in the *Gazeta Literacka* was asked to join the group as well.

Daniel disappointed his hosts: "I'm so tired, I beg you, do excuse me … I need to rest. Besides," he added, "I feel unable at this time to sit with other people in public."

"A death in the family?" enquired Frau Sohn with real sympathy.

"Several—several," he replied.

And, no sooner had he received his fee, than he had vanished from the reading room.

He practically jogged back from the Old Town to his hotel on Jerusalem Avenue, not stopping, not looking about him at the city, which he had never seen before. Crossed the empty lobby of the Sobieski Hotel, rode up to the seventh floor, lay down fully clothed on the double bed. In one hand the little envelope containing the ten hundred mark bills he had been paid, in the other the remote for the television.

At eleven at night, the telephone rang. Her neighbour, the wife of the jazz-writer, had rung the doorbell only a few moments ago, said Valeria.

He had up till now barely even considered the possibility that Valeria might find any trace of his infidelity. Now he was shaken to the core, whispered: "Yes? And? ... "

"Has she forgotten we have a baby?"

"Why ... why do you ask?"

"She rang so loudly that Max woke up!"

"Oh! ... "

There was a long pause. "Anyway—our fax machine is broken again—she brought me a message from Amadeo. He wants you to call him at home right away. He says it's very urgent, more important than ever before. Were you asleep already? What's going on with you? You sound so distant. How did your reading go?"

He ran up to the window, pulled at the handle—it couldn't be opened. There was a half-moon in the sky, high above the hotel. So speedy, he called to himself, so instantaneous, he crowed, was the effect of the phylacteries. So soon! Thank you, my God, Adonai, thank you!

He asked Spadafora Bonett to call him back, the hotel charges would be astronomical.

The lawyer was silent.

"Amadeo?"

"Listen, Daniel, I have some very bad news for you." What he had to say wouldn't take long: "The judge who replaced Señora

198

Aragon Rodriguez has decided against us this afternoon. He intends to lift the embargo in the course of the next few days." A fit of coughing or something like it interrupted his account. "Kirshman was entitled to continue to draw on Stecher Bravo's money, even after his death. All you were entitled to was what your uncle possessed in Venezuela, except for the 1962 yellow Chevy ... "

The heir had the sensation that the prefab building he was in was folding up and crashing about his ears—a house of cards. He stopped breathing. "Did you not ... show the chief, show your good friend ... the document you and I put together ... in Amsterdam?"

"Three days ago he came to my father's beach house, and seemed very satisfied with what I showed him. A new district judge must have arrived at this decision without my friend's prior knowledge, I assume. He said to me: Amadeo, this case will be settled in your favour, of that you may be certain! He said: I want to be your benefactor!" No sooner had he heard the news, says Spadafora Bonett, he had tried to call the Chief Justice right away, but his calls hadn't been put through. He must have tried about a dozen times. Decided thereupon to go round in person. He had got as far as the top floor, just outside the Chief Justice's offices, when security people stopped him. "I said I needed urgently to speak to the Chief Justice. They told me he had suddenly left the country."

Loew felt a chill about the temples and scalp, as though he had strips of ice round those places where he tied his *tefillin* every morning. He made an involuntary sound that resembled the groaning of a dreaming dog. He asked: "So ... we lost?"

"Don't give up! Never give up!" was Amadeo's response.

"Well then, what should we do?!"

A sound as of sobbing seemed to come from the other end of the line.

Daniel woke Valeria. "Everything happened exactly the way you said it would at the beginning. All my promises, for years ...

199

have been empty promises." He even considered making a clean breast of his affair with the neighbour, at the same time.

"I'm relieved you lost," said Valeria. "If you'd won, that wouldn't have deterred him in any way, Daniel, I was always really afraid that he might come to take revenge on us. Come and lie down with me. Press yourself against me."

"I'll be with you tomorrow … "

Helicopter noise clattered through the July night.

A squadron of jets shattered the air above the Warsaw hotel.

Not many days after Daniel had returned home, Amadeo Spadafora Bonett told his client that the freeze on the numbered bank accounts had been lifted. A further week later, he informed him that thanks to his circle of informants, he had managed to learn that one and a half million dollars, the bulk of the unfrozen assets, had been transferred: "And by no means to obscure little banks in Caribbean offshore havens, rather to the solid, confidence-inspiring branch of the Chase Manhattan Bank in Miami, Florida. Where the rest went, we'll find out too, never you worry. Meet me in Miami next week. My father has an apartment there. You can stay in it, that way the trip won't be that expensive for you. Do you know a lawyer in Miami? No? Too bad. We need someone to help us there. Just as well I've left my job in the administration, see, there's a good and bad to everything in life, and now I'm free to help you! We'll get a freeze slapped on the money on the American mainland too. Right will prevail! When are you coming?"

The same day, he received a letter from a major German publisher, asking whether he would like to write the definitive biography of Paul Celan, based on fresh, previously unused documents. And with reference in particular to the familiar and controversial accusations of plagiarism, some letters of a writer recently deceased in Jerusalem had turned up that shed new light on that whole affair. He declined. Dreaded the work, felt wary of the arduous research. The publisher, not inclined to take his no for an answer, wrote to him again. "You of all people," she wrote, "are the right man to intuit and give expression to Celan's special qualities. If money is an object, tell us the sort of sum you are thinking of—we will make every effort to meet your expectations."

Valeria threatened she would leave her husband if he actually went to Miami. The case was lost, surely he must see that now: "After all you've been through, all your anguish, do you really still think you have a chance? You should sit down at your desk and work. Work, Daniel, do you hear me? You've already wasted thousands of dollars on that mirage ... Is it never going to end?" And she began crying bitterly, which was something she hardly ever did.

There's not a single Western, he thought, in which the hero's wife is the first to quit, leaving her husband, while he fights for what is right. Valeria, too, he thought, wouldn't abandon him. Not at such a decisive moment of his life. Even so, in a whirlwind of momentary weakness, he dropped to his knees in front of her. "You're right," he cried, "you are so right. I was dazzled, these last years. I did everything wrong. It was as though ... I was bewitched. Now I can see it, I see it all too clearly. I'm going to leave this madness behind, I swear. And I'm going to accept the offer, the Celan book, why not, I'll start the reading in the next few days, do you hear me? We'll both leave the events of the past few years behind us, a long way behind, pull them off like a dead skin. I can't believe I was so blind! I am ... I will be ... myself again."

He threw his arms around his wife's legs, he laughed, they both laughed, he cried a little too. He pulled Valeria down beside him on the floor.

A week later, Daniel Loew flew to Miami.

23

MIAMI

O N THE SIXTEENTH STOREY, a view over the back of the city. Planes landing and taking off on the horizon. In the foreground, motorboats, sailboats, yachts, freighters, are criss-crossing the Bay of Biscayne. I am groping my way forwards, he thought, from hotel room to hotel room, from country to country, in my pursuit of justice. The journey from county to diocese, from village to village and town to town, took far longer in the days of Michael Kohlhaas, than with international jetliners. I am constantly out of breath, he sensed, just like that relentless horse-dealer of the sixteenth century, and my heartbeat is as erratic as on the day when I checked myself into hospital.

The room was subject to a continuous icy blast that could not be adjusted. His body trembled with fatigue. The drone never left his ears.

He was expecting Amadeo Spadafora Bonett to arrive the next day. A week had passed since the unfreezing of the assets. He went for a walk in the early evening, beside the bay. The pavements were still glistening from the late afternoon thundershower. The humidity caused the sweat to pour off him. He was reminded of Caracas, and of Panama City.

"Hey, man!" someone called out to him from the other side of the road, "you, yeah, man, you over there, white kid, man—your head should always look up, not down, man!"

The air smelled of salt, petrol and orange blossoms. In a little bookstore, he came upon a paperback copy of *Many Lives, Many Masters*, and snapped it up. Before going to sleep, leafed through Amadeo's favourite book. The words 'reincarnation', 'confidence', 'visualising', and 'psychic phenomena' flickered before his eyes.

He pushed a couple of pink wax balls deep into his ears to drown out the sound of the air-conditioning.

He spent the morning in the hotel pool. Above his forehead, the many stories of the Sheraton soared into the dependably blue Florida sky.

In the afternoon, he went to pick up Amadeo and Barbara from the airport. The three of them embraced like gravely wounded veterans after a lost battle. A car was hired. Daniel was in a great rush, they weren't to lose any time. Amadeo drove them to the north of the city, to Aventura, set down his wife in his father's apartment. He was no better a driver than he had been years before, when they had run over the cat on the steep slope. On the drive in the other direction, back to downtown Miami, he stayed in the overtaking lane, paid no heed to the speed limit of fifty-five miles per hour. They tore past orange and grapefruit plantations, past small landing strips for private aircraft, past yacht garages, where boats were stacked on storey after storey, to a height of six floors.

Daniel had arranged interviews with two law offices— Amadeo hadn't been able to do any of the legwork himself. From London he had got in touch with his American publishers; the Californian Robert Sparrow, not at all irritated or offended by him being out of touch for such a long time, listened to his story, and gave him the name of his own lawyer. Lloyd N Pickering in turn recommended a couple of colleagues in Miami, with whom he had had satisfactory dealings, and who, as he rather thought, had brought comparable cases to successful conclusions.

"Of course, two years ago we should have dangled before Señora Aragon Rodriguez the prospect that she would herself receive a substantial share of the now released moneys," observed Amadeo, as the car did a little slalom on I-95. "I understand that now. What crass mistakes we made, from the very start! Your furious reaction, not long ago, in the mini-city in Holland … it was perfectly justified."

"That's not much consolation! If only I hadn't agreed to take no further action at the time, the fault for that lies squarely with me. The second you joined the government, Amadeo, I should have gone looking for another lawyer to take on the case."

"Don't you be unfair to me now, in your desperation! Urosa Mateo made mistakes as well, in fact last week I had to sack him. I even suspect him, though I have no proof, of having been in league with the other side, up to a certain point ... Please try and understand me. My dream was this—my nation would be renewed from the roots up. And I myself, Amadeo Spadafora Bonett, would make a not insignificant contribution to this renewal!"

"Well, your idealism cost me my inheritance ... "

"No point in being gloomy or vindictive when things are getting tough. The case is far from over. I can't afford just to let it drop. That would mean I'd given three years' work for nothing! ... "

"Everything my uncle saved and accumulated and willed to me over decades has gone in the course of the past few years ... "

"Not gone," the lawyer corrected his client. "Your property has been siphoned into the pockets of people who were prepared to give a decision in favour of our opponents. I know of documents by which it appears that Kirshman has spent half-a-million dollars on our legal system, and at least another half-a-million more on his three lawyers. Over the years, he must have spent at least as much on the case as he would have had to give you."

Loew had the sensation that his heart and lungs and intestines were being turned inside out.

"Even the very highest government circles, and I have evidence for this too," Amadeo continued, "have accepted money from him. That was what prompted the landslide against us. Someone must have instructed the Chief Justice to unfreeze those assets, the Chief Justice thereupon instructed the local judge, and the local judge gave the order to the German Bank of Latin America to take off the embargo."

After a long time waiting in Dr Alan Pine's anteroom, they were ushered into his office on the thirty-first floor of the Peacock Centre on Chopin Plaza, not far from Miami harbour. The windowless room of the law firm of Cutler, Pine & Rengel was lit by neon light, in the middle stood a mahogany table, on the walls were copies of French etchings from the eighteenth century. Purebred horses and their riders and dogs gathering for the hunt. Dr Pine greeted them with the news that today was his fifty-first birthday. The visitors duly congratulated him, while the broad-shouldered, full-bearded man poured them Coke from a can into glasses stuffed full of ice cubes. He told them there was only one way of securing a further freeze of the assets now in the branch of the Chase Manhattan Bank: "You gotta post a bond!"

Loew didn't understand.

Amadeo explained the principle: "A sort of deposit ... We should put down fifteen, twenty per cent of the sum at issue with the court, in order to be able to compensate the other side in the event of our losing. If we win, the money is returned to us."

There was another form, added Dr Pine, an immediate injunction, a court order sent to the bank to freeze the account under contention. In this process, described as a 'garnishment' of the money, the plaintiff admittedly had to deposit up to one and a half times the sum of the suit as a security—in the case of Loew versus Kirshman, this would be a sum of over two million dollars.

"But I can't even afford one per cent of that kind of money," Daniel threw in.

"What's your job?" asked Pine with an expression of deep perplexity.

"Poet," Spadafora Bonett replied in Loew's stead.

"What university does he teach at? What guarantees can he supply me with? How would he be able to afford my fees?"

Amadeo stared at his glass, in which the ice was slowly melting.

"How is it possible," Dr Pine carried on, "to be a sane, healthy, white inhabitant of the northern hemisphere nowadays, and have so little money?"

From that moment on, the two lawyers disregarded him and merely talked to each other over his head, experts in the neon chamber, surgeons over a patient's hospital bed, in the moments before the operation.

By way of goodbye, Daniel and his lawyer were conducted up to the window of the anteroom, whose lower edge ran along the carpeted floor. The glass front was the fourth wall, creating the impression that the room was suspended in mid-air. The poet walked right up to it, with the sense of someone plunging into the deep: "Good fortune someone floating over the city," he thought, "Bad luck someone falling to his death."

"The next high-rise but one is the Chase Manhattan," Pine pointed to a sharply pinnacled building, "that's where the bulk of your money is held, gentlemen, and that's where you'll be able to collect it in a few weeks, once we've won our case. Think about it—you should put up the warranty. Maybe a relative can help you out, Mr Loew, or a friend of the family might loan you the money at a favourable rate. But I at any rate am raring to go for you!" And he gives his price: "Five per cent of the value, plus three hundred and fifty dollars an hour. As for our consultation this afternoon—just consider that as my birthday present to you … "

They spent twenty minutes looking for the rental car in the drafty underground car park, without managing to find it.

"I think our chances are slipping away," said the heir.

"A blue four-door Chrysler Paladio … It surely can't be that hard to find!"

"I'm not talking about the car … "

"You mustn't think that way. You have to be positive, Señor Daniel, *positive*! We haven't lost by a long way! I'm more optimistic than ever. Uriel will be prepared to put up the guarantee. Believe me." Amadeo insisted that his client move out of his hotel and move in with him in the apartment. "Surely you won't throw your money away on the Sheraton, when you could stay with us for nothing. That's what we arranged, wasn't it? Or have you got savings I don't know about? … You're a mystery, you are."

Spadafora Bonett's apartment in Aventura was the mirror image of his apartment in Panama City. It too was on the twenty-fourth storey of a condo block, it too was decorated with plastic flowers and full of brown, tinted, Perspex furniture. Here too the dining room functioned as the store-and-display room for bridal gowns from Amadeo's father's factory. The lawyer led his client out onto the wide, sunny terrace. On the smooth surface of a man-made lake, little boats with delicate white sails ran before the wind. A whole group of condominium blocks surrounded the lake, myriad apartments just like the one in which they were—mainly second residences belonging to well-off Latin American owners.

Spadafora Bonett disappeared into Barbara's arms.

Loew lay down on the lower bunk in Amadeo's former nursery. The bed was several inches too short. Soft, whooshing wailing sounds, the sound of tires on a nearby bridge, filled the air.

"What do you think is the most important thing in life?" the lawyer enquired of his client as they were sitting on the terrace by the light of scented candles.

" … the pursuit of the mystery of existence. In my work, in my poetry I search for … answers … "

Amadeo and Barbara exchanged glances, as though Loew had spoken to them in a language they had never previously heard.

"And what about you two," asked Daniel in turn, "what's the most important thing for you?"

Spadafora Bonett didn't have to think for long: "To earn a proper salary, so that we can have a healthy, happy family."

"Being healthy, that's my number one too," added his wife. "That, and I want baby girls. Four baby girls."

"Four?!" Amadeo blurted out, with a hint of shock.

"All right, then, three … " Barbara quietly conceded. They were silent. No sooner had Loew opened a bottle of Budweiser, than it was empty. Fire engine sirens came closer, a chorus of alarm. Three engines rushed along the lakeside road, drew up outside the entrance of one of the high-rise blocks glistening in the moonlight.

"In a building on Williams Island, where those fire engines are," observed Amadeo, "the apartments are three or four times the price of this one, even though they're only two hundred yards distant. On the left, you see, the eighth floor? ... " They watched the ladders being extended. Saw plumes of smoke grow thicker. Barbara brought a pair of binoculars out of the bedroom. They took turns watching the fire until it had been put out. "Incredibly expensive over there," the lawyer said again, "you can't get anything worth having for under two million dollars."

"What did you say the complex was called?"

"Williams Island."

The name had a strangely familiar ring to Daniel.

He woke at five. Sat down on the terrace, it was still dark, with the cordless phone. Called Valeria, told her he'd moved in with the Spadafora Bonetts.

"I found a poem of yours yesterday, in among some unpaid bills, no idea how it got there," she said.

"What poem?"

"I think you know."

"I've no idea."

"A draft, something you wrote last December. Still don't know? It's called 'Rough' ... "

He knew right away. His heart faltered. A few months before, he had written something in English that, he hoped, would satisfy the aesthetic tastes of his mistress, a hymn to her sexual appetites, nothing explicitly pornographic, but all the same a cascade of heady erotic and physical language of a kind that he normally didn't use. He claimed not to have the remotest idea of what his wife was talking about.

"And when I saw her at the chemist's this morning, our neighbour," she added, "I of course asked her about it. She blushed purple when I said: Daniel's new poems are really wonderful, don't you think, so different from before? ... "

He didn't say anything.

"You should have seen her face ... "

"I never wrote any poems for her! What makes you think it was something for that ... woman next door? I can explain ... everything to you ... " he whispered.

"That won't be necessary, sweetie. I'm taking Max ... "

Lips, gum, tongue, all felt like great pieces of blotting paper.

He called back. He called back again and again. She didn't answer. The early light broke above the flat surface of the lake. Which drew him, called him, tempted him to jump down, over the low railing.

The conversation with Dr Gilbert Wilmer, in the offices of Wilmer, Griffin, Paz & Hughes, took a similar course to the meeting with Dr Pine. Daniel's involvement in it lasted for no more than a minute. No sooner had the discussion begun in the black marble-clad office, than he got up, walked out, and went up and down the corridor.

"That won't be necessary, sweetie. I'm taking Max ... " he muttered to himself.

"Pardon me, sir?" asked the receptionist, as he passed her.

"Deposit the bond amounts I talked about with Mr Bonett, he'll explain everything to you. It's really worth it. I can win your case, it's so cut and dried, it's quite elementary—you're the sole heir." Dr Wilmer smiled happily as they said goodbye. "I'm sure you'll find someone to advance you what you need. I'll always be there for you! My terms are seven per cent of the sum at issue, and two hundred and seventy-five dollars an hour. Our first meeting today, of course, is gratis ... "

"What's the matter with you today?" protested Amadeo. "Positive, remember, stay *positive!*" Once again, they went looking for the blue Chrysler, this time under the Bayside Centre. Then Daniel suddenly remembered where he had come across the Williams Island address.

In the evening, he walked the few yards from Spadafora Bonett's apartment building to the wall around Williams Island. Crossed a little bridge. Reached a guard-post of the sort he might have expected to find outside some high-security establishment. A couple of female security guards in tight dark-blue trousers and dazzling white shirts asked him whom he wanted to see, whether he was expected. They took his passport, laid the photo page on a scanner hooked up to the Federal Bureau of Investigation.

The two overweight ladies wore pistols strapped to their hips. Closed-circuit television screens in the control room showed what was going on at a couple of dozen places in the Williams Island complex. The women repeated their question—whom was he hoping to see?

"Ms Eva Singer."

After a brief search, the younger of the two pressed one of four hundred buttons.

"Yes?"

"There's a gentleman here wishing to see you—a Mr Daniel Loew? El, Oh, Ee, Double-U," the uniformed woman called into an unseen microphone.

Ten seconds of silence. Only the quiet electrical crackle of the intercom was audible.

"This is a surprise. Let him in ... let him come up ... " Eva Singer's voice. Esther Moreno's voice.

He was waved towards a metal detector, and then he was handed back his passport and directed towards the middle one of three condo blocks.

Yellow-plastic ribbons marked KEEP OUT fluttered between the building, which had seen the fire the night before, and the footpath. On the lawn there were piles of charred briefcases and kitchen equipment, blackened sheets and withered plants in intact pots.

Daniel entered the building where Esther Moreno lived. The elevator slid up at great speed. Esther stood in the open doorway of her apartment. He had resolved to be coldly implacable with her. She threw her arms around him as he stood before her. He didn't return her kiss on the cheek. She looked different, sadder than he remembered her in Caracas.

"I knew you would turn up here one day. I knew it." She led him into a sunny room where he saw the painting *Leoncin in Winter*, the inherited piece she mentioned in the first minutes after their meeting in the dining room of the Hotel El Presidente. Out of the window he could see down onto the man-made lake. He thought he could identify the terrace of Spadafora Bonett's apartment.

"They're so ugly those houses on the other side of the lake, don't you think so?"

He could envision Valeria, packing her suitcases, dressing their son, leaving the house on Agincourt Road.

"I need to go very soon," said Esther Moreno, "to the opening of a conference, why don't you accompany me downtown, to the Hotel Crowne Plaza, that's where it's taking place … "

"No one in my life has ever done me as much harm as you have, Esther … I cursed you, then. I came to you today, really to tell you that."

"And that's all?"

"That's … all."

"You're saying I left you in the lurch. Let me remind you—in the days before the coup, I wanted to settle the matter of my apartment in Caracas, do you remember? That, whether you believe me or not, was the real reason for my trip. On the morning of the coup, the telephones were still working, I got a call from Julio Kirshman, who's a distant relative of mine, yes, that's right, and we've known each other from early childhood. He asked me whether I could do him a little favour. Then he told me about you, said we both happened to be staying at the same hotel, and so on and so forth, and everything that happened subsequently you know."

"I don't want to hear any more, Esther. If you hadn't ambushed me, if you hadn't betrayed me, then everything would have passed off differently, and better. I'm convinced of it."

"You gave me all the information I needed quite freely, without any trouble. If you'd been just a tad more cautious towards me … "

"How much did he pay you for the little service you performed?"

"Julio? Ha! He promised me five thousand dollars. I never saw a single cent of it! Now I really need to go, if you want to go on berating me, you'll have to come with me downtown. Otherwise I'll be late … "

Outside the front entrance to the building, a young valet drew up in a white limousine. "Will you do me a favour, Daniel? Please, I don't like driving at dusk, it's an automatic, that's OK, isn't it? Have you got your licence on you?"

As so often, he was surprised at himself. His curiosity was stronger than his firm resolve to show as much hostility as possible to Esther Moreno. He agreed, drove the car south down I-95, towards downtown Miami. The grapefruit plantations went by, and the little airstrips, and warehouses containing toys, kitchen equipment, spare parts for motorboats.

"You're furious with me. And why wouldn't you be. What's the state of things at the moment?"

"Ms Eva Singer. Working for the Navy and the US Coast Guard … "

"Who told you that nonsense? I deal in precious stones, a ring or necklace here and there, since my husband's death that's all I've done. And please don't call me that, I hate to hear my maiden name, the name of my father. I have no idea how your case with Kirshman is going, I'm not in touch with him. I urged him at the time to come to some arrangement with you, but he just laughed."

"Why the false date of birth in your passport? Why the different names and identities?"

"Why? Why? Isn't deception second nature for humans? Don't we need lies to help us survive? The conference that's beginning tonight is a gathering of Jewish children who hid during the war, they're coming here from all over the world for three days, to exchange memories, to get to know each other, six hundred of them. Those hidden children only survived because they lied, because they pretended to be other children, because they assumed different identities, because they dissembled, because they denied their origins, their language, their religion. That's the only way they managed to survive. Their lies helped them to survive. I'm a founding member of the American branch of the Union of Hidden Children of the Holocaust. Friends of mine in Poland, who went underground when they were little, asked me to be a sort of ambassadress for hidden children in the United States, and I persuaded myself to take on the assignment. Careful, Daniel! You're driving much too fast!"

After a long silence, Loew said: "I've … lost the case."

"Are you really sure?"

"What are you suggesting? ... "

"Perhaps your lawyers, whoever they are," she resumed, "won a long time ago, and just pocketed it all. Or they split everything fifty-fifty with Julio. People are like that. Believe me, I know. What brings you to Miami?"

He claimed his American publisher was planning to bring out a volume of his complete poems, at the same time pondering whether Esther Moreno's suspicions could possibly be true— had Amadeo won the case, and paid out half the money to Kirshman?

"But ... you haven't written that much in your life."

"Enough for a *Collected Poems*."

"I haven't deceived you, Daniel, quite the contrary. Why do you think Julio left the money in the numbered accounts, instead of moving it all out immediately, once he knew you knew? Didn't you wonder about that? He left it all in Panama, because I told him you were giving up. 'Julio,' I said, 'he's giving up, he promised me. Besides, he doesn't have enough money to hire a lawyer in Panama. Save yourself the trouble and expense of switching accounts. Believe me, I said to Julio, he's completely happy with the few crumbs you left him, and he'll leave you in peace now.' And no sooner did he learn a few weeks later that you'd managed to freeze his accounts, he was livid. He went around cursing me for weeks, for months, I'm not exaggerating, really. Your uncle should have left it all to you in his lifetime ... "

"And what about Dr Johannes? What part did he play?"

"That geezer? Of course I exploited him for my purposes, without him realising. Obviously he liked me quite a bit. But no, he wasn't in on it."

"Francisco Shatil? ... "

"Calling Shatil was Julio's idea, not mine. He was meant to show you how hopeless your campaign was, how doomed to failure from the very outset ... You must stop thinking about then, Daniel, life goes on, you should look forward, not back ... How is your wife? Are you still together? Did you have your child, or children?"

They reached the Hotel Crowne Plaza, Loew drove the car right up to the entrance, turned off the ignition, and handed his passenger the keys.

"I'm going to stay the night here," she said, "so that I don't have to drive home in the dark. Call me tomorrow, I'll be back in Aventura late afternoon. Please come visit me, will you promise to visit me?"

"I ... I don't want to have anything more to do with you. Esther. Eva. I'm a changed man from the one I was then."

She caught her dress in the door, as she got out. He helped her work the hem of it free, and watched her for a long time afterwards. On the long, red-carpeted passage that led to the bank of lifts and the international conference on *The Hidden Children of the Holocaust*, she didn't even look round once.

As he went out on the street, on the corner of First Avenue and Third Street, to start looking for a bus station, he saw a credit card shimmering greenish by his left foot. He picked it up. He read the name Ernest Samson. He didn't take his find to the hotel reception desk, but simply pocketed it.

24

SAMSON'S CREDIT CARD

THE FOLLOWING MORNING, his hosts are still asleep, he walks the mile to Aventura Mall, through the humid heat. The gates of the great shopping centre open at eight. He buys books, video cassettes, fairy-tale tapes for his son. Buys Valeria a four-hundred-dollar Tissot wristwatch. He gets himself kitted out with undershirts and pants and a couple of dozen pairs of socks. Finds a charcoal-grey linen jacket, imported from Italy that fits him like a bespoke garment. He pays for each of his purchases with the Mastercard he found the day before, issued by a branch of Barclays Bank in Manchester, England. As soon as the slip is put before him, to confirm payment, he copies Ernest Samson's signature as closely as he can. The dissimilarity between original and forgery strikes none of the shop assistants. He studies the motions of hands, shoulders and neck of the various men and women who wrap his purchases and take his payment, the way they blink their eyes. Can they tell his dishonesty? Do they guess that he's paying his bills with a stolen credit card? Samson evidently hasn't yet become aware of his loss, hasn't got in touch with the credit card agency. Loew imagines what profession the man might have, perhaps he's the director of a provincial art gallery, one of those hidden children, and after the war he emigrated to England? Or the owner of a garage? The boss of a car-repair firm, specialising in Jaguars and Land Rovers? Ernest Samson, import-export business in Latin America? Or just a poor sap? An impoverished painter, a starving poet, only able to keep his bank account open with the help of successful friends, friends who made it possible for him to travel to Miami, to attend the conference?

After concluding his shopping spree, Daniel wanders from ATM to ATM, first within the mall, and then in the wider area around the Aventura shopping centre. He finds a dozen machines; each one allows him to try three attempts at guessing the four-digit code number that would allow him to withdraw cash. After the third attempt, each time, a warning sentence is flashed up, saying the ATM will keep the card if a further attempt is made. Of nine thousand nine hundred and ninety-nine possible combinations of numbers, he tries twelve by three. He has no success.

Weighed down with paper and plastic bags, he enters Amadeo's apartment. Last night he spent hours lying awake, with violent palpitations. He wants to get back to his family, the only two people truly dear to him in the world. He must try to reach some kind of reconciliation.

Spadafora Bonett is standing by the door to the terrace, moving his upper body rhythmically back and forth, head and arm tied up in phylacteries. He turns east for morning prayers, towards Jerusalem, where the first and second Temples stood, on Mount Moriah, and where in the time of the Messiah, the third Temple of the Jews will be built. He speaks the Psalms, the Benedictions, the Shema Israel: 'Hear, O Israel—the Lord is our God, the Lord is One.' He doesn't allow himself to be distracted.

The guest retreats into the children's room with the bunk bed, hides and stows his purchases away in his suitcase.

"I thought we were friends," the lawyer complains once they're reunited round the breakfast table. "But you behave towards me like a stranger. Where were you last night, for example? Where were you this morning? What are you doing, running off like that? We wanted to take you to Fort Lauderdale, some cousins of mine from Panama who sell bridal gowns here, were giving a great party. We got back at three, I hope we didn't wake you? Too bad you weren't there. A rock band played for us, live, on the beach. There were loads of pretty girls. Everything you might enjoy … That, and the best kosher white wine from California—Napa Valley … "

"I'm afraid I have to go back to London ... tonight. My wife called. An emergency."

"My God, what happened?"

"She wasn't able to say ... on the phone ... "

"Is Max all right, please God?"

"The boy's fine," he sets Barbara's mind at rest.

"I hope you're still laying *tefillin* every morning?" Amadeo enquires. And after a pause: "You can't go now, you know, definitely not, not before we've planned our next move. I flew to Miami for your sake, remember? You can't just slink away now. We fight on, yes? *Venceremos! Many Lives, Many Masters!* I won't allow you to chuck everything overboard, at the critical moment!"

He didn't want to quit, absolutely not. But he had to go, "and as quickly as possible."

"We'll fly to Caracas together, that's the logical next step. And we'll bring a civil suit against Kirshman. This isn't over, you know, please, Señor Daniel!"

"What did happen at home?" Barbara asks. "You can tell us."

"The magicians came, but none could tell
The language of flames on the wall ... "

"You talk in riddles, friend," Amadeo shakes his head. "What magicians? What flames?"

"Belshazzar's Feast ... " Daniel replies, "Heinrich Heine ... "

"Who?"

The heir books his flight. He gets one of the last seats going on the evening plane. Since his original booking was for the day after next, and no changes are possible on the cut-price ticket, he has to pay full fare. The airline employee asks for the number and expiry date on his credit card.

"Sir? Are you still there? Your credit-card number?"

He hesitates for a moment. And then doesn't take a chance on giving the number of Ernest Samson's card.

"It's really silly and annoying having to break off at this precise juncture," moans Amadeo Spadafora Bonett. "But in any case— my return flight here from Panama, and sundry documents I obtained for you in the course of the last several months, and had to have verified and notarised by various offices, all that set me back over seven hundred dollars … "

Daniel has eighty dollars in cash in his pocket. They decide to go to the nearest ATM machine together. This time, he inserts his own card into the machine, and taps out his own four-figure secret code. Green letters on the screen let him know that his English bank will not approve the sum he wants to take out. He scales down his request from seven hundred to five hundred dollars, then three hundred, but it's only when he gets down to one hundred dollars that the machine agrees to give it to him. They drive on, looking for more ATMs. Amadeo is surprised by the precise intuition his client displays when looking for further cash machines. "I almost get the sense," he murmurs, "that you know the location of every cash point in Aventura!"

After finding their way to five separate cash points, Loew is able to pay his lawyer the desired seven hundred and eighteen dollars.

"There's one consolation," Amadeo says, as they're back on the terrace together, in the late afternoon sun, "which is that Julio's behaviour towards you can't bring him any happiness. There is such a thing as divine justice in this world. His apparent victory won't make him happy. Something terrible is bound to happen to him or his wife or his children one day. He or someone close to him will be horribly punished."

"I'm afraid I can't think in those terms, Amadeo, and I don't want to."

"Well, whatever—we mustn't stop here!" Spadafora Bonett continues. "We must fight the case to a conclusion! Don't disappoint me. When will I see you next?"

"Soon. That's my hope at any rate … I will do all I can … not to disappoint you." He asks Barbara to bring out the binoculars one more time. And looks across at the central apartment block on Williams Island. Looks for some point of reference on the nineteenth floor. Thinks he can make out the outlines of the Chagall, the banks of the Vistula, the low, snow-covered houses of Leoncin.

"What are you looking for?" Amadeo asks.

"I'm looking into the future."

"No, I mean now, with the binoculars. What are you looking for with the binoculars?"

And then he sees Esther Moreno, in her bedroom. The curtains are half-drawn. She is sitting on the bed. She is on the phone. Can it be that she's crying? But it could equally be that she's laughing. Her overloud, pearly laugh.

25

THE WONDER RABBI

DANIEL'S KEYS DON'T FIT in the lock of his apartment. He rings, knocks, rings again. He tries the neighbours' bell. They don't open either. He leaves his bags on the doorstep. Sets off to the locksmith by the Belsize Park tube station, with whom over the years he has struck up a cordial relationship, albeit one entirely based on the installing and changing of locks, and the furnishing of spare keys. Henry Zarfati, born in Tunisia, raised in England, is of Sephardic extraction. He lives on the perimeter of London, out by Heathrow airport somewhere. The father of five sons, he is a devout man. Every morning he wears phylacteries. He doesn't open on the Sabbath or on high holy days.

"Honestly, women!" Zarfati, powerfully built, with dyed jet-black hair, giggles softly to himself. " ... Women!"

"And men?"

"Not as full of deceit as women ... " He reaches into a deep drawer that makes metallic clangs, for new locks for his customer's apartment. "You should be glad your wife has played such a trick on you—you'll get a couple of days' peace at least."

During his lunch break, he shuts up shop for an hour, walks round to Agincourt Road with Daniel, and installs two new locks. While he works, he hums Sephardic melodies to himself.

Daniel is sitting on his suitcase.

Zarfati interrupts his work: "Are you afraid she might not come back?" he asks. "You mustn't be. She just wants to give you a little shock!" He goes back to singing. "Did you ever hear tell of the wonder rabbi, Rav David Hanania Harari?" he asks then. "Lives in Manchester, travels the whole time, I can get you a telephone number for him, if you like. Go to him, ask him for advice, if you're looking for advice. I've never been to him myself, but I know people he's helped, for whom he's worked miracles, great miracles even. You pay him a small amount of money, maybe ten pounds, not more. People on death's door have returned to life and health, infertile couples have gone on to have children. Someone who was kidnapped in Mexico was found at exactly the place where Rav Harari suggested he might be hidden. Not long ago, a nail bomb in a car blew up outside a Jewish school in Manchester. At the very moment when the children normally leave school—"

"I know, I read about it."

"No, listen, you'll understand—on the very day of the explosion, the clock that set the time for the school bell happened to lose three minutes. You won't have heard that part of the story, I'll bet my shirt. So the school bell only rang after the bomb had gone off, doing a great deal of damage incidentally. If the children had been outside the gate at the time they should have been, there would have been carnage and loss of life."

"I read about it."

"Yes, but you don't know the name of the headmaster."

"That's true," Daniel concedes.

"The headmaster is Reb David Hanania Harari."

Loew burrows around in his wife's office, in one of the metal cupboards that contain her drawings, chalk sketches, bales of material and sewing gear, he comes upon the little cardboard box where she keeps her papers. There is her passport, in among a pile of money, unpaid bills, photos of Max. She won't have gone far then! Perhaps she could even be in some place where people know who she is? Maybe she hasn't even left London! Their mutual friends have no idea where Valeria and Max have gone to, or else they've been sworn to silence. Barton, to whom he brings two reddish stones, washed smooth by the Florida surf, urges him to stay calm. The family will return to him in the very near future. The blind photographer says: "She just wants to give you a scare! I can understand that, can't you?"

Beside the sewing machine he sees parts of a coat, on which his wife was working obsessively in the weeks before his trip to Miami. If she had gone for good, she would never have left these components of a work in progress.

He avoids any meeting with the woman next door or her husband. There's an awful lot of noise from the removal firm, as they put the possessions of the odd couple away in tea chests, drag away cupboards from recesses and dismantle shelving.

He calls his mother. "Have you spoken to Valeria at all recently?"

"I predicted everything," she sighs, "just exactly the way it went on to happen, don't forget that. No, I've heard nothing from her … The person I feel sorry for in all this is the little boy … "

For the first time in months, he calls his father. "I'm sick, Daniel," says Jacob Loew, "didn't you know that? Did your mother not tell you? All this chasing around after money means you forget your own father! I'm sorry about your wife. If you want some advice from me, why don't you come and see me. Will you come and see me?"

Three days have passed since his return from Miami. Daniel has heard nothing from Valeria.

On the southern edge of the city, he goes and buys food and household articles, as much as if he had a large family waiting for him at home. The shopping cart is full past the rim. He pays with the stranger's credit card. The total bill is one hundred and eighteen pounds. The girl on the desk apologises—the payment hasn't gone through right away; she has to call the Mastercard central number. He doesn't know what to do—should he offer his own card instead? And then, what if she should notice that the two names are not identical?

She dials a number, waits for a reply.

Five customers in line behind Daniel send him angry looks. The cashier is now calling into a microphone: "Miss Whitehall to cash register eighteen, please," and from every corner of the vast store it echoes back. "Miss Whitehall, please!"

The Mastercard central office replies. The cashier reads out the name, "Samson, Ernest," and reads out the numbers, followed by the expiry date on the card. She holds the little piece of plastic jammed tight in her hand. Loew squeezes out between the little conveyor belt and the overloaded shopping cart. He upsets a packet of air-freshener and a couple of tins of Ovaltine. He walks quickly away. Hears loud shouts behind him. Doesn't turn round. Vanishes breathlessly into the underground car park of the shopping centre. Spends fifteen minutes hiding in a pitch-dark corner before climbing into his car.

On that same evening, he gets in touch with the secretary of the wonder rabbi. He needs some urgent advice, he explains, on the matter of an inheritance. The rabbi's assistant interrupts him. He himself has no interest in what it is he wants advice about. Everyone is welcome to speak to Harari. He proposes a time on the following afternoon, in London: "Rav Harari will be staying in London for twenty-four hours … "

Not far from the Golders Green tube stop is Rodborough Road, a short one-way street. On the first floor of a small prayer house, there is a square yard, roofed over. Women, men and children are sitting on folding chairs like patients in a doctor's waiting room. On the walls are pictures of renowned Sephardic rabbis and yellowing photographs of Rav Harari's grandfather and father. A young woman enters the rabbi's consulting room with a joyful expression and upright walk. She leaves it in floods of tears. An old man, with wild hair and ancient tattered clothes emerges from the room behind the drawn blinds moments later, with shining eyes. A girl has last-minute nerves about whether to go in or not. She gives her place to the man after her, someone who has come here after working hours in the uniform of a Royal Mail postman.

Some supplicants only spend two or three minutes with Harari. A sixteen-year-old girl reappears after fully a quarter-of-an-hour. Her delicate features give no particular clue as to her state of mind.

There are thirty people ahead of Daniel, waiting to set out their worries, fears, medical symptoms, legal difficulties, disputes with neighbours to David Harari. All the time, new people climb the stairs into the little yard, and take seats on the wobbly chairs. They are silent, look fixedly in front of them.

He moves (tired after an hour of waiting) to a different place in the yard. Through a chink in the blinds, he manages to see into the carpeted, narrow rectangular room.

He jots down in his notebook: "On the narrow side, a wall clock with Hebrew letters—Aleph as one, Beit equals two, Gimmel three, and so on. On the floor is a square fan or heater, coloured pink. Volumes of Talmud and Torah on high shelves. In a silk caftan, the rabbi, bowed over a desk covered with piles of paper, newspapers and magazines. His long hair spilling out from under a soft hat, mingling with his wild beard. His side curls reach down to his shoulders. He tells his visitors to sit on a red bench with high sides. It looks not unlike an electric chair. In his right hand Harari is holding a silver cigarette lighter, which he keeps clicking open and shut, the way a hero in a Western might, while the supplicants speak to him. He clicks it open and shut continuously. While giving his replies, he never takes his eyes off the Hebrew wall clock."

Daniel gets up.

In the evening air, he has a sudden sense of experiencing one of the definitive moments of his entire life.

The moment is truly fortifying, he senses tremendous alertness and strength, more than he has felt for years.

As if a blind man could see, or a deaf man hears, a mute learn to speak, so revivifying is the insight that jolts his body at that moment.

I will no longer wait to be told what I must and must not do.

Henceforth, I will be my own prophet.

He runs out of the yard of the prayer house.

Once back home, he climbs the steps to the attic, to his office. He looks at the little black-and-white photograph put up beside the window. On it, his smiling uncle is holding his little five-year-old left hand in his manicured right. A slim man, always clean-shaven, bespectacled from early youth. Every day he would put on a fresh white shirt, and always wear a tie, even when it was very hot. His hair cropped short, military style.

He lays the tips of his fingers on the place where Alexander's hand and his own form a little tangle of hands.

"Four years," he says softly to himself, "have passed since the day of your death, Alexander Stecher Bravo.

"After ten years, in the summer of 2002, the case of the inheritance, the case of my inheritance will lapse.

"I have six more years."

Pushkin Press

Pushkin Press was founded in 1997. Having first rediscovered European classics of the twentieth century, Pushkin now publishes novels, essays, memoirs, children's books, and everything from timeless classics to the urgent and contemporary.

Pushkin Paper books, like this one, represent exciting, high-quality writing from around the world. Pushkin publishes widely acclaimed, brilliant authors such as Stefan Zweig, Antoine de Saint-Exupéry, Antal Szerb, Paul Morand and Hermann Hesse, as well as some of the most exciting contemporary and often prize-winning writers, including Pietro Grossi, Héctor Abad, Filippo Bologna and Andrés Neuman.

Pushkin Press publishes the world's best stories, to be read and read again.

*